Joël

The Merivalkan Chronicles: Book One

LUKE H. DAVIS

Permission to quote in critical reviews with citation:

Joël
By Luke H. Davis

Print ISBN 978-0-9984000-5-1

www.dunrobin.us

Dedicated in memory of
St. Athanasius,
champion of orthodoxy

Whose bold truth of the past
inspired this story of today

AUTHOR'S NOTE

What you hold in your hands is a story, albeit not the end-all and be-all of the Great Story.

These are not the Four Gospels. Rather, this project began with a dream of what the entry of Christ into our world might look like in another world, another place, with all the shock value and wonder of what would happen if God Himself pursued us in person, in living color and intermingled deeply into our human dilemma. In the spirit of the Biblical Gospels, yet with enough differences from those books, the person and work of Jesus Christ is meant to come through in bold color.

I say "in the spirit of" because this is not intended to be an event-for-event matchup of the life of Jesus but rather a creative re-telling of the Incarnation of Christ. There are some things that don't make it into this novel. The birth of the Savior (or even the presence of Mary and Joseph's equivalents), Jesus' baptism, transfiguration, the depth of Old Testament anticipation of Christ, and many of his parables and miracles, for example, are missing. This is not to say these events are unimportant. The issue for me as an author was what moments I must emphasize for the sake of story and character development. Writing a fictionalized portrayal of Jesus' ministry is different from experiencing Holy Scripture. My writing stands well under the Bible, which is the only supreme, completely trustworthy standard for faith and practice. There are also matters the Bible de-emphasizes that I bring into fuller detail (the psychological asides and wonderments of Joël's believers and detractors, for instance). All of this merely underscores that my effort, while ideally engaging in its own way, is a pale reflection of the wonder of the Gospel story. Read this book you now possess, please! But do not allow it to be a substitute for God's Word.

I don't believe for one second that a novel is birthed in a vacuum. So many people over the years have brought me to this point. My parents, Ralph and Barbara, pressed the story of Christ into my heart from an early age. My college history professor and dear friend, the late Dr. Louis Voskuil, inspired me to see history as an outworking of the story of God's world that groans for redemption, and elements of that reality pulse through the lines of *Joël*. Much credit for how to write a setting of a unique world goes to L.B. Graham, author of the *Binding of the Blade* and *The Wandering* series, whose intricate establishment of time and seasons led me to structure the world and time of Merivalka along similar lines. Thanks, L.B., and once again, it's a bummer you're now half a continent away.

Jason Wilkins, friend and colleague, deserves highest praise for his reading of the initial drafts of this work. His feedback and encouragement has been most helpful. He was first to say with entire faith that "I think you've got something here." Thanks a ton, Jason, because this book wouldn't exist without you.

My daughter Lindsay—who is and continues to be a treasure—deserves many thanks for locating a beautiful image for the cover design, which Ciarra Peters used as inspiration for the stunning drawing that is the final cover image. Deep thanks to both young ladies.

I am also indebted to the writings of Philip Yancey and to his relentless literary pursuit of the doctrine of grace. The idea of grace flowing to the lowest part, like water, is vintage Yancey. Few authors have challenged my faith the way he has.

My wife and children patiently bore with me as I labored through a book markedly different than my past works. They did so, as they always do, with grace and dignity.

Luke Davis
Michaelmas 2017

"The price had to be paid in full,
but the price was paid by him.
His law stood;
his love stood.
The only possible solution
was to receive the punishment
in his own person."

Addison Leitch

Joël: Characters, Places, Events, Items, and Culture

Ahntunen → seer (prophet) of the Second Dawn, which began after an invading race of giants were mysteriously destroyed (ahn-TOO-nin)

Akran → a coin; the national currency of Merivalka; an inscription of Vuoristad is on every akran (AK-run)

Alisa → sinful Vale-dweller woman who lives in a thatched cottage outside of Selanna (ah-LEE-suh)

Avalukk → a lock-pin set in a long u-shape made of iron or brass; a guidepiece is inserted through holes in its pronged ends and locked in place by an indention in the ring of the lock's owner (ah-vuh-LUCK)

Avenue of the Commonwealth → chief street running through the eastern portion Selanna; where Joël's shop is located

Baudin → servant of the royal entourage of Kronjva; footman for meals (BAW-din)

Besno → seer of the First Dawn, which began after the Great Ruin; Besno prophesied concerning the Rhoken and inscribed the principles of the Revered Way on the Wall of Iniquity that surrounds Vuoristad (BEZ-no)

Bludge → term of annoyance; a "bludge" is a person or animal that keeps bludgeoning into the natural order of things; for instance, a duck that waddles into a market and chews on some food for sale would garner that nickname (blugž)

Bolsterpiece → an iron ring connecting four evenly spaced small pillars, upon which a pan might be place over a fire for cooking in an oven or out in the open (BOWL-stur-pēs)

Borga Reiji → aunt of Kaleva, Henrik, and Saku Reiji; resident of Kampo (BOR-gah RAY-žee)

Branström → city northeast of Selanna [BRAN-strem] known for its wine and farming (BRAN-strum)

Breath of Lord Creator → the mysterious third person of the Supreme Being of Merivalka; Joël promises and grants the Breath of Lord Creator to his followers

Brightide → the Merivalkan spring season, marked by much rain during its early phase

Canute the Eighth → king of Kronjva; his father, Martin the Second, had defeated Merivalka to bring it under Kronji control (kah-NOOT)

Capital Road → travel way that connects the cities of Stahlgard and Selanna

Conclusion of Wills → a legal term that refers to a verdict rendered by the Council of Nobles; in Selanna, a guilty conclusion of wills in a criminal case requires a three-fourths majority

Council of Nobles → any Merivalkan town or city's governing authority; the chief elected official of the Council is the Lord Steward

Cornetin → Kronji soldier serving under Vermeulen's command (kor-NĚ-tin)

Dagarata → younger sister of Prince Dewulf; Duchess of the Dalwa, the central region of Kronjva (da-guh-RAH-tuh)

Dalvig → one of the chief Messengers; leader of the *myrioi* (DAHL-vik)

Dasenpfear → both a fruit and the tree from whence said fruit comes; a staple of the Merivalkan diet, it is used in cooking meats, poultry, and fish; it is also used in desserts and some brewing and winemaking; the dasenpfear is the symbol of Merivalka as the original dasenpfear tree sat at the base of Vuoristad; wood from the dasenpfear tree is used for the Gathering bonfire at the midpoint of each of the four seasons. (DASS-un-fār)

Dewulf→ prince and heir to the throne of Kronjva and member of the Alvfinnur royal family; honorary admiral of its royal navy (de-WOOLF)

Dirnik Vanhanen→ member of Selanna's Council of Nobles; oversees business and commerce; highly resistant to Joël (DEER-nǐk vǎn-HAH-nǐn)

Edvin→ rug maker; member of crowd during Joël's feeding miracle (ED-vǐn)

Ehrma→ a race of fierce giants that briefly ruled Merivalka at the end of the First Dawn; their supernatural defeat eliminated them and brought Merivalka independence once more (AER-muh)

Eider duck→ a duck that lives in rivers and pools in the Merivalkan countryside, it has a distinctive call (EYE-dur)

Elaenor Nurmi→ young lady; best friend of Kyria Halmo (EH-lay-nor NURR-mee)

Elbart Laukanen→ Lord Steward of Selanna; resistant and hostile to Joël (EHL-bart lau-KAHN-in)

Elks Hill → an imposing mound north of Selanna where several key events of Joël's activity take place

Eno → servant of the royal entourage of Kronjva; personal attendant to Dagarata's family (Ā-no)

Evening Prayers→ the worship assembly that meets on the last day of each week; labor is suspended and people gather at sundown in a local *kopanos*; Evening Prayers consist of prayer, song, reading and exposition of a portion of the Stories, and—when required—other matters such as funerals; When a seasonal Nave falls on the last day of a week, Evening Prayers are suspended in favor of the city Gathering.

Faith, The→ The religion of Merivalka, encapsulated in several articles of belief that are held consistently if not always fervently: (a) mankind fell into a state of disgrace through the Great Ruin when Magnus and Merta drank from the waters of the Dark Pool; (b) Lord Creator still provides for his creation and loves his people even though the Ruin has touched everything, and no one may come to the Mountain of Vuoristad; (c) the seers of the past told and wrote the essence of Merivalka's history and religion in tales known as the Stories; (d) in the Stories, there are prophecies of a Rhoken, a Courageous One to come that will cause the Great Ruin to work backwards; (e) in the end, Merivalka will be redeemed and restored to a glory greater than its original, and mankind will return to Vuoristad once more.

Foundryman, The → One of the public houses in Selanna, located in the west-central part of the city

Gard→ one of Kyrt's hired hands (GAHRD)

Gates → entry points into the city of Selanna; there are three main gates: (a) the Western Gate, which opens to the road to Stahlgard; (b) the Coastal Gate, which opens to the road to Branström and the coastline running northeast of Selanna; (c) the North Gate, which opens to the road leading past Elks Hill and continuing onward to the Toiva River and—beyond that—to Vuoristad

Gathering→ a celebration, bonfire, and time of worship in cities and towns across Merivalka; Gatherings occurs at the Nave of each season in the main gathering square of a municipality; they consist of the lighting of dasenpfear wood in the parpallo, a time of song, and a reading from the Stories by one who volunteers from among the people

Germund Mustonen→ member of Kaleva's fishing crew (GEHR-mund moo-STOW-nin)

Gheren Nylund→ priestly assistant to, student of, and kinsman of Umlar (GEHR-in NEE-lund)

Gilles→ Kronji soldier serving under Vermeulen's command (GILL-us)

Great Market Road → the main thoroughfare in Selanna, cutting through the central portion of the city

Great Ruin→ the moment when Magnus and Merta disobeyed Lord-Father's command and instead drank from the Dark Pool when tempted by Tuona; both that incident and the disgrace that followed are known as the Great Ruin

Harvestide→ the Merivalkan autumn season

Helene→ Kyrt's wife; suffers from a blood disorder (he-LEEN)

Henrik Reiji→ younger brother of Kaleva (HEN-rik RAY-žee)

Hiiri→ known as the Mouse; one of the major star constellations; though considerably smaller than Kori or Miekammi, Hiiri shines more brightly than any of the *kuvim* in the Merivalkan sky (HEE-ree)

Holy King→ second person of the Supreme Being of Merivalka; uncreated son of Lord Creator

Honeyflax ale→ a sweet, smooth, thicker fermented drink made from bee honey and flax grains

Ilari→ young boy in Selanna; knowledgeable about coinage (i-LAHR-ee)

Ileska Reiji→ mother of Kaleva, Henrik, and Saku Reiji; resident of Kampo (i-LES-kah RAY-žee)

Ilma Linna→ Ivar's wife (ILL-muh LINN-uh)

Iron Bow, The→ public house owned by Olav Halmo; it is the site of Joël's final parable

Ivar Linna→ member of Kaleva's fishing crew; Mirko's brother (EYE-vahr LINN-uh)

Jaarko→ guard who serves with Niilo at Selanna's North Gate (YAR-ko)

Jara Voncanon→ maternal grandmother of Elaenor Nurmi; legendary battle-matron and archer (YAR-eh von-CANN-un)

Jehre Nurmi→ father of Elaenor (YEHR-reh NURR-mee)

Joël → traveler to Selanna who begins working there as a repairman of various broken items (žo-EYL)

Kaleva Reiji→ young man; fisherman; first person in Selanna to whom Joël speaks and the first of his followers (KAL-uh-vuh RAY-žee)

Kampo→ a small settlement north of Stahlgard on the western coast; known for its fishing industry and especially for its eel-chocked waters (KAHM-pō)

Karno→ one of Kyrt's hired hands (KAHR-nō)

Kings' Lane → the chief street running through the western portion of Selanna

Koiri→ known as the Dog; one of the major star constellations in the Merivalkan sky (KOY-ree)

Kopanos→ smaller worship house for weekly worship of Lord Creator; in smaller towns like Gelta, there may be only one kopanos, the *vikarloge*; in larger cities like Stahlgard or Selanna, there may be several to accommodate a larger population (ku-PAHN-nis)

Kralsten→ a term for a nation or people who live under the rule of another nation; it is uncertain how this term developed, but it is not used very often except for official assemblies or written statements (KRAHL-stun)

Kronji→ people of Kronjva (KROHN-žee)

Kronjva→ a coastal nation that has subjugated Merivalka and is the leading kingdom in the Northern Realms; it is sixty nautical miles southwest of Selanna (KROHN-žvah)

Kuvim→ constellations in the sky that can be seen from Merivalka (koo-VEEM)

Kyria Halmo→ young lady; most dedicated female follower of Joël (KEE-ree-yah HAHL-mō)

Kyrt→ farmer who lives several miles outside Selanna; he is the first person to encounter Joël on the latter's travels (KEERT)

Lakihalle→ translates to "hall of law"; seat of government in Selanna and residence of Elbart (LAH-kee-hall-uh)

Lakkaa→ the end of the work day in Merivalka (lah-KAH)

Lars Domi→ a young tailor; injured early on, he recovers (LARZ DŌ-mē)

Lasjen Kulmala→ general of Merivalka's standing army; member of the Council of Nobles (LAS-žin kuhl-MAHL-uh)

Leafbitter→ a type of sharp lettuce, similar to our arugula

Leena Halmo→ Kyria's mother (LEEN-uh HAHL-mō)

Lilja→ woman present at Joël's feeding miracle (LEEL-žuh)

Lord Creator→ Supreme Being of Merivalka; equivalent of the Christian God the Father

Ludvig Reiji→ deceased father of Kaleva, Henrik, and Saku Reiji; well-respected fisherman (LOOD-vig RAY-žee)

Magnus→ first man (MAG-nuss)

Malmfyr→ a cured edition of Merivalkan pinewood; normally used in the construction of a *vikarloge*, malmfyr is made from the stripping of branches from ancient pine trees so that the resin will collect in the main trunk, hardening the pine and making it more durable for building

Martin the Second→ King of Kronjva who conquered Merivalka during his reign forty years before the events of this story

Matleena Reiji→ wife of Henrik (mut-LEEN-uh RAY-žee)

Merivalka→ island nation (Finnish for "White Sea") (mair-uh-VAHL-kuh)

Merkkijo→ an eighteen-stringed harp made from malmfyr wood (mehr-KEE-yoh)

Merta→ first woman (MEHR-tuh)

Messengers→ angels; glorified beings fashioned by Lord Creator

Miekammi→ known as the Swordsman; the largest of the major star constellations in the Merivalkan sky (mee-uh-KAHM-mee)

Mirko Linna→ member of Kaleva's fishing crew; Ivar's brother (MEER-kō LINN-uh)

Myrioi→ the angelic army of thousands under Dalvig's command (MEER-eh-oy)

Nave→ midpoint of mornings and evenings of the Merivalkan day, as well as the midpoint of each season

Niilo→ guard at Selanna's North Gate (NEE-lō)

Nobles→ property owners and members of the upper class of each Merivalkan municipality

Nobles' Lane→ the chief street beginning at the northwestern edge of Selanna and looping toward the Western Gate

Northern Realms → a region of nations and confederations in the White Sea; Kronjva is the strongest nation in the Northern Realms and holds other nations like Merivalka subject in its empire; peoples and tribes such as the Ehrma and Torchers live in various areas of the Northern Realms

Olav Halmo→ Kyria's father (OH-laf HAHL-mō)

Olli→ servant at the Lakihalle (OH-lee)

Osku Virtanen→ wealthy young man who asks Joël about eternal life (OS-koo vur-TAH-nin)

Quartermaster→ transporter of supplies and other items to farms and estates outside of a city which still lie within that city's region; each city has a chief quartermaster who oversees the work of supply distribution and payments

Parpallo→ a fire pit when the dasenpfear wood is lit during the midseason Gathering (par-PAHL-low)

Pavender→ rainbow-scaled fish common to the waters of the White Sea near Merivalka

Pentii Koiviunemi→ owner of the Red Raven public house (PEN-tee koy-vyoo-NEY-mee)

Perttu Domi→ crippled boy; nephew of Lars (pur-TOO DŌ-mē)

Petric Seppänen --> member of Selanna's Council; skeptical but very open-minded about Joël (peh-TRIK suh-PAIN-in)

Pietari→ Alisa's male live-in partner (pee-uh-TAHR-ee)

Rauha Reiji→ wife of Saku (RAU-huh RAY-žee)

Red Raven, The → One of the public houses in Selanna, located in the northwest corner of the city off the Nobles' Lane

Revered Way→ the principles and commandments written by Besno on the Wall of Iniquity surrounding Vuoristad

Rhoken→ Courageous One; a messianic figure predicted in the Stories (RO-kin)

Sakari→ table-servant at the Red Raven public house (sah-KAHR-ee)

Saku Reiji→ youngest brother of Kaleva (SAH-koo RAY-žee)

Sanni Linna→ Mirko's wife (SAH-nee LINN-uh)

Seasons in Merivalka→ Each of four seasons is divided into three parts: Early, High, and Late. Each season roughly corresponds to elements of it. Our spring would be Brightide; summer would be Suntide; autumn is Harvestide; winter is Snowtide. Season portion beginnings correspond roughly with the midpoint of our months. For example, Early Suntide would begin around June 15; High Suntide would begin around July 15 with the Gathering bonfire occurring around July 30th or 31st; Late Suntide would begin around August 15. The midpoint of each season is called the Nave.

Selanna→ capital of Merivalka; port city on its southeast coast; place where Jöel settles and works (seh-LAHN-nuh)

Shadow-Realm→ the dwelling place of Tuona and after-life of those who reject Lord Creator

Sigrid→ daughter of Dagarata (TSIG-rid)

Sivvlaka→ the Dark Pool; located at the base of Vuoristad, its waters supply all of the Merivalkan rivers but the Dark Pool itself is off limits to humanity by the sovereign will of Lord Creator; it is the site of the Great Ruin (siv-LAH-kuh)

Snowtide→ the Merivalkan winter season

Solvik→ one of the Messengers; serves as Dalvig's lieutenant in the *myrioi* (SOHL-vik)

Sotakran→ larger value coin made of white gold; equivalent of one thousand akrans (sow-TAK-run)

Springbuck→ a golden-brown colored wheat; bakers in Selanna tend to toast the grains before making springbuck bread, which has a nutty and bold aroma

Stahlgard → coastal city northwest of Selanna that guards the western maritime approach to Merivalka; hometown of Elaenor Nurmi's mother's clan (SHTAL-gard)

Stories, The→ tales of Merivalka's history and beliefs; these are told and written down by seers who are the mouthpieces of Lord Creator; the Stories are viewed as the inscripturated divine word of Lord Creator

Stroika→ the national game or sport of Merivalka; how it developed is a mystery, but it bears a close resemblance to the Gaelic football of our day (SHTROI-kuh)

Sugarflax ale→ a crisp, lightly sweetened fermented drink, made with three parts flax grain to every one part of plum juice

Suntide→ the Merivalkan summer season

Survanki→ the Great Bear; chief god in the polytheistic pantheon of gods in the Kronji religion (sur-VAHN-kee)

Tarmo→ lieutenant of the guards at Selanna's Coastal Gate (TAHR-mō)

Time→ Though clocks are not a feature of Merivalkan life, time is marked by a general sense of the hours, with following designation: sunrise, morning nave, midday, afternoon nave, *lakkaa* (end of work day), sundown.

Toiva River → the main river that flows through the central portion of Merivalka; its origin is the Dark Pool at Vuoristad

Torchers→ a war-like race who invaded Merivalka after the Ehrma were defeated; the Torchers in turn were decimated by the inspired Merivalkan forces; those Torchers who remained intermarried with several Merivalkans to create the race of the Vale-dwellers

Tuona→ fallen Messenger; chief of the demonic beings; lives in the Shadow-Realm (too-OH-nah)

Umlar Korhonen→ high priest of Selanna; member of Selanna's Council; hostile toward Joël (OOM-lahr kohr-HŌ-nin)

Vale-dwellers→ interbred race of Merivalkans and the Torchers after the latter were repulsed by the Merivalkan defense; they dwell in huts in the wilderness between Stahlgard and Selanna, viewed as castoffs and "half-breeds" by others; they follow a mixed religion of the Stories interwoven with Torcher beliefs

Vermeulen→ a captain in the Kronji guards; sympathetic to Joël (vuhr-MULE-in)

Vikarloge→ translates to "vicar's lodge", serves as the rectory to the priests of Selanna and the chief *kopanos* (there is, by the way, a vikarloge in every town in Merivalka), and also functions as a school building for the children of the city (VEE-kahr-lož)

<u>Vilius Halmo</u>→ young man; fletcher; brother of Kyria; wants to believe the best about her but skeptical about Jöel (VILL-ee-us HAHL-mo)

<u>Vuoristad</u>→ translated as "the Mountain of God"; located near the northwest coast of Merivalka, it is the mountain residence of Lord Creator, the Holy King, the Breath of Lord Creator, and the Messengers; all citizens of Merivalka—indeed all people—are barred from the Mountain due to the shame of the Great Ruin (voo-OR-eh-shtad)

<u>Wall of Iniquity</u>→ edifice of stone twenty feet high and twelve feet thick that bars humans from entry to Vuoristad since the Great Ruin; as an act of Lord Creator's mercy, Besno the seer taught Merivalka during the First Dawn and inscribed the principles of the Revered Way in the Wall itself

<u>White Sea</u>→ ocean that completely surrounds Merivalka

<u>Winter's Liberation</u>→ feast and celebration of victory over the Ehrma; it takes place roughly ten days into Early Snowtide each year

THE GREAT RUIN

From time immemorial, the place was remembered simply as Vuoristad—the Mountain of God.

Known—or rather believed—to be where Lord Creator resided, Vuoristad towered over land and sea on the northwestern wastes of Merivalka. In days gone by, it was said to be many things. It was the rocky spire from which flowed all rivers that ran like silvery fingers through the land. Over rocky terrain, verdant hills, and lush valleys, these tributaries turned into brooks, creeks, and rivulets; some gathered strength over the golden farmland and turned back into rivers as they approached the coasts of Merivalka, against which lapped the waters of the White Sea.

It gave life, this mountain, this peak, one that legend insisted was more ancient than the remainder of that vast island. Indeed, the very soil of Merivalka seemed to be alive. Seers and prophets down through the ages swore that the earth whispered history back to its people, entreating yet warning, hopeful yet mournful.

Yes, the people of the land hoped for more. And yes, they mourned what had passed.

More than that, they mourned the curtain of cloud that wrapped itself around Vuoristad like a grey cloak that looked more like a burial shroud, and for the wall that ringed the Mountain, as well.

They mourned the reason that the cloud and wall existed.

And most of all, they bewailed that—if the Stories were to be believed—their race was the reason for that pillar of gloom and that stone barricade, both of which hid Vuoristad, and Lord Creator, from them.

How could it be that, so soon after the beginning, it came to this?

It was said for years that the time in which the world emerged was like a wedding feast. Indeed, the formation of Merivalka was like the nuptials binding Lord Creator to his children in everlasting joy, said Ahntunen, Seer of the Second Dawn. Lord Creator crafted the universe in stunning detail; no mark of beauty was insignificant. From the mist swirling on the waters surrounding Vuoristad, the ground rose forth, over time sprouting grass, trees, rivers, and hills. In the vast expanse of the heavens, those shimmering ministering spirits known as the Messengers danced and frolicked, and wherever their feet touched, stars emerged in the darkness. Lord Creator flung the burning sun into space, twirled snow from the frost-clouds in the sky, and brought forth animals leaping from the soil of Merivalka itself. And against the swath of the created order appeared Magnus and Merta, the first man and woman.

And there, in the midst of the color, the dervish movements, the laughter, and the joy, a single figure moved amongst the celebrants. The Holy King himself, Son of Lord Creator, swept through the masses of life with smooth and quiet footsteps. His piercing blue eyes and generous smile practically lit up the world as he passed through the albino leopards, sleek dogs, regal reindeer, and snuffling pigs, among others. Touching each creature with his firm yet gentle hands, the Holy King whispered to each one. In response, a sacred light arose in their eyes. Moving through the newly formed pack of souls, the Holy King continued until every single being was blessed, coming at last before Magnus and Merta. With a light stroke of his hands against their cheeks, he also breathed upon them, their hearts quickening to his hallowed exhalation.

The world was glorious for several years after its inception. Magnus and Merta had several children who farmed the land, built sturdy houses and huts, made musical instruments and authored songs, and constructed ships for sailing and the gathering of trout and pavenders in the White Sea. Many evenings, Magnus and Merta would walk hand in hand toward Vuoristad, and they would close their eyes to the warm breeze that enveloped them and listen to the voice of Lord Creator.

It was like a dream that would never end. All was from the hand of Lord Creator for their good and benefit. Nothing was illicit, nothing forbidden from the touch of their hands or their mouths.

Nothing, that is, except the Sivvlaka, the Dark Pool.

The Dark Pool spread itself upon the north side of Vuoristad. The most forceful river, the Toiva, rushed from the eastern end of the Dark Pool, down a rocky crag before plunging into the heart of Merivalka itself. The waters of the Dark Pool itself could mesmerize the unprepared traveler or the ordinary bystander. The waves that lapped against the rocky edge of the pool showed the name itself was no deception; both the surface of the waters and the foam itself looked like a shiny cut onyx.

The mystery was how something like the Dark Pool which was so cimmerian could be that beautiful; the greater mystery was the command from Lord Creator himself, *I grant to you, my treasured creatures, everything in the land and all that stands on Vuoristad. But the waters of the Dark Pool are not given to you for drink, nor shall you touch the surface or foam thereof.*

And why? Both Magnus and Merta asked that question even as they gave full yet quizzical obedience to Lord Creator. The berries from the vines that grew in sight of the Dark Pool were obviously watered by Sivvlaka itself. All that was good in the area of Vuoristad had its genesis from those enigmatic black waters. So why was this reservoir that would refresh any thirst barred from human hands and lips?

All that was required was an answer.

Or a temptation.

Magnus and Merta almost didn't see it, the shadow that crept amongst the beautiful dasenpfear trees that ringed the base of Vuoristad. These wooden guardians, graced with soft white leaves edged in purple, brooded silently as the couple walked in the vicinity of the Dark Pool. The ripples bobbed against its shore as Merta let go of her husband's hand, her head cocked and her eyes staring into the middle distance. The shadow had advanced, cutting the distance to Magnus and Merta in half in a matter of seconds.

The nebulous form nearly glowed against the reflected light from the pool, sending a glossy cobalt tessellation throughout the grotto that Sivvlaka called home. Merta turned toward Magnus.

"What is it, my love?" asked the man.

Merta pointed at the waves near the edge. "Those ripples right here. The ones that do not foam as much as the other waves. It's like they are pulling away from the side, as if they notice us approaching."

"That could be what Lord Creator intended," said the wary yet curious Magnus who came to his wife's side. "Why should the water come any nearer to us? It's as if it knows we're here and doesn't want to provoke us."

Merta stared, her eyes affixed to the surface of the waters. "Almost as if it wanted to return to Lord Creator, or at least closer to the mountain's edge."

"Or perhaps," a voice whispered from the darkness, "it is being pulled back by its Maker even though it desires the hand of another."

Magnus and Merta spun around. The dasenpfear leaves fluttered as a cold breeze whisked through the grotto. "Who is that?" asked Magnus, a film of sweat oozing from his forehead.

"I think the question is 'who are you'?" the voice hissed, a throaty chuckle throbbing in the grotto. "You must be here for a reason, true?"

Merta took a few steps in the direction of the voice, pulling the fabric of her tunic around her neck as a defense against the chill. "We always come here. To meet with Lord Creator."

"If you consider 'meeting' to signify a talk with a being you cannot truly see, a form you cannot clearly discern, a person you cannot relate to," hummed the voice as a tail of steam passed between Merta and Magnus.

The man drew himself up to his full height. "I ask you again ... who are you?"

The voice broke into a series of pops and hisses, as if thousands of bubbles had exploded at once, and the lurid vapors gathered into a pillar that rose between the two humans. "My name should ... ah ... not concern you as much as what I have to share with you. I couldn't help but overhear your question, Magnus, from before."

"And how do you know my name?" Magnus asked defensively.

"Again, not your concern," spoke the cloud, "but the reason why the waters pull back from you should highly interest you both. Perhaps the waters know what you do not, if you would only take and drink."

"We are not to do so!" Magnus barked back.

The cloud turned purple, nearly black, before returning to its cobalt hue as another chuckle burst forth. "Humans, I am trying to save you. But it takes faith. It takes trust in the truth."

The voice paused before continuing. "As you are now, you need not remain any longer. As Lord Creator is, so you may become. But as I said, it takes faith. Open your hearts, my children. Do you not see that Lord Creator has put the truth before you but is satisfied that you be blind to the strength you might have? The All-Knowing One realizes that a drop of the Dark Pool upon your lips means infinite knowledge and wisdom, and a life that will never end."

Merta turned toward her husband and whispered, "Is it possible we were never told? Could this be?"

"Why would Lord Creator have to gain from it?" asked Magnus in desperation, even as the sparkles of Sivvlaka's foam beckoned him to come near.

Merta, too, looked at the lapping waves. "Can we really live with ourselves," she gasped, "if we never know for sure?"

They stepped toward the Dark Pool. In seconds, the blue cloud disappeared; two pairs of hands stretched forth; and on the summit of Vuoristad, time stood still.

Dalvig threw his lance in disgust, storming across the throne-room of Lord Creator Himself. "My Sovereign," he exploded, "I would never accost you for what you decided, but neither I nor my *myrioi* can fathom why we are not riding down Vuoristad and bringing justice upon Merivalka!"

The words, so stinging, so full of heat and anger, boomed in the throne room. They did nothing, however, to cause the Maker of all things to flinch. The unapproachable light enveloping the royal seat pulsed once, then twice, deliberately, before finding voice.

"Justice? My dear Dalvig, what justice do you think is appropriate?"

"The sort that defends the word of Lord Creator Himself! You yourself even said that in the day of which mankind drinks of the waters of the Dark Pool, they shall utterly die."

"So I said."

"You promised they would die."

"So they shall, so they did."

"And yet Tuona has plunged your creation into unspeakable ruin, and the humans live on. Will not the Sovereign of all things do what is right?"

"So I shall, and so I am, Dalvig."

"Then why are my hands and the hands of the *myrioi* restrained? Why does Tuona roam free back to the throes of his Shadow-Realm?"

"Why must it be, Dalvig, that there can only be life or extinction? Why do you think my promise can only be kept if the humans are wiped out?"

"I speak not from bloodthirst, Lord Creator, but because you have promised. And your promises must be kept, and justice must be perfect, or Vuoristad falls and all that is can be no more."

"And the promise will be kept," said Lord Creator with a hint of a rumble in his majestic voice, "and you are right. They *do* deserve everlasting destruction, worse than any can imagine, even you, Dalvig."

Dalvig bowed low before the throne, saying nothing.

"Justice must be done," continued Lord Creator. "In truth, the darkness and ruin sweeping across Merivalka is accomplishing that in devastating measure. No longer shall the race of Magnus know wholeness and perfection on this side of death. No longer shall their farms yield grain in fullest measure. No longer shall their ventures at sea be free from danger or peril. No longer shall commerce be marked by spotless trust and honesty. And no longer shall love and friendship be pure and unstained. All is broken, all is brought to ruin."

"It is over, then," said Dalvig. "Tuona has ruined your world, Lord Creator. It is over."

"No," came the sound of a voice, choking through what seemed like tears, from the window near the corner of the great throne room. It was from this window that one could look out over the entire scope of Merivalka, past the shoreline to the vast expanse of the White Sea. At that window sat one who wept, and who wept bitterly.

"My King," said Dalvig, "why do you refuse to believe all is lost?"

The Holy King, Son of Lord Creator, balled his hands into fists before rising from his seat by the window. So fiercely had he turned his fingers inward that when he drew near to Dalvig, the *myrioi* commander could see bloody scratches in the King's palms.

"Because, Dalvig," the Holy King spoke in a tremulous cadence, "there is another way. In fact, it is the only way it could happen."

It took a moment before the enormity of those words cleaved Dalvig's heart. "My King ... no!" The Messenger turned to Lord Creator and approached the throne with long, flowing strides. "This cannot be!"

The light surrounding Lord Creator pulsed once more. "Dalvig, you are right when you say justice must be done. My world cannot exist without that foundation. But cannot generous mercy flourish alongside stalwart justice?"

Dalvig looked from Lord Creator to his Son, the Holy King. He looked at the hands of the King and saw the scratches; he looked at the King's brow and saw a film of sweat.

"You know what this means, my King," Dalvig whispered hoarsely, his throat dry.

"I know," replied the Holy King, clutching his heart.

Dalvig reached down and picked up his lance from the floor before he looked to Lord Creator. "By your leave, my Sovereign."

"Dalvig," said Lord Creator, "tell the *myrioi* what is to happen. And be assured it is not to happen now, but in the ages to come."

"We wait, my Lord?"

"Yes, until the fullness of time."

Dalvig bowed before the throne. "My Sovereign."

"For grace and kingdom, Dalvig," came the voice of Lord Creator.

Dalvig rose. "For grace and kingdom."

Dalvig bowed once more, slightly, and turned to leave the throne room. As he passed by the Holy King, he placed his hand gently upon his shoulder. He had opened the door to the Great Hall when he suddenly turned around, facing both Lord Creator and his Son.

"Why," the Messenger implored, "do we love them enough to do this?"

The Holy King lifted his face, meeting Dalvig's gaze squarely as his tears splashed to the emerald floor before he spoke his answer. His words were quiet but powerful, resounding throughout that glorious chamber.

"We love them," he declared, "simply because we love them." And he said no more.

THE ARRIVAL

1

The bustle of the market was the lifeblood of Selanna during the High Brightide days. The frigid winter was behind them, and the rains of Early Brightide dissipated as a dream that had run its course. The city center buzzed with energy as a young lady strode past the swerving carts and darted around a horse and rider headed toward the Hall of the Law, known as the Lakihalle. Kyria Halmo looked back at the dappled gray beast, its mane dyed purple to match the rider's livery, which bore the embroidered symbol of the dasenpfear. Looking past them toward the city walls, Kyria noticed the wind had picked up in the past hour, for the banners fluttered stiffly over the crenellated battlements.

Another day, another wind coming in from the White Sea, thought Kyria as she walked past the public house owned by her father. The Iron Bow boasted the finest smoked pavenders in Selanna, with choice ale to boot, and the wares garnered by her father gave their family a comfortable standard of living. Certainly, there was enough discretionary income this month to spend a little more on the leafbitter, beets, and carrots that were splayed across the tables by workers from farmers up to twelve miles away. They normally sent messengers ahead to tell Kyria and her family of their impending arrival, and so Kyria had high expectations of a magnificent collection for the coming days.

In this, she was not disappointed. Not only did she find plenty of the leafbitter alongside the carrots, there were more beets than she assumed would be there, and radishes and onions as well. The family could look forward to plenty of delicious additions to evening stew for days to come. Kyria thanked the farm servants and pressed several akran coins into their hands as payment. Carefully placing the vegetables in her basket, she turned back down the main thoroughfare, back toward the Iron Bow to inquire from her father if he would be working through the entire dinner hour that night. It was then Kyria thought it best she reverse course and stop at her brother's shop instead. Vilius

1

was widely known as the best young fletcher in the city, and between the army's archers and the adventuresome souls who enjoyed a good hunt in the countryside, his establishment was always an industrious one.

But Kyria had no chance to enter in and admire the shafts and feathers that were the pride of Vilius' displays, for her brother was coming through the door into the street. So swiftly did he exit the doorway that he nearly knocked her down.

"Kyria!" he exclaimed. "What are you doing here?"

"Coming to ask if we should expect you at Mother and Father's tonight for dinner," Kyria replied, catching her basket before the container slipped from her grasp. "What's going on? Where are you heading?"

Vilius nodded in the direction of the White Sea. "To the Lakihalle. Elbart is making a proclamation. One of his captains peeked in the shop and let me know. Said that I'd have a natural interest in it."

Kyria lengthened her stride as she followed her brother down the street. She wore breeches, so she had no fear of tripping over her feet in a dress. But Vilius was notorious for covering ground at a maddening rate of speed. Only by breaking into a trot was she able to reach him before they arrived at the courtyard outside the Hall. Whatever the news, it was clear they would be listening from the periphery. A goodly portion the town had arrived. More than seven hundred people swarmed the area, keeping a wide berth around the parpallo, the great pit on the dais where the bonfires were lit at the height of each season in worship of Lord Creator.

Kyria caught a whiff of the local bakeries' activities as she and Vilius waited for the Great Steward and his counselors to come forth. The earthy, inviting smell of rye bread all around made her all the more aware of her own growling stomach. She wondered if her friend Elaenor had several loaves available on her return home. Before she could think further, a flourish of trumpets broke into her ponderings, and the crowd cheered as Elbart Laukanen and his company emerged from the Lakihalle.

The man had been Great Steward for ten years, since the death of his kindly father, Arno. While Arno's warm eyes danced with happiness, Elbart's gaze was continually cordial yet wary. His black, flowing hair was pulled back in the traditional braid for public addresses, and even from where she stood Kyria could make out the ashen streaks that had crept into those well-maintained tresses.

"My citizens!" Elbart's voice carried over the crowd, heard even above the boom of the sea waves. "I have come forth to place before you two matters of great importance! Firstly, I have been in council with the priests of Selanna and we have come to agreement that next week's Gathering of Brightide Nave will proceed with additional public prayer and petition for our nation. This is due to the second matter, one of preparation as a people united at a critical time for our land."

He paused as the assembly waited, then went on. "For forty years, since the days of King Martin, we have lived as those who are kralsten, subjects and tenants to the nation of Kronjva, King Canute, and their Prince Dewulf. In ten weeks, a delegation of Kronji with Dewulf himself will arrive by ship in our harbor. Although we have not found our lack of independence to be an easy thing, I am calling upon our entire citizenry to be gracious and considerate hosts."

"However, this does not mean to be unprepared for the sake of our security. To that end, I am ordering a general mobilization of our standing army to keep the peace. This will mean that our local blacksmiths and fletchers will be required to make a number of weapons to supply for our troops, as we need to enhance our capabilities."

"I must also bear the reminder," Elbert continued, his volume increasing steadily as a murmur ran through the crowd, "that we must look to what is required of us in these days. However, that is not to ignore what has been said in ages past. We as a people, under the yoke of our past yet hopeful for better things, know of the prophecies in the Stories."

Steadying herself, Kyria grabbed her brother's arm. Vilius made no reaction, possibly because he was deep in thought about his newly increased workload and the greater riches he would gain. But Kyria knew he had to be asking the same questions. *Why is Elbert fortifying the army? And why now does he mention the ways of the Faith?*

"The Stories," Elbart went on, "tell us confidently and certainly of the Rhoken who is to come. We do not know the day nor the hour this Courageous One will inhabit our shores, but there can be no doubt that the Rhoken will come at a critical juncture in our life as a people. And our time as subjects under the Kronji ..." Here he stopped for a second, clearing his throat as the crowd stirred with anxiety and hope.

Elbart continued. "It is just such a moment. I am not saying we should look for fulfillment if none exists presently, but we should seek Lord Creator with additional hope this season as we maintain our abiding Faith. Bear this news to your fellow citizens who have not heard the tidings, and may Lord Creator keep you all this day!"

The Great Steward turned, pulling his large, sweeping cloak to himself as he and his counselors marched back toward the Lakihalle. The crowd erupted in conversation and questions almost immediately, some of them calling after Elbart to return. But the doors of the Lakihalle closed behind the Nobles, leaving the throng with their inquiries.

Kyria turned to her brother. "What did that mean?" she pleaded with him.

Vilius shrugged and then stretched. "You're asking the wrong person, Kyria. It does mean, though, that with my increased labors, you shouldn't expect me home early for dinner anytime soon."

2

Two days after Elbart's mysterious proclamation, a traveler appeared out of a mist among a grove of trees, walking southward as the sounds of the Toiva River rumbled behind him to the north. On a clear day, one could almost see the city of Selanna in the distance. The traveler's path wound near some of the finest farms in the area. For a moment he stopped, placing a large heavy cloth satchel on the soft grass. He took a small container and sprinkled his hands with water collected from the Toiva. He proceeded to rub the liquid over his face and neck, which had received their share of the sun. The traveler wore a simple dark green tunic with cream-colored pants and dark boots. With his satchel, he also carried a walking stick as thick as a man's wrist. Looking southwest, he saw several men running wildly through the fields of rye grain, whacking their sticks into the tall stalks at no one in particular. From the strident tones of their raised voices, it appeared they were severely upset.

The traveler decided to leave his path and approach the men in the fields. It was a couple of minutes before he drew near them, but whatever success the men had hoped for, it seemed they hadn't achieved it. They cursed and screamed before throwing down their sticks, one after the other, collapsing in the grain.

One of them—clearly their chief—held up his hand as if to quiet the other two. Whatever it was they listened for, however, was not forthcoming. As the traveler continued to draw abreast of the triad, the leader lowered his hand and nodded welcome.

"Strange journeyman," he said, his red cheeks contrasting with the corn-hued shock of hair on his head. "I bid you welcome. I can only hope you didn't hear the unseemly nature of our words during this chase."

"Think nothing of it, friend," the traveler kindly replied, switching his walking stick from right hand to left and stroking his facial stubble with his free digits. "I was walking by the river when I noticed your chase. Might I be of some help?"

The two helpers looked warily at him before looking back to their master, who smiled with equal parts humor and exasperation. "Karno and Gard were helping me flush out a black hare who has been playing havoc with our crops."

"Miserable bludge keeps makin' off wi' smacks of the spring beans," said one of the servants, who identified himself as Gard. "Won't be any hope a' good wares for market a' this rate. All we ca' hope for is stovin' in their heads."

"Not just one, to be sure," grumbled Karno, running his hand through his sweaty mop of red hair. "Black hares never work alone. We're overwhelmed this season, I'll tell you."

"Do they come around this time of the day," asked the traveler suddenly, "or is there any pattern to their arrival?"

"That's just the thing," the landowner replied. "There's no end to it. Even nighttime brings no respite."

"Mmmm," the traveler hummed, closing his eyes to the breeze floating by. When he opened them, he looked around before suddenly blurting out, "Is this entire plot the extent of your crop?"

"Yes," came the master's response, which affirmed the direction lay toward the east.

"I think there might be a solution," said the traveler, striding toward the cache of spring beans and river sprouts, "but I will need to see the edge of your garden plot."

"Our plot?" replied the other three men, jogging briskly to keep up with the traveler's flowing steps. They wanted to ask him what made him an authority on the activities of black hares on Merivalkan farms, but something held their tongues.

They had arrived at the edge of the garden, which was barricaded by a wooden fence. "As you can see," said the master, "there is a barrier, but those hares find a way under or through it. Any help is welcome, although I don't know what you can tell us that we don't already know."

"Well, there is one thing," the traveler said, handing off his walking stick to Karno and stepping toward the rye fields that surrounded the property. "We have all these stalks of rye grain that can be put to good use." He pointed to the obsidian soil. "The hares are coming in over the soil, and the soil itself is disguising their movements. What you need is a way to mark their steps. Black hares fear several things, but one is when they know they can be found out."

"An' how ca' we do that?" asked Gard.

The traveler pulled several heads of rye off a nearby stalk into his hands. Rubbing them vigorously, he knelt and spread a fine dust of crushed grain on the soil surface. The powdery material looked practically white against the coal-like ground.

"Come on," said the master, and he, Karno, and Gard began pulling stalks and crushing grains in their fingers for the next twenty minutes until a line of pulverized rye dust stretched for yards in a line parallel to the garden. The four men then stole back around the corner of the fence and waited.

"Now is the hard part," said Karno.

The landowner tapped the traveler on the shoulder and whispered, not wanting to give away their position to any nearby animals. "By the way, how do you know this will work on black hares?"

The traveler winked, a mischievous sparkle in his eye. "You wouldn't believe me if I told you."

It was ten more minutes before they heard a rustle in the rye field and suddenly a large male black hare poked his nose through the stalks. Seeing no impediment to a good theft of spring beans, the creature stole across the soil bed with the vegetables in sight. So focused was the hare on the prize that he never saw the line of grain powder below. Slipping as the crushed rye appeared underfoot, he scrambled and stumbled over his own paws, clearly alarmed by his lack of footing and that every step was now marked by a whitish print. Forgetting his hunger, the hare darted back into the fields as if he had seen a vision of death.

The farmers charged out from behind the fence, whooping with joy. The master clapped the traveler on the back and pumped his hand with gratitude.

"My thanks to you, sir!" he gushed, grinning from ear to ear. "Is that a trick for all black hares?"

"Indeed," replied the traveler, fingering his walking stick and pulling his satchel over his shoulder. "They find it impossible to find their footing with fine grain on their feet, and they instinctively dislike having their steps marked. Black hares depend on stealth, and since that one knows he is watched, I doubt he'll bother you much longer."

"Well, I am grateful for your help, and I apologize for not trusting you initially. Please allow me to introduce myself. I am Kyrt. And seeing that you appear to be on a long journey, could I trouble you to come to dinner and stay with us for the night as a show of hospitality and thanks?"

"I do not want to trouble you," replied the traveler. "It would be just for a night. I intend to reach Selanna by evening tomorrow."

"Are you travelin' there?" asked Gard.

"I desire to dwell there."

It was Karno who spoke next. "Doing what?"

"Being useful, in whatever capacity."

Kyrt scratched his head in amazement and confusion. "Going to Selanna. Knowing mysterious truths about the habits of black hares. And you just happened to appear from over the hill to the north." He laughed heartily. "Where exactly are you from?"

The traveler smiled and shrugged. "As with the hares and the rye, you probably wouldn't believe me if I told you."

"Being as that may," declared Kyrt, "you are most welcome here." He extended his hand to the traveler and gripped it strongly. "At the very least, may I know your name?"

"That I can tell you," the traveler responded, his clasp just as firm. "My name is Joël."

3

The harbor of Selanna was arguably the busiest place imaginable following the proclamation of Elbart from three days before. As the stiff wind buffeted the shipyard, builders, fishermen, and apprentices alike scrambled to ensure that no material went flying around. Just a month before, a storm gust tipped over a newly constructed mast that toppled onto a young tailor selling his material at the docks. Lars survived the blow but sustained numerous injuries. He had just been released from the city infirmary.

The loosely bound sails fluttered before the wind's assault, but the weather-hardened men of the docks pressed on with their daily routines. On the far corner of the harbor, in the formidable shadow of the West Tower, a fisherman tugged at the nets on the pier, lifting and twisting them in his arms before tossing the gnarled pile into the boat. Stretching after his labor, the man smoothed the long sleeves of his wool overshirt. Normally in Selanna, the High Brightide days meant an increase in warmer temperatures, but the ocean gale only brought cold and wet to those by the waters. For his sake, Kaleva Reiji was only too happy to layer his clothing as a buffer against the damp chill.

His brothers drew near. Henrik and Saku were soaking wet from the recent foray onto the White Sea, but any irritation they felt was stayed by the fact that their morning haul of fish was exceptionally generous. It had taken their group much time to clean and mend the nets, but these labors were worth every coin they'd earn. It made waking up before dawn and heading out to sea just after first hour a sacrifice they were willing to offer time and again.

Saku jumped from the pier onto the deck plank, bearing tin buckets in both hands. He deposited them in a storage trunk by the ship's wheel before turning around and repeating the process with the other buckets. Henrik drew out a stack of paper from a pouch and looked over some things he had written. "This is quite good," he said, eyebrows raised. "I think our work this month has turned quite the profit if our normal buyers continue stockpiling our haul."

Kaleva had lain supine on the pier, placing his hands in the water to free them from the residue of the nets. He lifted his head, gulping in the marine air before pushing off and standing on his feet.

"Thanks be to Vuoristad," Kaleva smiled, rubbing his hands from the salty fluid. "More delectable feasts, sturdy clothes, and well-cobbled shoes for your wives!"

"That is hardly the work of the Mountain," said the dubious Henrik. "But it should be several weeks of living well and not fretting over our basic needs."

"Kaleva never has to worry," Saku quipped, "for such is the life of a bachelor soul. I say we have an additional assignment for the Gathering of Brightide Nave."

"Our brother speaks the truth, Kaleva," Henrik added.

Kaleva waved them off impatiently as he jumped onto the deck and pulled the nets to the stern of the boat. "Our brother speaks of anxiety, dear Henrik. Neither of you are, in any way, playing matchmaker for me at the Midnight Promenade."

"Matchmaker is beyond our vocation, Kaleva," replied Henrik.

"It is our wives of whom we speak," continued Saku, "for they have that way of women, the talent and knack to find you a comely maiden of noble character. A wife to share your bed for life. A true love."

"This ship at sea is my one true love these days, Saku," Kaleva shot back, his nose wrinkling. "But I know you will not shutter your hopes, so by all means wear out your wives with another mission. If only you were more meticulous with bathing once in a while."

"Ho, there! You in the boat!"

Kaleva turned from his brothers in the direction of the voice. A man of medium height, light brown hair, and a set of curious blue eyes waved toward Kaleva from the thoroughfare that ran parallel to the docks. Clad in a black tunic with grey pants, he grasped a walking stick in his hand. Kaleva peered down at him, desperate to recognize the individual but failing to do so.

"I see you, sir," Kaleva called down. "How can we help you?"

"I have just arrived here in Selanna from some distance away. It is my first day in the city and I had some questions about how to get around."

Kaleva's brow furrowed. It was unusual for Selanna to attract new travelers. And while the population of the town was cordial with one another, it was odd to have someone so cheery and sure of himself come here in their midst. Shaking himself free of these questions, Kaleva shouted down, "One moment, traveler, and I'll come down."

In a few seconds, Kaleva had joined Henrik and Saku, who also drew near the stranger.

"I should explain," the newcomer said. "I have come here to dwell for some time and so that means looking for a place to live and work. I can see this city is quite industrious, but surely you could tell me the best way to get started. Is there someone to speak to about a building where I might live and work a trade?"

Kaleva looked sideways at his brothers before answering. "Well, if your desire is to live here, the place to get started is right over there." He pointed one block away, to a two-storied building with high-pitched roofs. "There is the Lakihalle, of course. There is one on the Council of Nobles, Dirnik by name, who oversees land transactions, business leases, and the like. He would be the one to meet with if you are looking for a place to establish commerce."

"Thank you," said the traveler. "That is most helpful."

"As a matter of interest," Henrik said loudly, "what is it you were thinking of doing?"

The newcomer appraised Henrik with a kind yet penetrating eye. "I have a number of interests and constructive abilities. It is likely most proper to see what the greatest need of the people might be."

"You believe that if you establish a shop of some kind, that people will come to you?" asked Saku.

"Forgive my brother," Kaleva said, putting up a hand, "but you must understand our slight bewilderment. Normally, visitors to Selanna come by sea, as part of a royal delegation or on a trading ship. From the looks of your walking stick, you haven't come by sea. From the way you're dressed, it's clear you don't wear the traditional garments of Stahlgard, Gelta, Marvik, Branström, or any of the smaller villages I'm aware of. This makes you somewhat of a mystery. And yet you've come here to Selanna wanting to dwell in the city and make your living."

"One has to eat and sleep somewhere," the newcomer replied.

"I'll grant you that, sir," Kaleva replied, "but you understand my concern. I'm not anxious for the safety of the city folk, for you carry no weapon and have no look of spy or enemy about you. My worry is that you come here out of nowhere, it seems. I'll just say that the Selannan citizens will be asking questions."

"A man comes here from nowhere," said Henrik, "means he is running away from something, or has no other choice, or is here for a reason that would baffle everyone."

The stranger smiled and nodded, looking down while leaning on his walking stick before straightening up to face them again. "Or maybe it's a baffling choice that will keep others from running away from something."

The three brothers recoiled from the cryptic yet powerfully spoken words. "What did you say?" Kaleva asked.

"Never mind," replied the traveler. "It was just something that came to mind. I thank you for your help. My name, by the way, is Joël." And here he extended his hand with a searching look.

It suddenly occurred to Kaleva this was more than a show of gratitude, and before he could help himself the words came unbidden. "Kaleva. I am Kaleva."

Henrik and Saku gave Joël their names before bidding him well. And with a tip of his walking stick, Joël turned and ambled slowly up the street toward the Lakihalle.

4

For centuries, citizens of Selanna and its surrounding vicinity were content to be governed by the Council of Nobles, of whom one held the prime position of Great Steward. Elbart was not known for an organized regimen of Council meetings, but the recent news that Prince Dewulf and the Kronji would be arriving soon served as a catalyst for more conciliar discussion. The Council met in the central chamber, where the men sat on chairs keystoned by the Steward's Chair. Elbart listened with deep concentration to the fervent entreaties of Lasjen, the general of the army of Merivalka, as the experienced soldier outlined the initial progress of the increased armaments and the fortifications of the three major battlements. As Lasjen ended his detailed report, Dirnik Vanhanen rose and swept to the center of the room. He held no notes in his hand. His memory was such that he rarely spoke with a page of facts in front of him, although many of his detractors believed Dirnik made up the facts as he went along.

"Fellow Councilmen," Dirnik began, "We as a city have little more than two months to prepare for the arrival of Prince Dewulf and the Kronji delegation. As you well have heard from Lasjen's account, the mood of our citizens as this day approaches is of utmost concern. He has rightly declared that the spirit of our people—given a more highly armed force—could be more defensive and grim in nature. This might be at the core of people's hearts, but we must be careful to publicly project a warm and welcoming spirit to our visitors. To that end, I have proposed to the Great Steward that the Grand Market Road be refurbished and decorated at all speed. All shops should bear tapestries and banners of festive colors. Although it would be difficult to have all things put forth in crisply coordinated fashion, I believe that what matters is the presentation of a vibrant city center, bustling with commerce and full of life."

One of the Councilmen, Petric Seppänen by name, raised his hand. "Dirnik, is this just to be on the Great Market Road or should we expect other shops to participate?"

"I was thinking the main lane, Petric."

"But to commit to only one avenue of the city risks much," replied Petric. "The Kronji delegation will certainly wonder why other shops lack for decoration. I know it is a considerable burden in both time and cost to expand the adornments, but shouldn't we commit to one side or another and not merely settle halfway?"

"You mean the mill and the brewery along the river? The mercantile near the *vikarloge*? Your own establishment?" Dirnik kept his frustration in check, but he couldn't help feeling miffed at Petric's deliberations.

"Certainly the questions of a tin merchant—one whose family has a sustained place in the history of Selanna—merit some consideration, Dirnik?"

Dirnik cast a glance at Elbart, who rose from his seat as if to address Petric. Before anyone could offer support or protest, however, the door to the central chamber opened wide, its hinges creaking at the speed of their dislodging. Striding resolutely into the chamber came a stranger wearing clothes none there could identify, gripping a walking stick and catching Elbart in his line of sight with his piercing eyes.

"I appear to have startled all of you," the stranger uttered, taking a satchel from his shoulder and placing it on the ground, nodding toward Elbart. "I apologize for the interruption, as it seems to have broken the conversation amongst you, so I'll be brief. My name is Joël, and I have traveled a great distance to come here and dwell in Selanna. How long I will remain is anyone's guess. I can assure you that it is urgent I not only find a residence to rest my head at night, but I must also locate a place to set up a business."

Dirnik, clearly upset that Joël had barged in, stepped forward. He slowed his breathing as he approached Joël, not wanting this intruder to notice his frustration.

"Your presence here is fraught with mystery and intrigue, O traveler," the nobleman said frankly in the well-lit hall. "You wear gear more attuned for sojourning than working, and your clothes bear the crest of no other city in Merivalka. Those truths by themselves raise enough suspicion. You come here wanting to settle in Selanna, but how do we know you are a friend of Selanna, or of Merivalka, for that matter? And what trade would you take up? What is your skill? What are your habits? And most importantly, from where do you come?"

"A man of many questions," replied Joël, reaching into his satchel. "I admire that. Surely your faith in Lord Creator must be great to speak so boldly in the world He has fashioned."

"Hold, stranger," Dirnik ordered, holding out a stiff palm. "Before you reach in the satchel, our guards will come forward and search it. I realize you probably got past the platoon outside but we must be doubly sure." He gestured for two soldiers to come forward, and one of them grabbed the bag and began rifling through its contents.

"My question," declared Elbart, as he descended from the Steward's chair on the dais, "is why this bludge speaks so forthrightly and confidently in our presence. Sir, you stride into our hall with questions, when it is we who must grant permission for entry. At best, your regalia, if you can call it that, exhibits no loyalty to Merivalka. And your declaration of Dirnik's belief betrays a confidence in the Faith that must be tempered with more humility. You seriously cannot believe we would feel no reservation to one who displays no genesis to his person, no rationale to his beliefs, and yet practically demands dwelling and citizen benefits of labor. So to help us define how we might choose, Joël, where are you from?"

"O Steward," one of the soldiers said, "there is a crust of bread, some spring beans, and a bag of akrans within."

"I see," said Elbart. "Traveling, eating, and spending. Tell me, stranger, from where to you get these possessions?"

"I don't think you'd believe me," replied Joël with a resigned smile.

15

"The granting of your request may rest upon your conduct in heeding our own."

"In fact," said Joël, "you will find the information impossible to believe. Not all will, but you will. It is enough to know that I come with every intention of being a peaceful inhabitant of this city. Because it is right that everyone work for his bread and seek the good of the city, I wish to set down productive roots at this time. The location in Selanna is immaterial. It is enough to be among the people of this city and this land and to engage in productive commerce. As I walked through the city, I noticed several vacant shops—not many, mind you, but several—that merely need a proprietor enter in, refurbish the interior, and set about with diligence whatever the future brings."

"You speak boldly, Joël," said Petric, stroking his beard with an air of curiosity rather than defiance. "How did you know to come here and speak your request?"

Joël lifted his walking stick and set it across his shoulders. "For that, I must give thanks to Kaleva, the young man down at the ship docks who was kind enough to recommend Dirnik to me for this endeavor. To be fair, he was somewhat suspicious as well, given my arrival and ensemble. But in the end, he was most helpful and kind."

Petric looked at Dirnik. "Well, sir, this is your area of expertise."

Dirnik swallowed hard. He had no desire to see his previous monologue derailed by this intrusion, but the sooner he was rid of Joël, the better. "Very well, stranger. Did you have a particular location in mind?"

"There are two or three that are rather large and spacious," replied Joël, "but the interior area would be too much for my meager needs. I did have my eye on the small tucked-in shop off the corner near the East Tower. The one painted rich brown with red trim around the windows, on the Avenue of the Commonwealth?"

"For being a new arrival, you seem to be familiar with your surroundings," muttered Dirnik.

16

Joël shrugged. "I was merely trying to pay attention as closely as possible."

"That is hardly the best part of town, sir," said Petric. "Surely you would be able to profit from a more advantageous location."

"And this is hardly the time to bring that up," hissed Dirnik, as Elbart shot a warning look at Petric.

Joël held up his hand. "Making a profit is not my agenda. Surely one can utilize the gifts and abilities that Lord Creator bestows without money being the primary goal. If I can live, serve, and offer myself to those around me, shouldn't that be enough?"

"And in what way would you 'offer' yourself to the people?" Elbart pressed him, drawing near and positioning himself two feet from Joël. "What unique trade would you propose that could make you stand out within the bustling enterprise that is this fair city?"

Joël said nothing at first, content to lock eyes with the Great Steward for several moments. When he spoke, he moved past Elbart, barely brushing his arm, and stood within the throng of nobles. "It occurs to me that while there is much that is made, created, and constructed, there are many among those creations that become broken or decayed. And while it might be tempting to do away with tattered curtains or broken chairs or chipped pottery, not everyone can afford new items. No, I think what is in order is a place where people can come in, pay whatever they think they are able, and have such an item repaired. Surely there is a place for that."

"Repairing broken furniture?" Dirnik spluttered. "Chipped pots? Torn fabric? Are you mad?"

"I have a feeling you'll be asking that final question many more times over the coming months, sir," replied Joël, not even looking at Dirnik. "But that is what I intend to do. And I do not consider it madness but mercy. For how does this world have any hope unless we believe that Lord Creator himself will make what is broken and ruined new again?"

"And what does a traveler from afar, from an unknown place, know about the Faith?" a voice rose from the chair next to Petric's. The white-robed figure from whom that question had come darted across the space until he too was face-to-face with Joël. "You come here to ply a trade unheard of, and you justify it with words of the Faith, practically tying it to the Great Ruin and the hope we wait for as a people? Could you possibly be any more flippant in your reasoning?"

Joël said nothing in response, merely tilting his head to the side and looking at Petric.

Petric coughed and said, "This is Umlar Korhonen, the high priest of Selanna."

Fixing Umlar with a rigorous stare, Joël brought his walking stick to his side. "Respected one, I speak not out of disdain but on behalf of the truth. Surely one would expect that if Lord Creator will bring deliverance, then that restoration encompasses all things. And certainly we could see that renewal even in the small places and the ordinary patches of our days. Why would I be in error to view this humble work as the activity of Lord Creator writ small?"

Umlar's eyes flashed, but when he opened his mouth to respond he could not find voice for his objection. Looking around confusedly, he saw the same disbelief on the faces of Elbart and Dirnik. Only Petric, it seemed, bore a look even approaching agreement.

"Not to force the issue," continued Joël, "but I desire to begin my labors as soon as I can. So may we settle matters for the shop here today?"

Dirnik rubbed his hands together as if anticipating a negotiation battle. "There is no direct owner of that property of which you speak, stranger. The blacksmith who worked there died three years ago and the family sold the structure to the Council. Any negotiations must go through us."

Elbart nodded. "And as we have much to debate today as a Council, it would be wise to wait until we are finished."

Placing his walking stick on the floor at his feet, Joël opened his satchel. "I think we can arrive at a settlement, men. You get your money; I get a chance to be a dweller and producer amongst you. Name the price."

Dirnik and Elbart shared a brief glance before Elbart gestured that Dirnik make the first offer. Joël's weatherworn tunic did not give a flattering picture of his accrued sustenance, nor did the paltry bag of *akrans* within his satchel give them much hope of Joël's chances.

"Twenty sotakrans," Dirnik demanded as the noblemen, minus Petric, grinned broadly. "The family received ten sotakrans from the Council's treasury, and it has sat unused. If you wish to not buy it at that price, I am certain there are others …"

He never got a chance to complete the sentence. Joël reached into an inner pouch of his satchel notched with four buttons. Pulling thirty white gold coins from the hidden cavity, he placed them in Dirnik's hands as the open-mouthed nobleman watched with a glassy, bewildered look.

"Thirty sotakrans," declared Joël as he picked up his stick. The equivalent of thirty thousand akrans, I assume. Twenty coins for the full price of the shop, with ten more as an affirmation of good faith regarding my intentions among the citizens of Selanna. By your leave, I'll take possession of the shop now, if none of you mind."

Silence reigned in the hall except for Petric, who stepped forward with a sweep of his hand. "By a good will, sir, I will be happy to see you to your new abode."

The two of them, noble and traveler, left together. The doors closed behind them and, as if the sound released the tension in the room, the Council immediately broke into worrisome chatter. Elbart took Dirnik by the arm and drew him toward the south wall.

"This is indeed a troubling thing," the Great Steward whispered stridently.

"What was I supposed to do?" Dirnik pled, frowning and looking down upon the mysterious pile of coinage in his fingers. "Expel him for daring to pay a time and a half what we demanded, three times as much as what Pentus' family gave us?"

"It's not the money, but the mystery," said Elbart. "He might appear harmless, but until we know more about this Joël, I say we be more circumspect in our actions toward this man. Recall that none of us truly know where he is from or what his long-term plans are."

"So the welcome you suggest, sir," replied Dirnik, "is more restraint than open hand."

"For more than just him," the Great Steward mumbled before he found his voice and reconvened the Council to order.

5

This day, thought Elaenor Nurmi, promised a slew of sales and activity that would see no break. Kyria had mentioned she would be there late afternoon, requiring seven loaves of rye bread as her grandparents would be eating with them this evening. *Grandparents,* Elaenor thought, brushing a tear from her eye. That entire generation of the Nurmi family had perished before Elaenor's tenth birthday. For the last nine years, Elaenor's parents had been the eldest members of their extended clan. Her father's parents had died when Elaenor was six. Poppa Nurmi had developed pleurisy during the Snowtide months and perished before he could see another Early Brightide or his sixtieth birthday. Mamma Nurmi had followed him nine months later, although the family never discussed if it was illness, a broken heart, or matters that Mamma took into her own hand.

Elaenor's mother's side of the family had hung on longer, surprising given the colorful, swashbuckling nature of the Voncanon tribe. Elaenor's mother had grown up in the lookout point of Stahlgard, where Poppa Voncanon had been a commodore of the naval fleet there. It was in the last rebellion that he had lost his life at sea in a legendary and tragic defeat to Prince Dewulf's armada. Mamma Voncanon was no less hardy. After joining the Nurmi family in Selanna during her husband's fatal excursion, the Voncanon matriarch had taken to the battlements when Dewulf's ships invaded Selanna Harbor. For two days, her sixty-four-year-old arms tirelessly sent arrow after arrow hurtling toward oncoming Kronji forces with remarkable accuracy. It took a Kronji swordsman to scale the side of the West Tower and cut her down. So great was Jara Voncanon's bravery that the vanquished Selanna forces sang a lament for her soul at the Gathering of Harvestide Nave two weeks later.

Tearing herself away from the memories of the past, Elaenor accepted the akrans from several customers for the orders of loaves they had purchased. Kyria entered the door and waved at Elaenor, who returned the greeting with a weary smile.

"Nice to be extraordinarily busy," Kyria quipped as more customers clamored for rolls and loaves. "Need any help?"

"Thank you," replied Elaenor, as she wiped her hands on her apron. "The arrival of Prince Dewulf and the push for more cheery business has done its work. Listen, Father just got a tray of fresh bread out of the oven and we have no room on this cooling board. Can you take some of these loaves and place them on the low-table by the window?"

"Gladly," said Kyria with a shake of her head, scooping up a half-dozen rye loaves and taking them toward the window. Several passersby waved their greetings to her and she nodded back. Her attention to their greeting, however, distracted her long enough to miscalculate the distance to the table, and she accidentally kicked one of the legs. The loaves fell out of her hands onto the table, which collapsed to one corner as the struck leg snapped in half and crumpled.

Kyria froze, aghast at her clumsiness and embarrassed this should happen in her best friend's shop. Jehre Nurmi came charging out of the oven-room, past the chagrined Elaenor, when he saw the red-faced Kyria holding only one of the six loaves she had meant to transport to the hamstrung table.

"I'm ... I'm sorry, sir," Kyria whispered, wide-eyed with the blood pooling in her face. "I accidentally kicked the leg, and ..."

Jehre waved off her apology. "Think nothing of it, Kyria," he said. "It's an old table that I bought years ago. I'll have to find a new one, but it shouldn't be much trouble." He looked up from the table as a customer, dressed in a royal blue tunic with tan breeches, opened the door to the shop and entered in. "Greetings, sir."

"A good afternoon to you, as well," said the customer. "I was wondering if I could purchase some bread to have with dinner this evening."

"You most certainly may," declared Jehre, gesturing toward the cooling board at the sales counter. "Those loaves have just been pulled out of the oven, a mixture of white bread and rye. My daughter Elaenor can assist you."

"And what of these?" asked the man, pointing to the floor and the loaves next to the capsized table.

"That would be my fault," Kyria muttered sheepishly, kneeling by the fractured table leg and scooping bread into her hands. "My clumsiness."

"Kyria," Jehre responded soothingly, "I told you not to worry. We can get another table placed there."

"If you don't mind," said the customer, placing his walking stick aside and kneeling on the floor along with Kyria, "did you mean this leg here?" He ran his finger along the grain of the wood on the snapped piece.

Jehre looked more closely and Elaenor came from behind the counter. The leg had both snapped and angulated; the break was not a clean one.

"As I said," Jehre reminded, "we can always put another one in here. The wood is very soft."

"It's pine, is it not?" asked the customer, his eyes going from the table to Jehre. "Raw pine instead of malmfyr? Soft enough where the break is. Less than ideal but not so bad as to stay beyond repair." He stood up and offered his hand to Jehre. "Allow me to introduce myself. My name is Joël, and I have recently moved into the old shop on the Avenue of the Commonwealth, by the East Tower. I repair items of any sort, and with your permission I would love to make an attempt with this table."

Jehre looked at Kyria and Elaenor. "I'm happy that you'd desire to do so, Joël, but the table needs replaced, not fixed."

"All the same, I do have materials at the shop by which I can at least try," replied Joël. "If I can get this table to my shop this evening, I can work on it tonight, allow it to dry, and then return it tomorrow."

Jehre, stunned at Joël's confidence, hesitated briefly before nodding his assent. "Good sir, if you truly believe it can be done, then by all means I will grant you that opportunity." Wiping his hands on his apron, he continued, "I should ask, do you need help carrying it?"

"I should be able to handle it by myself," replied Joël, "although I'd need to return for my stick and satchel."

"You shouldn't have to do that," Kyria blurted out, her recent stumble suddenly forgotten. Eager to help, she approached the two men. "I can carry the stick and satchel if you wish to carry the table."

Jehre rubbed his hands together. "This has turned out to be quite the event. I, for one, am looking forward to seeing your handiwork, sir." He gestured to his daughter. "Elaenor, why don't you accompany them and carry along a pair of loaves? Joël," he said, placing his hand kindly on the man's shoulder, "please accept this bread as a down payment of thanks. If you are going by the shipyard, chances are Elaenor can buy some fish for you to have with the bread for dinner tonight. That is, provided your stove is in working order."

"You are most kind, Jehre," said Joël, clasping his hand. "Expect the table back here tomorrow, good as new."

"I have to say, Kaleva had a beautiful supply of pavenders this evening," Joël remarked as he lit the fire in the stove. "Your father was right to send us by the harbor."

Elaenor smiled as she laid the bread on the table in Joël's kitchen while Kyria set the walking stick and satchel by a chair in the corner. The maidens looked about the shop, which had a rather austere feel to it. Joël had laid the table by the north wall, which bore a series of hooks and bags hanging over a compilation of buckets and boxes.

"For having recently arrived here, you've been busy collecting what you need," Kyria noted aloud.

"Some nails, a chisel or two, and other odds and ends," replied Joël warmly, "although I won't be needing that." He looked carefully at the splintered table leg and ran his finger across the runes of the wood. "I believe this will work. Kyria, Elaenor, could you help me?"

"We'd be glad to," the pair echoed, startling each other.

24

"There is a pile of leafbitter there in the kitchen, along with an old iron pan left behind by whomever lived here before. I am going quickly to the harbor. I'll be right back. In the meantime, there is plenty of wood sitting on the back porch. So, once you manage to get the stove heated up, place the leafbitter in the pan. After the leafbitter simmers for a bit, it will of course produce a pale green oil. When there is enough oil to fill this cup," and here he pointed to a mug on the kitchen table, "take the pan off the stove and pour the oil into it. Leave the wood burning, of course, and if I'm not back yet, please begin to fry the fish in the pan with the remaining leafbitter. I'll eat the fish after I'm finished with the table."

"Whatever are you going to the harbor for?" asked Elaenor as Joël stole away from the house into the twilight.

If the ladies had not seen it with their own eyes, they would not have believed it possible. Joël returned in five minutes with a handful of mud from the shoreline, which he deposited into the mug of leafbitter oil. After wiping his hands somewhat clean on a towel, he took a small wooden stick and whisked the contents together to make a paste.

"How did you know that would work?" asked Kyria, amazed, as Joël procured a brush from a bag on the wall.

"The saltwater from the White Sea mixes with the mud by the shoreline, and that salty mire has a way of blending with leafbitter oil." He brushed the paste into the damaged table leg, pushing it into the gaps and then smoothing it over the runes. "When used as a paste, it will adhere to wood and expand to fill the empty and splintered spaces. It should dry and be as strong as if one fastened the leg with a nail."

"Why is it no one knew this in the entire city?" gasped Elaenor.

"In truth?" Joël responded as he wiped his hands again on the towel. "What do you normally do when you have damaged goods?"

The young ladies looked at each other and shrugged. "Normally," said Kyria at last, "we build something new and throw what is broken away."

"Why?"

25

"What do you mean, why?"

"Why do you throw it away, Kyria?" Joël pressed as he tossed the towel into a wooden pail.

Kyria's heart trembled, her voice catching for a moment. "Isn't it obvious? Because they are broken."

"And because they are broken, does that mean they must remain broken?"

"It's just a table, Joël," Elaenor offered, defending her friend.

"Just as Merivalka is just an island?" Joël countered. "Just as humans are just humans? Because something is broken, must it stay that way?"

Kyria looked down at her hands. "Merivalka, Selanna, people. Those are different from a table. If we are broken, even if only in spirit, isn't hope something we must wait for? Isn't that what we've always been taught?"

Joël smiled warmly and walked toward her. "Would you wait for it if you had to? What if you could approach it yourself?"

"For someone who seems so wise and insightful," she said quizzically, "you seem to forget we cannot approach Lord Creator. We as a people are barred from the Mountain, and we cannot go there."

"That you cannot deny," Elaenor piped.

"I do not deny it," said Joël. "You cannot go to Vuoristad. But why would hope depend solely on your movement to Vuoristad? Could not hope draw near to you?"

Something in Joël's voice struck deeply within Kyria's heart. She looked at Elaenor and saw her friend felt the same. A shaft of hope, mixed with both warmth and worry, pierced her soul. When she looked back at Joël, he rubbed his eyes and waved his hand.

"Well, I know that you came here for anything but a lecture. I've kept you too long. I am sure you have other places to be, like dinner with your families. Elaenor, please thank your father for the bread and tell him I'll return the table in the morning. Kyria, thank you for frying the fish. It will make for a delicious supper."

Kyria and Elaenor said their goodbyes and moved toward the door, Kyria remembering she was due home for dinner. "Thank you, Joël. And I apologize if I was inappropriate in my response."

"Think nothing of it," Joël replied before closing the door. "I am sure we'll have more things to speak of in the days ahead."

The next morning, Jehre entered the door of his bakery. His wife had gone ahead of him to heat up the ovens, so he wasn't surprised to see the door unlocked. What did give him a pleasant shock was the sight of the old table back in its place. Laid on top of it was a note on parchment:

My friend Jehre,

Thank you very much for the delicious bread. I shall most certainly return for more in the coming days. I trust the table will be as strong and sturdy as ever. No charge at all for the repair. Your kindness in giving the bread was enough.

Joël

6

The next night brought stiff winds blowing over Selanna's harbor into the center of the city. With some difficulty, Vilius Halmo opened the door of his fletching shop and closed it carefully behind him, easing it shut as he braced it against the gale with his hand. Threading the hook-pin through the avalukk holes, he joined the ends of the hook together with the guide piece, turning it to a locked position with the indention in his ring. His stomach rumbled, but Vilius sensed a hunger that went beyond food, a thirst that superseded drink. Tonight he needed to remind himself of what he deemed important.

Turning westward, he moved away from the area of the Lakihalle and made for the tower near the Western Gate. While most citizens preferred the majestic view from the Coastal Gate or traveling though the North Gate to the countryside, Vilius had sentimental reasons for wanting to peer out from the Western Gate. So deep in though was he that he did not see the man turn the corner in front of him, walking stick in hand.

"Excuse me, sir!" exclaimed Vilius, perturbed by the near-collision and by the intrusion of his thoughts. "You seemed to be hurrying though!"

The man lifted his head, displaying a kind set of eyes and a forgiving smile toward Vilius' cry. The flickering flame from the lane-lamp above illuminated both faces when the man nodded suddenly.

"I am truly sorry, my friend," he replied. "I was returning from a dinner at the Foundryman and decided to take a circuitous route back to my shop. I apologize if I detained you from your destination."

"I suppose it's nothing to worry about," Vilius relented, his voice less strident. "It's not as if the streets are bustling after sundown. I happened to be working late, so I'm surprised to find anyone out at this hour."

"Because of preparations?" asked his counterpart.

"For Brightide Nave tomorrow?" Vilius asked. "Maybe, although that wasn't my concern."

The man's smile broadened. "I think I may know why you are! Are you by any chance related to Kyria?"

Shocked by the stranger's powers of recognition, Vilius nodded slowly, warily. "I am." He extended his hand cautiously. "Vilius Halmo. Kyria is my younger sister by five years. How do you know her? And how did you know me?"

The stranger shook his hand. "It wasn't because she told me directly. My name is Joël. I am a recent inhabitant of the city and happened to meet Kyria during an incident at her friend's bakery. You seem to have her eyes, plus you were rubbing your thumbs and forefingers together in unison when we nearly collided. Kyria has that same idiosyncrasy."

"Elaenor's place, eh?" Vilius responded, unnerved by Joël's incisive detection of his characteristics. "I trust the incident wasn't one of an overheated oven?"

Joël laughed. "No, I managed to repair a table from the bakery. Kyria and Elaenor were most kind to accompany me back to the shop when I took it. I mend anything that is broken. That's my trade."

"Since when?"

"Within the last week, Vilius."

"Hence my inability to recognize you."

"Few do," said Joël. "I seem to be somewhat of a mystery. Speaking of mysteries, you appeared to be heading that direction with some purpose in your step. May I ask why?"

"I was heading to the Western Gate. I felt the need to stand in the tower and oversee the view in every direction."

"You are able to gain access to the tower?"

"I am not a soldier, but I am the descendant of soldiers," Vilius sniffed. "And I am a supplier to Selanna's standing army, so I do have some privileges of entry that the ordinary citizen does not enjoy."

"Can you see a good distance from the tower?"

"It's a tower for a reason, Joël. Were you seriously wanting to climb up there?"

"You have the privilege of entry, whereas I do not. It seems to be a moot point, wouldn't you say?"

"Ordinarily, it is. But you can enter if you are with another who has such privilege."

"Is that a reporting of fact or an invitation to come with you?"

Vilius sighed, growing somewhat weary of Joël's questions. "I wasn't expecting company tonight, but I can't imagine any reason to disallow you the view." He pointed. "It's a short walk and we'll get there just past Virtanen's mill down this lane."

The White Sea pounded rhythmically against the base of the wall below as Vilius drew a deep breath of the salty wind into his nostrils. The guard positioned just east of them watched Joël with keen interest but seemed to believe he was no threat. Vilius looked out in the distance over the waves before looking to his right, past Joël, toward the coastline that led toward Stahlgard.

"Which view is better, Vilius?" asked Joël.

"I beg your pardon?"

"Which view do you prefer?"

"Both are precious to me," Vilius said thoughtfully. "I love the smell of the sea, but I despise what lies beyond it. I look back at the land behind us and I think of how strongly we must defend it. We've won and lost bitter battles as a people. I would give of myself to equip others so that we can gain our freedom back."

"By supplying for the archers?"

"That is the work of a fletcher," replied Vilius. "That is the work of this fletcher. And pardon my brutal honesty, but it does seem to be more pertinent to the life of our nation than repairing broken table legs and cracked pots."

"Those are small items to one's everyday sight, I will admit," Joël responded with a slight glint of steel in his voice. "But do you think it's not a worthy activity?"

"I've never given it much thought, Joël. I see the results of my work or what my work can become. That seems to fix a certain value to it. Your items will be broken once again. Why labor to repair them when you can make something new?"

"What if Lord Creator did that?"

"Excuse me?" Vilius sputtered, shocked at the intimate, easy way that Joël referred to ruler of Vuoristad. "I don't understand what you're asking."

"Just a question. What if Lord Creator started over with someone else than those He created? What then? What about you? What about other Merivalkans?"

"I still don't see the point."

"You were saying your work has more value by starting over to make something new rather than transforming what is broken. What if Lord Creator did that to this nation and abandoned it?"

"It seems," said Vilius, "that He already has, else we wouldn't be under the grip of Kronjva. And why are you pressing that issue?"

"I am merely following where your beliefs lead, Vilius."

"Well, at least my beliefs and identity seem pretty clear," Vilius retorted, pushing off the wall and drawing himself to his full height. "In the meantime, all I know about you is that you are Joël, that you refuse to throw away items that should likely go on the refuse pile, and that you arrived here in Selanna just days ago! Aside from those things and that I know you are wearing a light blue tunic with black trousers, while needing a stick to travel around, I know nothing about you!"

"For which there is no reason to grow alarmed."

"I'm not alarmed, Joël!"

"The tone and pace of your voice suggests otherwise, Vilius," Joël said gently.

"Just what would you know of Lord Creator, of what we experience in this city? Can you answer me that?"

Joël placidly looked at Vilius before gazing out to the White Sea. "I would know more than you might imagine or care to imagine."

"Then what about where you came from? Can you at least dispel that confusion?"

"From beyond these walls, Vilius. And that is all I will say. More detail would only be both confusing and unbelievable. All I can tell you is I've come here wanting the best for this nation, for this city." He paused. "And for you."

"Then perhaps you'll consider my desire for freedom, for the good life, for the path of happiness. I don't know who, other than the Kronji, would deny us that."

"You have no idea how close you are to what I desire, Vilius."

"Truly?"

"And yet, you have no comprehension of how truly far away you are at the same time."

Vilius' eyes narrowed. "What?" His voice dropped to a thick growl, yet Joël wasn't shrinking away.

"Do you use Lord Creator for your freedom," Joël spoke calmly, "or do you believe he grants you freedom when you most need it?"

"What I believe," Vilius replied flatly, "is that if you're going to insist on passing this night in speaking riddles, perhaps I'd be better off enjoying this view by myself."

Joël waited, ensuring that Vilius' dismissal was complete. "Very well, Vilius. It was at least good to make your acquaintance tonight, even if my company might not have been the most pleasant." He moved toward the trapdoor leading to the tower stairs. "I'll let myself out."

Vilius noticed he was gripping the iron rail on the battlement, his knuckles turning white. Releasing his hands from it, he called out, "Joël?"

Joël looked up from the stairs through the door opening, his stick propping the trap open. "Yes?"

Vilius shrugged. "My apologies for being short with you. But to be honest, I found your questions both unnerving and less than helpful. If you would continue living and working here in Selanna, you should use better discretion when you open your mouth. This city is a cordial community, but there are limits. There are traditions. And there are certain desires and expectations of our nation's life. You wouldn't want others to turn against you because of the words you pose to them."

Joël shrugged back. "That is for them to decide. Good night, Vilius."

Vilius watched Joël shut the door and then turned back, sweeping his eyes over the ferocious and glistening waves that beat through the dark below.

"You wouldn't want me to turn against you, either," he said to no one in particular as another wind gust blew over the battlement.

7

The city center of Selanna was a bustling hub in the two days that followed, a feverish pace marked by a spike in purchases of fish from the harbor wares, fruits and vegetables from the tables lining the Great Market Road, and clothing from the tailors. Indeed, so furiously energetic was the teeming mass of humanity throughout Selanna that the contrasting calm that settled over the city at suppertime on Brightide Nave Eve appeared practically eerie. By tradition of the Faith, all citizens ended their commerce, returned home, and joined in their families for a quiet, reflective supper before an early bedtime.

It was a brisk yet sunny day when the citizenry awoke, and within an hour of morning nave, the streets were alive with streams of people striding toward the courtyard by the Lakihalle where the parpallo, the ceremonial fire pit, was already stockpiled with trunks and branches of dasenpfear trees. The Council had given the order to fling open the city gates an hour earlier than normal so that those from the surrounding farmland might enter Selanna, as well. A crowd of over ten thousand gathered as near to the courtyard as possible, awaiting the arrival of the Council and Umlar, the high priest.

Kyria, Vilius, and the rest of the Halmo family had staked out a place in the eastern portion of the crowd. Looking around, Kyria saw Elaenor's family on the other side of the square. Turning left, she discovered that Kaleva had wormed his way into their midst. Greeting him with a polite nod—and not wanting to appear too exuberant on an obviously solemn day—she whispered, "Good to see you, Kaleva."

"You as well, Kyria," he replied. "I take it the fish were plenty for your needs a few nights back?"

"Not for me. For Joël, actually."

"Ah, Joël. Mysterious fellow, but I like him. Did he put a new leg on that table?"

34

"That's the thing," Kyria whispered, dropping her words lower as some nearby shot her warning glances. "He repaired the old leg."

"Repaired?" Kaleva muttered. "How?"

"With some of that saltwater on which you sail and the mud by your blessed harbor," came the voice of Joël directly behind them.

They turned, startled, and Joël raised his hand. "Hello," he said quietly. "I didn't mean to startle you both. Do you mind if I stand here with you?"

"By all means," Kaleva replied. "I assume this is your first Gathering here in Selanna?"

"Here in Selanna, yes, although I've seen plenty of Gatherings all over Merivalka."

Kaleva's brow furrowed.

Umlar walked before the Council, clad in a simple white robe with a golden sash. Elbart followed the priest, carrying a silken cloth wrapped in a silver cord. Behind Elbart came Lasjen with his sword strapped to his belt, then Dirnik, Petric, and the rest of the Council. The murmuring of the crowd settled to an awed hush as Umlar took one of the two massive torches, already lit, and Elbart took the other. When the Council had surrounded the parpallo in a semicircle opposite the crowd's own swarming assembly, Umlar spoke out loud, his voice carrying over the crowd and above the waves pounding in the harbor to the south.

"To the King of Heaven, Lord Creator, Ruler of Vuoristad and Maker of Merivalka, we make our prayer!"

The crowd, stirred by the opening words, answered as one: "Lord Creator, hear our plea!"

"We come in the stain of our long-standing corruption," continued Umlar, "to stand once again before the fire of cleansing. To you, his people, I ask: Do you seek Lord Creator with all your heart?"

"We do!" they shouted together. "Lord Creator, have mercy!"

"Do you seek him with all your mind?"

"We do! Lord Creator, have mercy!"

"Do you seek him with all your soul?"

"We do! Lord Creator, have mercy!"

"Do you seek him with all your strength?"

"We do! Lord Creator, have mercy!"

Umlar cleared his throat and went on. "To you, Lord Creator, we give thanks and praise for being a God who hears our confession. We bewail the manifold evils we continue to commit, and we ask that as this fire consumes this wood of the symbol of our nation, even now you would in your mercy consume our failings, as well."

"This we pray," chanted the crowd. "This we believe. This we hope."

Umlar looked northward, beyond the city gates, his eyes fixed, as in all Gathering he had led before, on the distance where he knew Vuoristad stood. He gestured to Elbart and both men tipped the torches into the woodpile. The oil-stained trunks and branches ignited, sending a sweet and smoking blaze toward the clouds. He nodded to the director of song and the pipes of the musicians began to play their pained yet sweet tune. He opened his mouth and let the words of the songs flow forth as the assembly and the nobles joined with him.

> *To you, our Maker, we raise our song,*
> *And give to you, the Ageless of Kings*
> *To praise you with your Messengers strong*
> *This canticle that loudly rings!*
>
> *In Sivvlaka, the Dark Pool of gloom*
> *Our ancestors did stumble and fail*
> *And Merivalka plunged into doom*
> *Our manifold sins we all bewail!*
>
> *To you, we pray, Great Judge of all*
> *To send the Rhoken, Deliverer true,*
> *And save us from our corruption's pall*
> *That Merivalka might be made new!*

Our subjugation surely will end,
Our enemies brought low to dust
The One Courageous that you shall send
Will bind our hearts in hope and trust.

The song's final notes lingered in the air as the assembly quieted. Umlar strode to Gheren, his assistant, who held the Book of the Stories forth. Taking the volume and turning to the assembly of thousands, Umlar raised the leather-bound book heavenward.

"The Stories of our nation, the Word of Lord Creator given through his seers to his people!"

The people responded, as they had done down through the centuries: "To Lord Creator we give thanks!"

"To those assembled," Umlar responded, "I ask that one among you draw forth to speak the promises of Lord Creator to his people."

It was almost certain, Umlar knew, that one of the merchants or tradesmen of the town—one of the more religiously devoted anyway—would draw near and ask to take the book for the privilege of the Reading. The story of the Great Ruin would be followed by a promise of hope from Ahntunen or one of the seers, and then the reader would pass the book back to Umlar himself.

Except this time, no one—no one!—came forth!

A silence of several moments came over the crowd. Citizens looked at one another, wondering why the delay prolonged. It was as if a force beyond sight was holding back anyone from coming near the fire.

Kyria and Kaleva, head bowed, suddenly felt someone brush past them, shuffling through the assembly. Looking up, Kyria saw a familiar person approach Umlar, walking with stick in hand.

"I will declare the word of Lord Creator," said Joël, to the surprise of all the nobles and most of the crowd.

Placing the Stories on the raised petrified stump that served as a lectern, Joël looked over the assembled thousands. He could sense the rage from Umlar, Elbart and others behind him. He clearly saw the confusion on the faces of the citizens, wondering why a new dweller was so bold to come forth for this moment. But most of all, he felt his heart grow resolute, yet heavy. *This is it,* he thought. *This is the beginning.* He began to speak, never looking at the Stories, but calling forth as if he heralded a new Story.

"The Great Ruin is why this city assembles here, but does it bring forth any redemption if Selanna, and indeed all Merivalka, trades one sin for a greater one, exchanging one idol of pride for a more devastating one? Magnus and Merta made war on Lord Creator the moment they dipped their hands into Sivvlaka, but to place your hope in making war on your subjugators is just as wanton an evil as theirs! To place faith in a kingdom in which Merivalka is free, and yet to ignore the grace that can free you from your rebellion, this is to remove yourself further from the Mountain, not place yourself closer to it."

"You call out the words of the seers of the past, and the Stories which call you back to Lord Creator, the words which speak of the Rhoken and the deliverance he will bring. Yet will you follow the Rhoken wherever he will take you? Will you believe him? Or will you believe your own image of what you think him to be?"

The crowd stirred. Joël could sense Umlar stiffening behind him, yet he knew the high priest had made no move to remove him from the stump. The unseen resistance remained steady. Joël continued.

"You tell the Stories from years past and remember the words of Ahntunen as the Second Age dawned, when you were liberated from your captivity to the Ehrma. And yet a deeper, more sinister captivity holds you here, one that Gatherings and the torching of trees can bring to mind but never take away. You have escaped one prison, but another remains. And yet not all is lost. Grace remains. Hope remains!"

Out of the crowd, several people began shouting, "He speaks truth! He speaks truth!"

Across the blazing trees, Elbart hissed at Umlar, "What are you doing? Why does he go on?"

But even Elbart remained rooted where he stood.

Joël raised his hands slightly, his palms facing upward. "More than anything, throughout this land, you people crave the presence of Lord Creator, to feel his Breath upon you with joy. Well, that Breath has fallen upon me. He who reigns from Vuoristad ... He has chosen me and sealed my life to proclaim the grace and hope broken from time immemorial, to come to the captives and release them, to open the eyes of those who cannot see, and to open your hearts to Lord Creator's favor. Decry your sins, but do not attempt to purge them of your own doing. That is the true Story of these Stories. And today, that has been fulfilled in your hearing!"

Joël closed the Book of the Stories as the shouts of the crowd grew. As if released from a stupor, Umlar and Elbart, along with Dirnik, rushed toward Joël and grabbed him roughly.

"How dare you fill this stage with your curses, stranger!" yelled Elbart.

"Troublemaker!" cried Umlar. "He is not to be trusted, citizens of Selanna! He speaks as if he knows the Rhoken himself! Do not believe him!"

The thousands would not bear it, pressing toward the barricade that separated them from the parpallo dais. Some cried, "Let him speak!" Others screamed, "Let him go!"

Joël, for his part, turned to Umlar, Elbart, and Dirnik. His eyes were as bright as the sky yet fierce as a sea-storm. His voice was extraordinarily steady and filled with authority.

"If you would reject that Story, then you have not believed the others. These Stories bear witness about me."

He looked past them at the blazing pile of dasenpfear wood before turning back toward the cheering, adoring crowd. The mass of humanity parted as he walked through their feverish celebration. Kyria watched Joël stroll in the direction of his shop when she felt her brother's hand on her arm. When she looked at Vilius, he was trembling, his skin white as flour. He was pointing toward the dais.

"Kyria, what ... what is that?"

She followed his finger and saw the trunks and branches piled in the parpallo. Openmouthed, she marveled as the fire had abated, and all the wood was untouched by any fire or charring, as good as new.

THE CALLING

8

Late Brightide brought the longer, sunnier days of rebirth and renewal. Walking through the farmland surrounding Selanna, one could almost sense things growing. As the season turned to Early Suntide and the temperatures warmed, the White Sea grew livelier and the fishermen looked forward to the more abundant catches of their wares that came with these days. The Great Market Road was livelier than it had ever been. Clothiers, bakers, butchers, and merchants of all kinds were reaping higher profits than normal, although many noted those involved in weaponry gained the most. Even restaurants and public houses gained residual benefit; neither Kyria nor the rest of the Halmo family could recall a time they experienced such abundance.

The citizens of Selanna rejoiced in their good fortune, confident the Kronji and Prince Dewulf would find their shores to be those of a confident, proud, and rich people. Yet hidden in the midst of this energy, behind the exchanges and sales and good will of the community, the question hung in the air like a secret both frightening and thrilling.

Who was this Joël?

The sun had sunk beyond the horizon just moments before, but the human traffic on the Avenue of the Commonwealth had petered out an hour ago. A crowd sang lustily at pubs such as the Iron Bow or—closer still—The Foundryman. The notes were slightly off-key and occasionally bawdy, but the tunes were joyous and energetic. Pipes and fiddles drowned out most of the tone-deaf attempts and the result—at least from those who heard the songs from further away—sounded more like a lullaby.

Behind his shop on the Avenue, Joël plunged his hands into a basin of water drawn from his small well pump. Slapping his drenched fingers on his neck and bringing them over his face, he began to rub the dirt and grime from his body. He looked around at the scraps of pottery and wood piled in the trunk next to the back wall of his house, then looked up at the sky to behold the moon as it moved toward Vuoristad. Exhaling deeply, Joël took satisfaction in a day well spent over repairs of furniture, pots, and lamps, followed by a delicious supper of trout, dasenpfear, and Jehre's filling barley rolls.

A twig snapped beyond the back fence at the rear of the shop. Waiting for further noise, Joël heard something crash in the alley to the rear, and a branch from a tree flew into the air as a curse did the same from a nighttime visitor.

"Hello?" Joël called out. "Who's there?"

He had reached the back gate when a face appeared, red and obviously embarrassed over its owner's inelegance.

"Hello, Joël," the visitor panted. "I'm sorry for this clumsy surprise."

"Petric! Welcome!" Joël's face broke into a wide grin as he opened the gate and bade the noble welcome. "Come in! You know there's a front door that works just as well."

"I understand," replied Petric, flicking a small leaf that had lodged in his beard. "I just happened to be out walking and thought I would come by." He hesitated. "Actually, that's not entirely true. It's more like I thought I would come by, hence I went out walking."

"Come on through," Joël beckoned, leading the way through the small back yard, into the kitchen, and on into the main room. "Can I get you anything? Water? Ale?"

"Some water might do me well, Joël, thank you." Petric took off his hat and cloak, placing them on a hook on the south wall. "You've been busy."

"A little of everything," Joël called from the kitchen before returning with a tin mug of cool water and a pitcher. "I assume the receptacle is familiar."

Petric peered at the mug quizzically. "Yes, one of mine," he commented. "The imprint in the base makes that clear. It looks worn." He took a sip. "Did someone give this to you?"

"If you count fishing it out of the garbage, noticing the handle was loose, and then fire-molding it back on as giving, then yes." Joël spread his arms out. "I know it would be more proper to buy a new one for the sake of your accounts, but I felt as long as this mug had some life remaining, why not fix it?"

"Do you find that to be an activity which seems well-received?" Petric asked, sitting down.

"For the most part," Joël replied, taking a seat opposite the noble. "I think it's so much a part of Selanna's tradition, though, that people love having new things. It seems like a symbol of status that citizens want to spend money on new items, new goods, and so when a possession is broken, the last thing they desire is to repair it. But nonetheless, I am discovering there are those who do not think that way."

"Why do you believe that is the case, if you don't mind me asking?"

"Truthfully? If someone sees there is something about their possessions that is broken, they might be persuaded to repair it. And if that is true, then there might be things in life for which that is true. So if someone sees their own brokenness, they might seek true renewal, the life they absolutely require."

Petric drained the remainder of the water. Placing the mug on the table, he continued, "You are an odd fellow, you know that?"

Joël laughed, a hearty guffaw that filled the room. "I guess you could say I'm no ordinary citizen of Selanna, or of Merivalka, for that matter. But let me ask you a question. Do you normally frequent the back gates of people's houses to seek an audience?"

"Being completely truthful, I came to see you because you ... shall we say ... you intrigue me." Petric wiped his hands on his pants and leaned forward, his forearms on the edge of the table. "That reading at the Gathering of Brightide Nave. No one in Selanna knows a whit about where you come from, whom you come from, where your loyalties might be, and yet your words left the people wanting more."

"Wanting more?"

45

Petric lifted his mug, staring inside as if to confirm he'd left no water within. "Yes. It's called hope. No one has ever spoken like that in years. Certainly not in my lifetime or my father's lifetime. Some people—quietly, mind you—keep comparing you to Besno or Ahntunen. That is lofty company, Joël, amongst the prophets and seers of ages past."

Joël lifted the pitcher and filled Petric's mug. "But testing my prophetic utterances is not the reason you've come tonight."

"I told you why I've come. You intrigue me."

"And so the natural time for that is to come by night and the natural place is in a back alley?"

Petric nodded, knowing Joël had smelled out his motive. "I was close enough to the nobles when they rushed against you that day."

"When Umlar, Elbart, and Dirnik accused me of speaking curses and said I was not to be trusted?"

"What they said is immaterial, Joël. If they were completely serious about the substance of your words, there would have been a trial that day, as there should be in any utterance against the Faith and the ways of Lord Creator."

"The ways of Lord Creator might surprise you and others."

Petric's eyes danced, his lips curling into a stunned smile. "See, there you go again! Speaking of Lord Creator as if you truly know him! As if he's here in this room!"

"Wouldn't that be reasonable for the Maker of all there is?"

"Honestly, Joël, the more you say, the more you amaze me. What I have been wanting to make clear is I recall what you said to them that day."

"The nobles?"

Petric nodded, taking another sip. "You said to the assembly *'Decry your sins, but do not attempt to purge them of your own doing. That is the true Story of these Stories. And today, that has been fulfilled in your hearing!'* And then you said to the nobles, *'These Stories bear witness about me'.* "

"You thought that odd?"

"The words were a bit of a surprise. The fact they were accompanied by a miracle surprised me further."

"Miracle?"

"The trees ceased burning in the parpallo, you know."

"You are observant. Go on."

"I'll be blunt, Joël. What you said sounded ridiculous to me, except for the fact it seemed true."

"Seemed true?"

"You come amongst us, repair what is broken, and speak with authority. The nobles speak out against you, but offer nothing against you. You speak as one who has true authority, full authority, one who commands truth and respect."

"And from this you believe ... what?"

"I speak for myself, not the Council. But no one could say these things unless he was sent by Lord Creator in some way. That is why I came tonight. I confess I did not want to come in broad daylight. That would raise suspicions amongst the Council and, if prevented from seeing you, I'd never have spoken to you. But that's what I came to say."

"That you believe Lord Creator has sent me for some reason?"

"Yes."

"As a prophet? A Messenger? A proclaimer? A priest?"

"Does the role matter?"

"Why do you believe Lord Creator has sent me, then?"

"Whatever your role, I think you are here to bring us closer to Lord Creator. Because we have been banished from Vuoristad. You've come to show us a way back to Lord Creator. To help us see that, as you do with tables and pots and everything else, we must be repaired."

"What kind of repair, Petric?"

"I don't understand."

"What sort of change do you speak of? Do you speak of a table leg patched together so that the table can stand again?"

"That seems reasonable, if you will."

"You cannot will that, Petric. And the repair to a table might be small, and appropriately so, but even then, the table cannot repair itself.

It cannot make that transformation. It needs someone else to do that. Your brokenness, Petric, and the brokenness of all in the world, you can speak of it in any way—it is a wound much deeper and more fatal than a broken table leg. You might think your sin is small, great, or moderate—and I will tell you it is massively deep—but however you might view its depth, I will tell you the cure is beyond you."

"But Joël, we pray, we hope, and we trust the Rhoken will come. Isn't that what Lord Creator desires?"

"You speak of what Lord Creator desires, and that is most accurate, Petric. But how can you do what Lord Creator desires?"

"By doing it?" Petric said, finishing his second cup.

"How are you able to do it?"

"What do you mean, Joël? I told you ... prayer, hope, the ..."

"You told me about the elements of the Faith, like ingredients in a stew. But you've told me nothing about how that stew might be made."

Petric rubbed his head and his eyes. "Joël, I'm not sure I see where you are leading me."

Joël poured another mug of water for Petric. "My friend, you can speak of returning to Lord Creator. You can speak of sorrow for rebellion against Lord Creator. But unless you are cleansed by him for your rebellion and unless you are renewed by his Breath, you will be no closer to Vuoristad than a man on the other end of the world."

"How can that be?"

"Have you been listening to the Faith your entire life, Petric, and still don't know these things? Why else would it be, for someone to offer you cleansing and his very Breath of life?"

"Why indeed?"

Joël extended his hands, palms up once more. "Because Lord Creator loves his world. He loves Merivalka and the people in it, people who wander and are lost, people who love their own way above Lord Creator's own. And he would love you enough to send One to draw you back to himself."

"A nice hope for years in the future."

Joël poured himself a drink of water into a stoneware mug. "Have you seriously heard nothing I've said just now, or what I said during the Gathering?"

"I've listened both times, although I admit you say much that is hard to understand. We speak much of obedience, hope, and sorrow for our Great Ruin. Love, though, may be what we need. It certainly strikes a chord within me, if Lord Creator would love us as we are."

"The truth is even more wondrous and staggering than that, Petric."

"Why do you say that?"

"Not as you are, but in spite of who you are. And yet Lord Creator has acted, not to condemn, but to save."

Petric fingered his tin mug deliberately. "Why do you speak as if this has already happened?"

9

Two days later, the harbor area was full of members of Selanna's standing army, dressed in full livery, making their inspections. Fishermen kept to their duties along the shore, haggling for the most optimal docking rights remaining when the smaller vessels of Prince Dewulf's incoming fleet would temporarily displace their boats. With the Council of Nobles clamoring for more victuals on hand for the Kronji arrival, it fell to the fishermen to brave the strong waves on more lengthy expeditions.

Preparing for one such foray into the White Sea, Kaleva checked the sail on his vessel for tears before calling to his brothers and the rest of the crew that they would cast off in ten minutes. Henrik and Saku brought salt-packed wood-fired poultry and dozens of rye rolls on board, while Germund—easily the strongest member of the six-man crew—rolled a cask of water onto the deck. Noting the presence of only five of them, Kaleva asked, "Where is Ivar?"

"Beg your pardon, sir," said Mirko Linna, Ivar's brother, "but he was taken by fever last night. He will not be with us today."

"Much work for fewer hands," grunted Kaleva, "but nevertheless we have work to do. Let's prepare to depart."

The rest of the crew scrambled to their duties as Kaleva headed down the gangplank and onto the pier, wondering how to divide Ivar's duties among the men when a shout interrupted his ponderings.

"Hi there, Kaleva!"

Kaleva looked to the harbor walk and saw Joël waving to him as he approached the ship.

"Hello yourself, Joël! Good to see you, although I'm about ready to head out to sea."

"Which is why I came here. I was able to complete all my orders through last night, and since I have no projects scheduled for today, I wondered if I might join you on your fishing trip this morning."

50

Kaleva looked at Joël's clothing ensemble, which was clearly a different selection from the usual. He wore a twill shirt pulled over a thinner undershirt, with durable breeches and boots. There was no doubt Joël was dressed for a day at sea.

"Actually, Joël, your presence is an answer to prayer. One of my shipmates fell ill and we could use someone to replace him for today."

"I am sorry for his sickness but would be happy to join you. How can I be of service?"

"We have a battery of usual jobs: rowing out until we catch the wind and run up the sail, manning the anchor and the nets, sorting the fish after the catch, and cleaning and mending the nets upon our return."

"Well, then," Joël smiled, "if you are ready, I can help you make your way to sea."

Kaleva was pleasantly surprised at Joël's giftedness on deck. He noticed a couple of spots in one net that needed tightening, and before Kaleva could instruct him, Joël had threaded a sheet bend knot in both places to secure the nettle-hemp line. With Germund, Joël helped push off from the dock, and before ten minutes had passed, the ship was headed out to sea.

"Where else have you gone fishing before?" bellowed Germund, his smile creasing his ruddy face

"Nowhere in particular," said Joël, "although one can find several hundred eels near Kampo."

"Ah," remarked Henrik, drawing astride, "an eel is a fine meal. Eel stew particularly in the autumn."

"Henrik, you believe sawdust chased with oil is a fine meal," Saku barked at his brother over the roar of the waves. "Forgive my brother, Joël, but he has yet to clear all the expectations of gentlemanly conduct."

"It's the way of the sea," Kaleva called from starboard as he walked toward the center of the deck to take the wheel from Mirko. "It does strange things to all of us, but Henrik is lost for good, I believe.

Thanks to Lord Creator that before Henrik grew extensively uncouth, he managed to secure a wife for life's storms!"

Joël looked toward the south. "Speaking of storms, that might be trouble."

The rest of the crew looked intently in the direction he pointed. "What trouble?" inquired Mirko.

"That," replied Joël. "That low-lying cloud that looks no bigger than a man's hand."

"And here I had such high hopes for you, Joël," Kaleva laughed as a shock of foam sprayed against port side. "You know your knots and you can push off your boats, but I'm afraid reading the skies is beyond your ken!"

Germund slapped Joël on the back in a show of friendship before turning to Kaleva. "What, ho? Long lines today, captain?"

Kaleva shook his head. "No, the stone weights are working fine and we need a high volume before heading in. We'll get far out and drop both anchors and then lower the nets." He looked toward the cloud Joël had noticed and could have sworn it had grown in size.

The haul of six hundred pavenders with a smattering of trout was beyond what the crew had hoped, and it was with a volley of whoops and yelps they were able to drag the nets over the side of the boat and drop the salty, colorful mass of squirming fish unceremoniously onto the deck. It took the crew about twenty minutes to sort the fish into baskets, but all worked efficiently, and in due time they were sitting down to a brief lunch of salted chicken, rolls, and copious amounts of water.

"I could tear apart one of these pavenders in my mouth, that's how hungry I am," groaned Henrik.

"I told you," Kaleva chuckled, elbowing Joël, and nodding toward his brother.

"Kaleva," Mirko said tremblingly as he stood near the mast, "I believe our guest might be saying those same words to you, if you'd look at that cloud!"

"Don't be a bludge," Germund roared. "The chances are better we'd see a poor peasant fishing out here in a coracle than see a storm cloud on a day like today."

"Then explain this!" Mirko yelled back, pointing toward the east.

The entire crew scrambled to port side. The cloud had increased seven times over and was moving toward them at an alarming speed.

"That's a giant when it was a dwarf just an hour ago," Saku said dourly.

"Dark though it is," replied Kaleva, "we don't need to worry until ..."

He was interrupted by a jagged lightning strike from the rapidly approaching cloud and peals of thunder that rippled through the air.

"You were saying?" said Germund.

"Up anchor!" Kaleva snapped. "No time to waste. Germund, you and Henrik raise the anchor! That's a stiff wind coming! Mirko, secure the baskets and nets with Joël! Saku, with me at the wheel!"

Aghast, Kaleva looked again and saw that nothing was going to save them from the onslaught. "Curse this storm!" he bellowed. "How does one cloud become this? Nothing of this sort was to happen today!"

"That seems completely worth discussing, but at another time," gasped Saku, who was impatiently gesturing to Germund and Henrik to pull up the anchor. In two minutes, the ship was turning to catch the ferocious wind headed their way.

"It's a brutal affair, brother," Saku yelled over the winds, "but we'll need the wind to carry us back to shore."

"Wonderful," Kaleva grumbled. "Needing the storm to survive the storm. Well, let's hope the sail holds and we don't have to deal with a shattered mast, as well."

The boat, buffeted by the waves, managed to catch the wind. Kaleva took the wheel from Saku and peered ahead, desperately trying to see Selanna in the distance. He was calculating their arrival time when Germund roared from behind.

"Secure everything! Here it comes!"

And just like that, the waves and foam blew over the sides, the saltwater rush sending the men to the deck. Kaleva barely held on to the wheel as Henrik rushed to the mast for a better lookout, struggling to hang on. The cold gale cut through Kaleva's skin as he pressed against the wheel. Rain fell in sheets and the thunder crashed around them. Kaleva checked to make sure the entire crew was on board, but as he did so, a finger of lighting snaked across the sky, boring itself directly into the sail and slicing it open with a fiery incision. Henrik, as if hit with an ethereal punch, fell from the mast and slammed to the deck with a sickening crunch.

"Henrik!" Kaleva screamed. Saku, slipping and falling, dove across the deck in a vain attempt to reach their brother, but Joël managed to get to his side first. Placing a hand to Henrik's neck and his ear toward his mouth, he looked to Kaleva and yelled, "Alive! He's still alive!"

Kaleva was relieved, but practical matters remained. "Then leave him and get to the mast!" Despite the rain doing its part to put out the fire, the sail was in tatters and the boat was in danger of breaking up. "Saku will help you!"

Looking behind him, Kaleva saw Mirko nearly get washed into the White Sea while trying to keep water clear from the hold area. Turning back, he saw with relief that Saku had reached the mast and was gathering in the ripped sail. But Joël was nowhere near him. Instead, he stood near Henrik's prone body on the deck, his twill shirt soaked through, looking back to the south and into the vicious teeth of the storm.

"Joël!" screamed Kaleva. "What are you doing? Don't you care about helping us?"

As soon as the words were out of Kaleva's mouth, Joël lifted his hands upward, the thunder continuing to roll and the lightning strikes increasing in all their fury. With his jaw set and his eyes rooted on the clouds, Joël opened his mouth and called into the gale.

"Silence! Be at peace!"

Kaleva was about to open his mouth to rebuke what he viewed as Joël's useless command, but the words caught in his throat as the darkness abated instantly, the clouds vaporized, and a bright sunlight exploded overhead. The choppy waves slowed to a gentle bob, and the fierce squall vanished, replaced by a brisk and warm wind pushing them in the direction of Selanna.

Henrik picked himself off the deck, looked around, and found himself facing the open-jawed astonishment of his brother and every member of the crew, with the exception of Joël.

"What, may I ask, just happened?" Henrik screamed, half with joy, half with terror.

"Mirko, take the wheel," gasped Kaleva, placing the transfixed Mirko's hands onto the helm. "Germund, run up what's left of that sail. It might be enough to get back. If not, let's be prepared to row."

Skimming over the slickened planks, he reached Joël, clasping his shoulder with his left hand and Joël's left arm with his right hand.

"Joël," he whispered, wide-eyed and with his throat stinging. "Joël, what was that? Please tell me I didn't just see that happen!"

Placing his hand on Kaleva's head, Joël nodded before looking around at the others. "Why are you surprised? You needed help. Where is your trust?"

He walked off, headed for the short bowsprit at the front of the ship. Kaleva watched him, but he was aware of the murmurs taking place around him, all mingled with both relief and terror.

Finally, Saku came to his side. "Brother, that couldn't have just happened."

"We saw it happen, Saku. There's no denying it."

"But how? A tempest doesn't go from a frothing rage to a peaceful sun-kissed breeze in a matter of seconds! Kaleva, please tell me how this makes sense!"

Kaleva took another look at Joël, who was gazing toward the far-off outline of Selanna from the bowsprit. The sting had returned to Kaleva's throat, and he shook his head in amazement and confusion.

"I don't know, Saku, but until we find out more about Joël, I want you to make sure no one spreads this news around when we get back. That may prove exceedingly difficult, however. I don't understand this."

Saku nodded, eyes blinking furiously. "I'll tell them." As he started toward Germund, he asked, "Who does that?"

"I don't know, brother. Only the maker of the world can control this world." He paused before continuing. "What sort of man is this, where even the sea and storm obey him?"

10

The next evening, Kaleva sank wearily into a chair at the Red Raven. Having spent the day replacing the sail, cleaning the fish, and making the rounds to markets and public houses, he was relieved this would be his final stop. He pushed aside the guilty feelings that gnawed at him for eating here tonight, as Kyria would likely tease him for going anywhere but the Iron Bow. Still, he rationalized, the exchange of his wares for a free dinner was too much to pass up, and he enjoyed the Red Raven's musical ambience during supper. Tonight, a dark-haired maiden plaintively strummed her merkkijo to the delight of the patrons, who seemed to require a pensive tune as their meals' accompaniment.

Pentii Koiviunemi, the Red Raven's owner, had personally overseen Kaleva's transfer of trout and pavenders a half-hour before as they loaded the haul into the salt-bin. As per their longstanding agreement, Pentii ushered Kaleva to the prime table near the fireplace before taking his order of seared trout, buttered carrots, springbuck bread, and dasenpfear sauce.

"The usual for drink?" Pentii asked before leaving the table. Kaleva nodded his agreement before closing his eyes.

The music wafted through the room, the notes falling heavily into Kaleva's exhausted spirit. He knew the previous day at sea had stretched him physically. Every muscle in his body begged for relief, and he rubbed his right shoulder that he'd overworked pressing the wheel with difficulty during the storm. *That is why I can hardly move,* Kaleva thought to himself. *But there is something within me beyond physical exhaustion, beyond the bruising of a hard day on the waves. This is a disturbance of another kind.*

Why indeed was he so vexed? If anything, he told himself, he should be grateful for the rescue from certain death, for him and his entire crew. One minute, they were a heartbeat from their doom, and the next, they stood firmly on deck under a warm sun with a placid breeze taking them back to Selanna. So why did anxiety crowd his heart more than thankfulness? Why did Joël's sudden might terrify him more than gratify him?

"Kaleva?"

He jumped at the sound of the voice, not because he disdained interruptions, but because the reason for his worry happened to bear that voice. Kaleva sat open-mouthed and then rubbed his eyes at the sight of the man before him.

"Joël! Hello! What a ... a surprise!"

"Yes," replied Joël, who bore a large cloth sack with him. "I wasn't trying to startle you. I saw Henrik and Saku near the harbor and they mentioned you would likely be here this evening."

"My brothers, much to my amazement, told you the truth. I brought a portion of our catch from yesterday to Pentii here and I will get a complimentary meal in exchange." He looked at the bulky sack in Joël's hand. "What do you bear with you?"

"The reason why I was seeking you out. I appear to have caught you at a moment when you desire peace and privacy, though."

Kaleva looked at Joël, wondering what additional shock his new companion might be bringing with him this night. Pushing aside his angst, Kaleva gestured to the chair opposite him. "Actually, I could do with some company tonight. Would you like to join me?"

Joël eased into the chair and placed the sack on the floor next to Kaleva. "You misplaced this yesterday."

Kaleva looked at the sack, then Joël, suspiciously. "I found it hard to believe I misplaced an item half the size of your body, Joël. What's in here?"

"Your damaged sail from yesterday's excursion," Joël replied as Kaleva opened the top of the bag. "I noticed it had been flung into a pile and ignored as you asked Saku to get a new one from the cabin."

"That is our usual procedure, Joël. The sail was ripped down the middle. Don't tell me you tackled this as a project!"

"It took most of the day after breakfast, but I completed it about a half-hour ago. I managed to find some durable thread where the color best matched your sail. It isn't washed, and I know you might not want to use it as your primary sail, but if there is room for a secondhand one in case of emergency, this should be of service."

"You fixed the sail?" Kaleva sputtered with a pained smile.

"It's not meant to intrude on your needs, but merely to provide for your crew. I just didn't want it to be left in a refuse pile."

"Your ale, sir," a young table-servant said rather loudly as he set a glass of warm ale in front of Kaleva.

"Thank you," said Kaleva, who noticed Joël shifting in his chair. "Joël, would you like a drink?"

Joël looked at the servant before nodding to Kaleva. "I would like to break bread with you, Kaleva, beyond just a drink. But have you ordered?"

"I have, but we can add to my reward. Sakari, what do you have in the kitchen tonight?"

"Much of the fish from your delivery, sir," said the servant, "and we have some seasoned quail that other patrons have found quite delicious."

"I'll have the quail, then," said Joël, "and a small portion of leafbitter and spring beans with the same bread that my friend is presently enjoying. And ... that drink?"

"It's a sugarflax ale, Joël, and the Red Raven makes the best in the city. But don't tell Kyria I told you that!"

"We also have honeyflax ale, sir," the servant added, "if you would care for something smoother and sweeter."

"The honeyflax will be my choice," said Joël, who pulled several akrans from his pocket and handed them to Sakari. "That should compensate for my portion of the meal and provide some additional payment for you."

"Thank you, sir," gushed an overjoyed Sakari, who rushed off to place Joël's order.

"Making a few friends, are we?" Kaleva chuckled to Joël as he lifted his glass to his lips.

Joël smiled. "You prefer the sugarflax ale over the honeyflax?"

"It's a crisper blend, and I find it does well when joined with a meal of fish. That is not to cast your decision aside. Honeyflax ale is best paired with fowl, so you chose wisely."

Sakari returned with Joël's ale. "Shall we raise our glasses, Kaleva?"

"What shall we drink to, Joël?"

Tapping his glass to Kaleva's, Joël said, "To the hope of the future, and the renewal of all things."

"Like the sail?"

"A foretaste of things to come," Joël replied, sipping his drink. "But we can always return to that truth. We spent a great deal of time at sea yesterday, Kaleva, but you never got the chance to tell me about yourself and your family."

"Is that a request to share my story?"

"Or an entreaty. Why?"

"Something about you makes me think you know a good bit about me."

Joël took another sip of the honeyflax ale, said nothing, and gestured Kaleva to continue.

"As odd as it might be to hear this, I am a fisherman who is not a native of Selanna. Henrik and Saku were born here, but my parents moved here from Kampo when I was nearly a year old. So, like you, I have come from elsewhere."

"Indeed," Joël acknowledged. "And yet you have become a true Selannan."

"Yes, we were warmly received, I must say. I think it had more to do with my father's contributions as a fisherman. He not only was skillful at his trade, but he was very generous with his talents. He trained and advised others, even the competition. If another boat needed its nets mended, then he would help in any way he could. In truth, that has paved the way for whatever success Henrik, Saku, and I have had. Many fishermen and sailors tell us regularly of the kindness of Ludvig Reiji. His legend has become our legacy."

"A wonderful father is good to be proud of," Joël agreed. "Your use of the past tense betrays that he is no longer alive, though."

"Yes," nodded Kaleva. "He was lost at sea. There was a dispute of territorial fishing rights in the White Sea, one that Kronjva asserted with fervor and that we held just as firmly. This was about eight years ago. Legates from both nations arranged to meet in open water to mediate the squabble, and members of the fishing industry for both nations went, as well. Independently, and quite ironically, each side took along armed guards and archers in case hostilities quickened. Sadly, they did."

"And your father was a casualty?" Joël spoke with a great deal of heaviness, his voice husky with what Kaleva felt was sadness. And yet Kaleva suspected that somehow Joël knew every word he would say. Putting those thoughts out of mind, he continued.

"He was. A Kronji archer called out, claiming a Merivalkan archer had just fired past him. Needless to say, that unleashed attacks from each side. My father was trying to pull a member of his crew to the deck when a Kronji arrow pierced him through the heart."

At that moment, their food arrived, steaming hot on earthenware plates. Joël paused to say a prayer of thanks to Lord Creator before they ate, which they proceeded to do for several minutes before Joël spoke again.

"What happened once they noticed your father had been killed?"

Kaleva swallowed a prongful of carrots before going back to his remembrance. "There was a cease-fire after there were some deaths on each side. Our legates blamed them for firing first, while theirs blamed our side. Needless to say, nothing brought back the dead, but out of respect to those who perished, the Kronji and our legates struck a deal that would be the dividing point for territorial water claims. It didn't set our nation at ease, but there wasn't much we could do. Our standing army is built to defend our land, not to attack our subjugators. Still, those who hate Kronjva and pine for our own independence had more fire in their bellies for some time. Henrik would be one of those."

"He has not come to terms with your father's slaying," Joël surmised.

"I think it's his way of keeping Father alive, but he raises his frustration less often than before. Part of that is because our mother—her name is Ileska—has left to go back to our ancestral home. She now lives with our Aunt Borga in Kampo."

"Yes, Kampo," Joël repeated. "No wonder Henrik knew about eels at Kampo."

"Yes, we've had our share of eel stew. We take the ship there in Harvestide as a family vacation and manage to gain temporary access to some fishing coves off the coast."

"Then when this happened," asked Joël, "would you have still been in school?"

"It was during my last year," Kaleva said. "I remember Kyria was the first to comfort me when the news came. She was in school with me, although she is four years younger. Henrik was a year behind me, Saku three years. I would be apprenticed the next season under my father. Out of a sign of respect for him, the other fishermen in Selanna kept his boat docked in the harbor until I finished school at the kopanos. Then several of the men whom he had helped and trained offered to train me until I could manage the ship. Some of their sons, like Germund, joined my crew and others became willing to be trained by me or my brothers once they finished their education."

"So you have always had fishing within your spirit," Joël concluded.

"Something like that," Kaleva said as he bit into his bread and took a long drink of his ale. "Why did you put it that way?"

"Fishing means finding, discovering, and that begins with seeking what is not present at first, what needs to be found." Joël paused. "That can be useful in many ways."

"How so?"

"Not merely hauling fish from the sea, but also reaping treasures of faith within the lives of others."

"You've obviously mistaken me for the priests of Selanna, Joël," Kaleva grumbled. "Faith is not my strong suit. My convictions and beliefs are important, but I hardly see how I would be a standard of how to build up the same in others."

"Perhaps you should allow others to make that judgment," Joël replied, taking a bite of quail and turning to the girl playing the merkkijo.

"Speaking mysteriously might not make your point as forcefully, Joël."

Joël closed his eyes, listening to the music and swallowing the bite of quail before turning back to Kaleva. "Is it because I say strange things or because I do strange things?"

"Like yesterday?"

"You said so yourself."

Kaleva stared at Joël. "As I intimated when we met, not knowing your story will raise questions in the minds and hearts of others. Including myself, to be honest. But when you add to that an experience like when you quell the storm on the White Sea, that is both an occasion for cheer and terror."

"Why both?"

"Because if you are a man like me, I know I cannot destroy a tempest like you! And if you are not a man like me, then I don't know what to do with you, let alone know you! And here I have told you my story, and I know none of your own!"

Joël blinked at the forceful words coming from Kaleva's mouth. Quietly, though, he drank the rest of his ale and placed the last of his bread in his mouth.

"Not knowing my story now does not mean it will be hidden from you forever," Joël said, standing from his chair and taking his walking stick in his left hand. "It does mean, however, that there is much in store for you, Kaleva Reiji, and I have many things to tell you, but you are not able to bear them right now. Thank you, though, for telling me your story. And for your company."

"Thank you, Joël, for yours as well." Kaleva reached forth and shook Joël's hand. "And for your patience."

"Good night, my friend," Joël grinned. "And please pass along my thanks to Pentii for the excellent meal."

Within seconds, Joël passed through the assembled diners and disappeared through the door that led out onto the Nobles' Lane. Kaleva watched him depart and absent-mindedly took a gulp of his ale.

"Good night, Joël," he grunted. *Strange,* he thought to himself. *I was troubled by his arrival here, and now I am oddly more troubled by his departure.*

11

The Council of Nobles had called for a general feast to be held in the public houses, the market places, and anywhere else that could accommodate large crowds. The city green by the vikarloge was graced with tables to hold portions of the food and drink for the preparatory celebration, to be followed by a litany of worship around the parpallo akin to the Gathering of any Nave. With the Kronji due to arrive in Selanna harbor the next day, the mood was one of high anticipation. The workday had come to an early end, and as lakkaa occurred, the citizens of Selanna streamed as one body to the places designated for the feasts.

Kyria's father was determined to accommodate as many as possible in his establishment, but Olav bade his wife and children to attend the feasting elsewhere for the sake of a more public appearance. Kyria silently wondered how much of this was due to wanting more room for others in the pub or if he wanted the family to come back with any news or gossip of how the army might be preparing for the Kronji. Kyria sighed as she kept pace with her mother, Leena, who was also finding it difficult to match Vilius' easy strides.

The crowd had flowed toward the vikarloge area, the Lakihalle, and the harbor road. Vilius suggested taking some back paths over toward the city green, and soon the Halmo family was within sight of the vikarloge. The building itself towered above the green, with its malmfyr pine beams held together in post-and-lintel fashion. Hundreds of folk were already there, some eating, some engaged in traditional dances, and others talking around several mugs of dasenpfear ale around the layered bays of the stave frame. Kyria waved at Elaenor, who was seated with the rest of the Nurmi family. A brigade of volunteer servants was bringing around selections of roast meat and a variety of mouthwatering vegetables and fried potatoes. Kyria and Vilius sniffed the air and caught the scent of the dasenpfear and berry tarts that would serve for dessert.

"I can hardly remember the city so festive the past few years," Kyria remarked as Vilius ordered another ale.

"We have dances, we have pageants, we have plays," Leena said. "What's not festive about those?"

"I know, but do those draw in the thousands?" asked Kyria.

"Perhaps this is to match the force coming from Kronjva tomorrow," Vilius said coolly after a sip of his refreshed ale. "Although there now seems to be little stirring from the Council about standing up to them."

Elaenor approached the table with her plate of food in hand and caught every word of Vilius' reply. "Oh, Vilius, you're not spreading your cynicism."

"It's hardly cynicism when business has brought in the equivalent of three years' wages within a span of two months. But given that I've been told to taper my production ..."

"Still, you capitalize on the decrees of our nobles, and you end up better off?" Elaenor replied, rolling her eyes at Kyria. "It may be proper to hold back from complaining."

"I don't see your family's bakery suffering at all," Vilius said in return between bites of meat, his songlike voice masking his sarcasm.

"And here I thought we were joining together as a people tonight," Leena broke in, exasperated. "This meal has all the makings of undoing that before it starts."

"Indeed," Kyria said, giving Elaenor a knowing look as a familiar person drew near to their table. "Joël!"

"Good evening," Joël called out heartily to their group. "May I join you?"

"Of course," said Vilius. "It would be to our advantage if the storm clouds gather."

"Vilius," Leena responded, embarrassed. "How is that a way to greet a guest?"

"What do you mean?" Kyria said, quizzically.

"Evidently, the word is that you're quite the tempest charmer," Vilius grinned, although his voice contained a definite edge. "I know that Kaleva didn't want the word to get around but he has difficulty controlling the tongues of his crew. Apparently, our new arrival to Selanna can just speak the words, and behold!—the rain and lightning and thunder bow to him!" At this, Vilius spread his hands, wiggled his fingers, and bowed to Joël.

"Can't you show a little respect?" Elaenor snapped, looking apologetically at Joël.

Joël waved off the cloaked insult. "You seem to cover your own troubles with a blanket of bravado, my friend," he said to Vilius. "Shouldn't you at least be happy your friends survived a harrowing ordeal?"

"I wasn't there," Vilius offered, "so I can't say for sure. So please forgive me for holding off judgment until all the facts are in. I have other matters on my mind."

"Your fletching business, yes," said Joël. "Quite profitable. You must be proud of its recent expansion."

Before Vilius could reply, a flourish went up from the gathered band near the Lakihalle.

"There's our summons," Vilius groaned. "I hope you will excuse my presence with the family, Joël. I am asked to be alongside Lasjen and his commanders tonight as a guest of honor." He took up his plate and mug and began walking toward the canopy-topped washing table to turn in his dishes.

Leena reached across the table and patted Joël's hand. "I am sorry my son was so abrasive, Joël. He has not been himself since the Great Steward announced the increased supplies for the army. And he's been even worse after being told to stall his work back to normal levels. He is much like the entire city, filled with pride but with a seed of worry in us all."

"Neither of which," replied Joël, "is truly wholesome."

The thousands who gathered near the Lakihalle rivaled the crowd from the Gatherings at any seasonal Nave. The Halmo family insisted Joël stand with them, and they managed to find a place relatively close to the dais.

"Is it true?" Kyria asked Joël.

"About what?"

"What my brother said. About what happened on Kaleva's ship?"

"I am sure that your brother was not saying it in the best spirit, Kyria. However, he is not misinterpreting the story."

Kyria stared at Joël, looking for some sign he was joking. She studied his face but could detect nothing ornery or humorous. She was about to ask him if he was lying when the flourish of horns erupted again, signaling the arrival of the Council of Nobles on the dais. It was not, however, the music that stayed her question as much as what entered their line of sight. A man was struggling to carry a little boy as an older woman walked behind them. The trio was attempting to find some place near the front of the assembly and the first line of the crowd was berating them.

"I wonder what ..." Kyria began, but stopped as she saw Joël push through the crowd amid the shouts. She saw Elbart, Dirnik, Petric, Lasjen, and Umlar approach the barricade of the dais and look down.

"Move!" cried one man.

"You should have arrived here first!" called out a woman.

Kyria followed Joël through the mass of people and saw what he and others did. A little boy was lying on the ground. His crudely made crutches lay askew as a young man cradled him and tossed insults back to the crowd. The older lady, obviously the child's mother, covered her mouth with her hands. Elbart, his black hair braided again for public address, hurried over to restore order.

"What is this, Lars?" he asked the young man hurriedly. "Our assembly is about to begin."

"Beg your pardon, Great Steward, but m' little brother wanted to be near th' front, being crippled an' all. He can't see from th' back 'less I hold 'im. Please, sir, we apologize fir any trouble. I would be glad t' hold 'im, but I just got myself out of th' infirmary a li'l w'ile ago fir tha' mast drop on me in th' harbor."

"I have no issue with you being here, Lars," began Elbart, "but this is hardly the way to begin a solemn assembly. We have to ..."

Elbart stopped, transfixed. Joël had knelt in front of the little boy and taken his hand.

"Hello, son," said Joël. "What is your name?"

"Perttu, sir," the little boy said, fighting tears and shirking away from the glowering looks of Elbart, Umlar, and Dirnik.

"That is a nice name, Perttu," Joël replied gently. "How long have you been lame?"

"As long as I can remember, sir," said Perttu out loud, now oblivious to the gathered crowd. "I'm sorry for this disruption, like. I didn't mean to be a bother."

"No disruption, no bother," Joël smiled. "I'm glad we have met now." He waved the people away, creating a space around them. "Why are you crying?"

"I'm sorry, sir. It's just I see you. I know me. I feel bad. I'm such a bad boy. Wish I wasn't crippled like this. But I'm still a bad boy."

Joël reached forth and laid his hand on Perttu's head as the assembly fell to a hush. "You have done well, Perttu. You know what you truly need?"

"I hope I do, sir."

Joël looked at the people clustered nearby, then looked back at Perttu with a loving gaze. "Your sins are forgiven!"

A collective, horrified gasp went up from the nobles, a greater hopeful gasp from the crowd, and tears flowed from Perttu's eyes at the very mention of forgiveness. A furious Umlar pushed past the other nobles and scaled the dais barricade, coming nose to nose with Joël.

"Who do you think you are?" he griped loudly. "Who are you to forgive sins? Only Lord Creator can forgive sins! And do you see a wood pyre here? Do you see dasenpfear trunks and branches? Do you see a Gathering taking place?"

"I see a little crippled boy who needs forgiveness," Joël called out, ignoring Umlar and speaking to the vast throng. "And what this island cries out for is forgiveness. But in order that you might know that my words to this child have true force ..."

And here Joël knelt in front of Perttu again, placing his hands on the boy's knees.

"They can't move, sir," Perttu said quietly. "They're bent. Haven't moved 'em in years."

Joël made no reply. He felt the knees and moved his hands behind, feeling the tendons and muscles that were hopelessly contracted by years of atrophy. Pressing his hands against the skin behind the knees, he felt something loosen deep behind Perttu's joints. He looked at the child's face, and Perttu's jaw had dropped as his legs straightened. Power flooded the little boy's muscles and he wiggled his toes and bent his knees back and forth.

"It can't be," Lars said, looking on. The mother clutched her heart and looked as if she might faint. Kyria covered her mouth with both hands as tears slid down her cheeks.

"Now for the true test," said Joël, offering his hands and pulling Perttu to his feet.

Before the astonished and roaring crowd, Perttu let go of Joël's hands and took the first steps he had ever known himself to take. He hobbled on the first step, tottered on the second, and then began to walk ... to walk ... toward his mother! Before the cheering assembly, Perttu jumped into his mother's arms before being joined by Lars.

The crowd whooped and screamed with all their might. Hats flew into the air, and those nearby clamored to reach Joël. Kyria grasped his arm first.

"What ... How? I don't understand," she began. But her words were cut off by the flourish of the horns once more. The crowd swirled around them, trying to reach Joël but held back by uniformed guards. Umlar, agile for a man of seventy-five years, had bounced into the crowd and once again came face to face with Joël, with Elbart and Dirnik at his side.

"You!" Umlar screamed, flecks of spittle popping from his mouth. "Is there any form of blasphemy you are not willing to spew before the good citizens of this city, before the people of this land?"

"You are hardly the model of good citizenry, sir," barked Elbart. "We have arranged for our people to join as one, and you create this ... this carnival through your base and wanton actions?"

"Healing a child?" Joël asked, incredulous. "This is what enrages you?"

"The noble work notwithstanding," continued Elbart, "it still could have waited. Why is it that every time I see you, Joël, you are drawing attention to yourself?"

"Drawing attention is hardly the sole issue!" Umlar bawled, his eyes bulging and red. "This stranger, this upstart!" Umlar waved his hands to quiet the crowd. "You who gather here in unity of our nation and our Faith, know that this Joël has dared to forgive this lad's sins! Forgiveness, which can only flow from Lord Creator himself, and this spiteful bludge has taken our Maker's power and claimed it for himself."

Joël said nothing, but he calmly placed his left hand on Perttu's shoulder. The boy looked up at him, smiling, his eyes dancing with joy.

"You dare deny what you said?" Elbart growled, bumping against Joël as the guards pressed around.

"If you need to confirm what I said," Joël answered, "then why does it take armed guards to surround me as you verify my words? If you desire to worship Lord Creator and honor him as you do when this city gathers here, then why do so in the pomp and livery we see splashed across these streets, which brings glory, not to Lord Creator, but to yourselves? If you truly wish to follow and adore Lord Creator, then why did you need to do so while previously searching for an opportunity to throw off the yoke of Kronjva? And if Lord Creator offers forgiveness as freely as you seek in every Gathering at each seasonal Nave, then why do you reject that one can bring that forgiveness in his name?"

"Blasphemer!" cried Umlar.

"Traitor!" Elbart yelled.

Even Lasjen was not amused. He bulled into the cluster of bodies around Joël. "Such words you speak," he boomed in earshot of hundreds nearby, "are hardly the example of decency. You have disrupted this assembly once again with your disorder and have called into question your very loyalty."

"Isn't loyalty first given to Lord Creator and not the idol of political liberty?" Joël asked, bringing pained gasps from some in the throng, cheers from more, and jeers from others.

"You believe that we are to be subject to those who seek to enslave us?" Elbart roared.

"Enslave you?" Joël answered in a shocked tone. "You should ask first and foremost which servitude is more devastating, your subjugation to Kronjva or your slavery to Tuona?"

"The devil's own!" cried Umlar. "He dares to call us children of the devil!"

"You can place yourself in that ring by virtue of your own words, high priest, and Tuona would warmly embrace you. You debate and dispute if it is right to remain under the yoke of another people! I tell you that to do so is to ignore the light and easy yoke of service and love to Lord Creator, who offers forgiveness for your rebellion, and I come bearing that gift!"

At these words, Umlar, Elbart, and Dirnik howled ferociously. Lasjen reached through the roaring crowd and collared Joël, dragging him toward the dais.

"No! No!" cried Kyria. Out of the corner of her eye, she saw Kaleva, Henrik, and Saku scramble through the crowd, trying to reach Joël and free him, but in no time, they were stopped by the guards.

Lasjen had just lifted Joël over the barricade by the collar of his tunic and was barking orders to his lieutenants above the tumult. Before he could finish his commands, though, Petric swept in between the general and Joël.

"Lasjen, please! Stop! You cannot do this!"

"You're wanting him to foment a revolt right here, Petric?"

"He is correct," yelled Elbart. "He needs to be placed in the prison!"

"If the Council drags this man into the prison," Petric shouted over the bellowing masses, "in full view of these people, then the revolt will be uncontrollable! And do you want that on the eve of Prince Dewulf coming ashore?"

Elbart and Lasjen looked at each other, gauging the sense of Petric's entreaty. For his part, Joël stood apart from the roaring crowd, staring at the nobles as if awaiting their sentence.

"Umlar," Elbart ordered, taking the high priest by the arm, "calm the people and lead them in song and prayer. We are taking this upstart to the Lakihalle quietly."

"Great Steward, have you lost proper sense?" Umlar spluttered.

"Do as I say! You and Gheren complete the evening. We will stand back with Joël and then take him where we might continue our discussion."

Elbart removed his cloak, his skin moist against his tunic from the summer warmth. Three servants lit the lamps in the Lakihalle's court atrium, and the dark wood walls flamed with light, even though plenty of sunlight poured through the clerestory windows looking out to the White Sea.

Joël stood politely, walking stick in hand, as the nobles gathered in their low chairs. Only Petric wore a look that could conceivably be judged as kindly. Elbart took the middle chair arrayed on the platform raised three feet above the floor. Lasjen and Dirnik sat on either side of the Great Steward, and other nobles filled in the rest, Petric seating himself a few feet from where Joël stood.

Elbart rose from his chair, deliberately descending the steps toward Joël. "You, sir, seem to enjoy playing the gadfly's role, butchering the relative calm of our fair city and noble country. Causing a stir at the Gathering of Brightide Nave is one concern. When reports swirl that you have managed to mollify a storm on the White Sea, people are impressed but worry all the same. Now that a crippled child is healed, his family and others rejoice! But all you seem to concern yourself with is prodding our people's disturbance further with your vexing declarations."

Silence reigned in the atrium. When Joël did not answer a word, Dirnik leaped from his chair. "Well?" he angrily blustered. "Do you have nothing to say to these charges?"

"What indeed are the charges, Sir Dirnik?" Joël requested placidly. "I hear many recollections of what has been done. You yourselves were there at the Gathering when I spoke. You know what I said. About the storm, I do not deny it. Do you not trust the reports from the ship crew? And as far as little Perttu being healed, why is this cause for judgment rather than celebration?"

"It seems just your way to ask questions in response to our questions!" Elbart barked at him.

"Great Steward," Joël spoke evenly but firmly, "the only question levied against me in this room came from Dirnik; none came from you. But if I may, I find it disturbing that the love of Lord Creator shown to one of his children is a matter of such concern."

"Your insistence on placing yourself at the center of these proceedings, in a way that detracts and divides our people, the day before we are to receive our lords from across the White Sea!" Lasjen called out, rising from his chair. "No one denies the good that Lord Creator would do! But to do so now is unthinkable. And to do it through someone like yourself is impossible!"

Joël moved for the first time, taking three deliberate steps toward the general. Two sentries moved from the corners of the room and barred Joël's path.

"My general," he said finally, "why is that impossible?"

"You cannot speak seriously!" Elbart roared. "You must be mad!"

"I told all of you, just two months ago, that you would repeat that accusation toward me. Would a mad man do such things? Would someone enter a city, live quietly, repair items for others, and dwell in good faith with the citizens of Selanna? Would someone offer to board

74

a ship with a crew, help with the everyday duties, and calm a storm? Would someone stoop to heal a little boy who could not walk and offer him the cleansing grace of Lord Creator? If a man was mad, would he do all these things, and do them exceedingly well?"

"It is precisely because of what you did that we have no other option!" Dirnik snapped. "Who are you to forgive the sins of others? It is only Lord Creator himself who can grant absolution of our wrongdoings!"

"And why is that?" asked Joël.

"You heretic!" Dirnik growled, mouth agape.

"You have made your statement, sir. Why is it difficult for you to tell us all why Lord Creator is the only one who can grant forgiveness?"

"I, for one," said Umlar, who had just entered the atrium, "would be very interested to hear this from our young vagabond."

"Whether I am a vagabond or not is for history to decide," smiled Joël, "and you know not what you say when you assume my age, but I believe Dirnik can give an answer to my question."

"I, too, would like to hear it," Petric said, standing and fixing his eyes on Dirnik, "in the interest of giving Joël a fair hearing."

"Don't tell me you've come under his spell!" Elbart shouted at Petric.

"Dirnik, just answer," Petric said, nonplussed.

The insulted Dirnik tugged at his cloak and stepped down from his chair. "The truth is simple, so simple that this vagabond can see it. Only Lord Creator can grant forgiveness because it is only his to give! We cannot grant that!"

"We do all the time, Dirnik," Petric said calmly. "What if I want to forgive you for insulting me for saying I've come under Joël's spell? Can't I do that?"

"That's different," Joël corrected.

"As shocking as it is to agree with this madman, he is correct. That is a different matter!"

Petric joined them on the sunken floor. "Why? Why is that different?"

"Because if I insulted you, then I offended you in that action. You were the one offended, so it was your right to let go of the offense."

"Dirnik is correct," said Joël.

"But," Dirnik shot back, turning on Joël, "you are not!"

"I'm not?"

"Most certainly not, you apostate fomenter," Umlar screamed from his chair, "for you have no right to forgive the totality of that child's sins!"

"Because they were committed against many people?" asked Joël.

"Yes! But ultimately against Lord Creator!"

"Agreed, and you say that because ...?"

"Because the only one who can forgive all sins is the one who is ultimately offended by all sins!"

"Agreed."

"And the one who is ultimately offended by all sins is the Maker of all things!"

"Agreed."

"One who is over everything and everyone, and the one who deserves all honor and worship!"

"Agreed."

"Then why," Elbart shrieked, "do you dare befoul the air and stain our soil with your falsehood and your division?"

"I have neither befouled nor stained, Great Steward, nor have I spoken falsehood. As to the charge of division, I have simply done what I did because of everything that the high priest has eloquently claimed here and now."

"You are saying, then," Umlar spat, "that you are here in Selanna to show all of us the way back to Lord Creator, to demonstrate the path back to Vuoristad?"

"No," Joël replied. "I am here in Selanna, not to show the way, but because I am the way to Lord Creator."

The silence that hung in the atrium became heavy with shock. Even Petric could not quite believe what he was hearing.

Finally Joël spoke. "No further accusations?" He paused. "Then I shall take my leave. For now you know why I forgave Perttu his sins."

Joël turned and sauntered out of the atrium, into the vast expanse of the Lakihalle, and finally walked outside into a thunderous volley of cheers from the people outside. Not a single noble called him back, nor did any sentry or guard lay a finger on him.

Umlar glared at Elbart. "Great Steward, it is blasphemy that he even exists! He defies our Faith and acts as if he speaks for the Maker of our world! The idea is preposterous!"

"How can you possibly know that for sure, Umlar?" Petric offered, sweeping his hand in a dismissive wave. "We know one day that Lord Creator will send the Rhoken. How do we know Joël isn't the Courageous One?"

"Truly, you can't believe that, Petric!" gasped Dirnik.

"What I am saying is we shouldn't be too sure of what we think we know," Petric replied. "Joël comes into our city from nowhere that we know of. He is a decent and good worker. No one has complained about him. We all heard about his miracle at sea. Now we have seen for ourselves a miracle here in our midst! My fellow nobles, whatever we might say about Joël, his actions leave us no other option. You can curse him and shut him up for being a deceiver about what he can do and who he is, yet the way he conducts his life amongst the citizens of this city is not the life-path of a deceiver. Or we can take him at his word because we can find no fault in him. What you can't do is call him mad, because he certainly retains full control of his mind. But you must choose, for what is clear to me is that you cannot ignore him!"

"That is the very problem, Petric," said Lasjen. "At morning nave tomorrow, thirty ships will arrive here at Selanna from Kronjva. At a time when we are prepared in case simmering rivalries should fester, when we are trying to display national pride, good citizenry, and decent order, this Joël threatens to tear our needs apart. His actions do not serve the needs of our nation."

"Have we ever thought that what we believe our needs might be are in fact not the most important affairs, Lasjen?" asked Petric. "Perhaps Joël is calling us to something greater?"

"Greater than our life as a nation?" Lasjen shouted. "Greater than the glory of our prominence even as we hope for freedom? If Joël is serious about the needs of this people, perhaps he should be attentive to that!"

"Quiet, all of you!" Elbart grumbled, turning around and facing the window, which was now letting in the long rays of twilight. "None of this is needed at this point! It does us no good to have him showing off his powers when Prince Dewulf and his navy are here. They might view that as a threat we cannot defend at this point. But neither can we just bar him from the life of the city. He enjoys too much good will from the people, so we cannot have a large-scale rebellion on our hands, either. The people love him, and so we must find a way to honor the people. And speaking of the people, I believe it is high time the rest of you made yourselves present among them to reassure them of your leadership. Good night."

The nobles began filtering out of the atrium, and Umlar might have left as well if he hadn't seen Elbart signal him and Dirnik to stay. They came to either side of him, and he waited until all the others had left before continuing.

"We must find a way to honor the people, I said," he began, "but that also means we can find a way to turn the people against him and to our side."

"There are ways, Great Steward," nodded Dirnik.

"Yes, Great Steward," agreed Umlar. "There are ways."

12

"Have you ever seen anyone with that sort of talent?" Elaenor wondered aloud as their group strolled up the Great Market Road.

"Are we speaking about talent or power?" asked Kyria as they tried to keep up with Kaleva, Henrik, and Saku. "Because what we saw tonight seemed to be more of the latter than the former."

Kaleva stopped and turned quietly toward them. "I can assure you that having seen him turn aside a storm like it was a scrap of parchment, it's power beyond anything I've ever seen."

"I agree," mused Saku. "We've experienced what people would call Lord Creator's blessing when we've prayed. You pray a fever will break and it does. You pray that you will return home from a voyage safely and you do. You pray for food and drink so that you don't starve. But to see power like that is a scope greater than ever before."

"Why do you suppose he is here?" asked Kyria as they approached the city gates at the North Wall.

"Joël?" Henrik replied. "That is the most confusing question. We know he is here. He has done no harm and, from my view, he's done nothing but good. But there is a mystery about him that is unsettling."

"And yet we're still leaving the city, in the dark, to look for him," noted Elaenor.

"Let's make sure we can leave the city," said Kaleva as they drew near the gates. "Ho, Niilo! You drew guard duty tonight?"

"First watch, until midnight," a red-haired guard with sheathed sword and a blue cap called back. "And if you don't mind my asking, why are the lot of you wandering this direction at this late hour?"

"Trying to find our friend Joël."

"Joël? Oh, heard of him! Repairer, healer? And if the reports should be believed, wanderer."

"Wanderer?"

"Walked to the Coastal Gate, did he. That was the word. News passed down the line in the battlements when he was let out of the city so that no one would take a shot at him."

"Where was he going?" asked Kyria.

"They pay me more and I might have asked that myself Miss. Anyhow, gossip was that he was headed to the vineyards near Elks Hill. Don't tell me you're intending to chase him down?"

Kaleva waved his torch toward the gate. "Alert your superiors, Niilo, that we have need to go out and find Joël. We go, we search, we return with him, understand? Can you please let us out?"

"Your signal upon your return?" inquired Niilo.

"You don't trust us?"

"I do, Kaleva. But I also have an interest in the five of you not ending up with a Selannan arrow in your throats. It would be a shame to be killed by one of your own."

"Any enemy would approach from the sea," reminded Elaenor.

Niilo stared hard at her. "Any guard on the battlements would take no chances."

"Very well," said Kaleva. "What signal?"

"The call of the eider duck. Two coos should be enough."

He signaled another sentry to open the gate a crack and turned over a sandglass. "You have one hour."

"How do we know he'd stay at Elks Hill?" asked Henrik. "He might have headed in that direction but I wouldn't gamble on him staying there."

"It's a beautiful spot at night," replied Kaleva. "Elevated. Overlooking the city to the south and the Toiva Valley to the north. We'll go there and then, if we don't find Joël, we'll split up."

But the group needed no division, for when they approached the western rise of Elks Hill, they could see Joël from a distance in the light of the full moon. He was between two rows of vines, kneeling and with his face downward, the crown of his head pointing north. The quintet of friends scaled the hill until they were ten feet from Joël. His head dipped slightly, then rose, dipped, then rose, his breathing shallow, his voice coming in halting whispers.

It was Kyria who thought she saw something whisk away over the east side of the hill, and she tugged on Elaenor's arm and pointed in the direction of a dark vapor. The inky cloud moved fast against the outline of the vines, and what seemed to be a cobalt mist at first disappeared as soon as Kyria noticed it.

"What?" whispered Elaenor.

Kyria shook her head. "Noth--." She hesitated. "Nothing," she whispered. "It must have been a trick of the light."

Suddenly, Saku took one step too many and his foot crunched a stray twig in the grass. The noise roused Joël from his stillness and he turned toward them. "Hello, friends," he said quietly.

"Joël," Kyria said, stealing quickly over the remaining ground between them. "Joël. Whatever are you doing here?"

"I came here to pray," Joël replied, casting a brief glance toward the east, sweat peppering his face. "I needed to come here and find some quiet. I do so from time to time."

"You heal a little boy, and the first place you go is outside the city, away from the crowds, and pray?" asked Henrik.

"Yes, to pray," answered Joël.

"Joël," said Kaleva, stooping low in front of him, "are you well?"

"I think if you came here to find me, it's time to go back to the city," replied Joël, looking eastward again.

With surprising difficulty, Joël got to his feet, Henrik and Saku each taking an arm.

"You still haven't answered my question, Joël," Kaleva pressed him.

"Kaleva," Kyria said, "let's not burden him now. We can talk on the way back."

The group began retracing their steps back toward the city, the moon granting plenty of light for their return march. As they came within sight of the North Gate, Kyria came alongside Joël.

"Why were you praying, Joël?" she asked him.

"It's most appropriate to pray to my Father, don't you think?" he replied.

"Your Father? Lord Creator is the Father of all the living, isn't he?"

"He is," said Joël, looking back, "and yet, don't you believe he is mine, as well?"

Ignoring the question, Kyria looked closely at Joël. "You look spent, Joël! You're covered in sweat!"

"Quiet, everyone," Kaleva ordered. "We're coming up the gate path." He cupped his hands around his mouth and put forth the call of the eider duck. "*Ah-ooh!*" he cooed with a pause, followed by a second "*Ah-ooh!*"

There was a crack of wood, then a creak of iron, and then Niilo's face appeared in an opening in the gate. "You made good time," he announced. "Come on through."

"Thank you, Niilo," said Kaleva, pressing an akran into his hand as six forms slipped through the gate.

As he lay down in his bed, Joël pulled the linen sheet over his body, thinking back to his time on Elks Hill just hours before. The words and entreaties that spilled from his mouth to Lord Creator resounded in his heart. The warmth, however, was matched by the soberness in his depths, a dark chime of his soul that marked the words spoken to him by his unwanted visitor on that same hill.

"What makes you think, after all you will do, that they will follow you to the end? That you will be victorious? Why should you even love them?"

"Whatever you say," Joël had said, "is and always will be a lie. And I will always love them, to the end."

"The end doesn't have to come to you," the voice growled. "Take this bread and water I give you, that you see before you, and strengthen yourself. Or acknowledge my power and confess me as the ruler of this world. You will always have Vuoristad. Isn't that enough?"

"You are not the ruler of this world. And I accept nothing from you, for all that you touch becomes ruined forever."

"Such pain you are willing to endure," the form laughed derisively, "and such temptation you push aside, all so that a few of them might possibly believe. Why do you pursue such minions?"

"Pursuing those whom you deceived and pulled into rebellion and ruin?" Joël asked. "You know why."

"Yes," the darkness said in a gravelly, throaty laugh, "it is your nature to show grace, to cherish, and to pursue the unlovable. And that is your weakness."

Gripping his hands together and muttering entreaties to Lord Creator in between his breaths, Joël looked again at the nebula, which hovered before him. "That, O Adversary, is no weakness. To be cast from Vuoristad for pride and vainglory is weakness. To snuff out the candles of my dearest creation because you have no light is the deepest flaw. And to dare believe you have a path to victory ... well, you deceive only yourself."

"Be that as it may, they will reject you. And He must reject you. And all for love, you say."

Joël heard footsteps in the grass to the west but managed to croak out the final words to the retreating shadow. "Yes, as I said, I will do. I will love them to the end."

13

The red, green, and yellow banners that fluttered in the stiff breeze throughout Selanna's harbor posed a bright contrast to the cloudless blue sky that soared over Merivalka and the White Sea. A small crowd had gathered at the harbor thoroughfare, but the true party of note was the Council of Nobles as they took their stand before several of the piers. In the distance, they watched as several Kronji ships dropped anchor and placed soldiers and diplomats aboard for transport to shore. Only two longships went on toward the harbor, their crewmembers expertly and efficiently working details on deck upon approach. The mast of the first ship bore the bright gold and blue standard of the Giant Bear, the symbol of Kronjva, and at its helm was Prince Dewulf, the heralded admiral of the Kronji fleet.

The city folk who had turned out with the nobles stood in awe of the fleet, but especially the prince. It had been said he would be king soon, as his father Canute the Eighth was said to be in failing health. Although officially a diplomatic mission, the gathered assembly believed this visit to be of a decidedly different flavor. And, they also thought, so did Prince Dewulf.

Kaleva stood near the nobles, having been asked to assist in the docking of the ships as they welcomed the prince and his troops. It was just as the ship threaded between two piers that Kaleva looked behind him. There, about forty feet from him, stood Joël.

What is he doing here? thought Kaleva.

"Dockers, approach!" called Lasjen over the cheers of the crowd and the ocean's roar. Kaleva and other ship farers surrounded Prince Dewulf's ship and secured it, offering a sturdy deck plank constructed for the occasion. Sweeping down the board off the ship came the prince, who made straight for Elbart.

"Great Steward," Prince Dewulf crooned, "my thanks for your ready reception upon our arrival."

"Your Majesty," Elbart replied, his head bowed like all those around him. "It is our honor to welcome you to Selanna and to Merivalka itself. I trust your voyage was a smooth one."

"Not much wind, so there was more rowing than usual. My galley slaves are worn out and will require immediate food, water, and rest. I trust you have quarters prepared for me."

"There are many to choose from for your selected entourage, your Majesty. A number of inns near the Lakihalle, for example. And you shall have the chief of the guest quarters for yourself. First, may I introduce Lasjen Kulmala, general of our city guard and standing army."

"Hail and well met," Prince Dewulf grunted.

"Your Majesty," replied Lasjen with a slight bow. "This way, if you would. The Lakihalle is prepared for your arrival."

As the delegation moved as one following Dewulf, Elbart, Lasjen, and the others, Kaleva turned back and approached Joël. "You're away from your shop in the middle of the day, Joël," he said. "Hardly like you."

"So many people had their opinion of the visitors, I wanted to see for myself if their assumptions were true," replied Joël.

"They have certainly brought enough protection for the prince."

"And, it seems, for members of their families. Of course, it's only normal to protect wives and children."

"This is either for show or for other reasons I cannot understand," Kaleva muttered. "As it is, it doesn't look like we'll be heading out to sea anytime soon, so it will be counting money and mending nets for some time."

"Hey! Joël!" A voice called out above the excited buzz of the crowd. Both Kaleva and Joël looked in the direction of the sound and saw Vilius approaching them. Trailing him was Kyria, who wore a look of anxiety.

"Vilius, good morning," said Joël. "You and I must have the same idea to be away from business at this hour."

"Come now, Joël," Vilius responded. "You and I know why many gather here. Sizing up the delegation is a rather strategic element for today, don't you say?"

"I do not say that," Joël said. "I have no opinion that should impress you regarding our visitors. I simply wished to be here when they came ashore."

"No one is that apolitical. The only ones here are those with a vested interest in Merivalka's well-being."

"I would say even those who aren't here are in the same category, Vilius."

"Brother, please keep your voice down," Kyria whispered. "Are you trying to start a fight?"

"And if so," Kaleva added, "with the Kronji or with Joël?"

"Have you paid your quarterly tax to the Council?" Vilius said, looking directly at Joël.

"I have."

"It didn't strike you as somewhat exorbitant?"

"Vilius, please!" insisted Kyria.

"I simply paid my tax," replied Joël. "Am I under suspicion for actually having paid what is due our authorities?"

"Ah, yes," nodded Vilius sarcastically. "Yet who exactly is our authority?"

"You are complaining about the one who rules this land when the Kronji are here?"

"I'm wondering where your loyalties lie."

"You didn't answer my question, Vilius," said Joël frankly, as the crowds continued to gather around them. Some of the Kronji reserve guards overheard the argument and were edging closer.

"I am simply noting that we may be a subjugated people, but we could live under less burdensome financial conditions."

"Is it burdensome for everyone?"

"Fine talk from one who managed to pay above and beyond the full price for your shop! But you are not everyone, Joël!"

"Your last statement was more right and more wrong than you could possibly know, Vilius," replied Joël with a pained smile.

"Surely," continued Vilius as dozens crowded around them and two Kronji guards pressed in, "you are able to speak from your extensive experience how we should respond to our captors!"

"Vilius!" Kyria shouted, but any further reply of her was overcome by the chants and murmurs of the crowd.

"Is it right to pay tribute to Kronjva, or is it not?

The hush that fell over the crowd proved cold, icy. In that emotive frost, Joël never took his shining blue eyes off Vilius, only breathing softly, jaw set, hand gently gripping his walking stick. Finally he spoke above the whispers and mutterings.

"Could someone please show me an akran?"

"You're going to show us your answer on the surface of our national coin?" Vilius sputtered, but several citizens immediately plunged into their purses and satchels upon Joël's request. Finally, an older lady, her brown hair thatched with silver streaks, wobbled toward Joël, holding out her hand.

"For you, sir," she said.

Joël smiled and placed his hand on her shoulder. "My thanks, dear one. Stay here and I will give it right back." He held up the akran. "Is there an image of a person on this coin? Does the akran bear the image of King Canute or Prince Dewulf?"

"No!" shouted the crowd, eagerly.

"Oh, what is he doing?" thought Kaleva. "Whatever answer he gives, he'll either enrage the people, the merchants, or the Kronji guards."

"Does the coin bear an image of the Great Steward or any member of the Council of Nobles?" Joël continued.

"No," the people said with less vigor, their response marked by confusion.

"Then what is it we see on the coin?" asked Joël, holding the akran aloft.

"It's a mountain!" a little boy chirped, his eyes bright and his hands pressed together. "It's Vuoristad!"

Joël stooped and rumpled the lad's blond hair. "What's your name, young man?" he asked.

"Ilari, sir." The boy blushed, but it was clear he was enjoying the attention.

"Right you are, Ilari," Joël replied. He rose to his full height. "What little Ilari has noticed, I declare to all of you! What you see on the coins you use every day in shops and in the Great Market Road, you gaze upon but never perceive. You see with your eyes but you shield your hearts. What you give ultimately is not your coinage, your wares, your income, but your very selves! You have asked," he paused, staring at Vilius, "if it is right to pay tribute to Kronjva or not! All the while, the Mountain of God, Lord Creator's home ... Vuoristad looks up at you from your palms in the marketplace and the bakeries and the shipyard and the public houses every day. It might not be the most perfect rendering of Vuoristad, but it is enough that it should draw your thoughts and loves to Lord Creator. And does it?"

"How would you know," Umlar the high priest shouted out, "how the Mountain should look?" He had evidently drawn aft by a great deal of stealth.

"Believe me, I know, more than any of you," Joël firmly replied. "But the truth remains. You speak of freedom and throwing off yokes, and you ask if it is right to give over your monies to Kronjva or not. I tell you this: Whatever you give to your captors is one thing, but never forget that all you have belongs to Lord Creator, and if you do not give all of yourselves to Him, it is you who have lost your true freedom!"

Wonder gripped all those surrounding Joël, and his final words were followed by the crowd's roars, sneers, and exultations. Brushing through the people, Joël placed the akran back into the hands of the woman who had given it.

"Thank you, sir," she gushed.

"I give it to you," Joël said, "so that you might love the One who gives you all things." And he disappeared through the morass of bodies and made his way down the Avenue of the Commonwealth to his home.

14

Three days after the Kronji arrival, the initial pulses of excitement and wonder had begun to fade around Selanna. Although the Council of Nobles had assumed the delegation would want an elaborate tour down the Great Market Road or to see school in session at the vikarloge, much of the time was devoted to council meetings and an assessment of the wall and battlements. When the day came that Prince Dewulf announced a general holiday for his own travelers and guards, the proclamation was greeted with a high sense of relief from both Merivalkans and Kronji. Even the prince's cousin, Dagarata, had gone back to the longships where her own daughter was more comfortable playing on the deck.

It was on this day that three Kronji guards exited the Iron Bow as Kyria was stopping by to see her father. Prior to their arrival, rumors spread thick and fast that the Kronji soldiers were of a rough and brutish quality. But in the short time since their landing, Kyria had not experienced anything of the sort. Thus, when she came face to face with the armed guards, she felt no trepidation.

"Good day, sirs," she said, basket in hand for her market excursion.

The ranking man nodded toward her. "And to you as well, miss. As an inquiry, you wouldn't happen to know of a place where I could have something repaired?"

Kyria brightened at the suggestion. "Well, sir ..."

"Captain, miss. I am Captain Vermeulen."

"Yes, Captain," Kyria replied. She reprimanded herself for neglecting the fact that a group of Kronji soldiers could be addressed one way, but an individual address required the rank. "I am happy to say that as you have been to the best public house in Selanna, I can take you to the best repair shop in the city, as well."

"You seem rather confident in your statement, young lady," said one of the others, a red-haired private.

"I am biased, of course, regarding the Iron Bow," Kyria replied, "as my father owns and runs it. But I can also tell you that the repairman you require truly has no peer."

"Is there nothing he cannot do?" Captain Vermeulen inquired.

"Everything that has been brought to him has been done well. In fact, one could argue the repairs made each project better than new."

"Ha!" Vermeulen retorted with a playful grin. "We'll see if your friend is up to the challenge." He reached behind his head and pulled two metal sleeves from the pack he carried. "My armor greaves are in need of care. Both the buckles came loose and need reattaching. We come all this way with our Prince, but somehow, he overlooks the need of spare parts on board. Apparently, he believes that despite a lengthy time here, we will still be granted immunity from breakdowns in our ensemble."

Kyria looked at the greaves, mesmerized by the painting of the grave and scowling Giant Bear on the front of each. The brilliant blue background contrasted greatly with the golden glint of the bear's image. The intent of the dazzling color, Kyria guessed, was to blind opposing forces during an infantry charge.

"Well, miss?" Captain Vermeulen asked. "Is this a project worthy of your friend?"

Kyria looked at Vermeulen and his fellow guards. "If you will follow me." And she began walking southward.

Joël was finishing repairing a cracked cup as a gift for the newly mobile Perttu when Kyria walked through his front door, followed by three uniformed men with sheathed swords. The tallest and most decorated of the men held a pair of highly colored iron plate sleeves and he walked directly toward Joël, who was clad in a cream-colored work shirt and green twill pants.

"Your friend Kyria informed us that you can repair nearly anything in this city," said the soldier. "Allow me to introduce myself. I am Vermeulen, one of the captains of Prince Dewulf's army. The Prince has given us a general holiday today and we came across this lady, who has brought us here. As you can figure, I wouldn't be here in the shop of a Merivalkan citizen unless there was dire need."

"It looks as though your greaves require repair," Joël acknowledged, standing and looking at the gold and blue iron contraptions, well equipped to protect any fighter's shins from impact.

"Yes, the fronts are not the issue," said Vermeulen. "As you can see, the buckles for the straps are faulty and need new clasps. When do you think you might have them done?"

"A matter of minutes," Joël responded, clapping his hands together and beckoning Vermeulen into the kitchen.

"Minutes!" The three soldiers and Kyria shouted in unison.

"My friend Kyria wounds me with her unbelief," Joël laughed. "She's seen me repair plenty of items. No, Captain, the problem is not faulty clasps."

"Of course they are. See how the hook can't even reach the metal loop. It's faulty."

"It's true they do not reach, but it's not a faulty clasp. The hook has become rusted here at its base where it slips into the sleeve of the leather strap." Joël held the strap of the greave close where the soldiers and Kyria could all see it. "It's nothing out of the ordinary. Water, rain, the elements ... they've all conspired to do this. What is needed isn't a new buckle but to clean the rust from this one. That should loosen the hook and give it better range and help it attach to the loop of the clasp."

"And how do you intend to do that?" asked one of the other soldiers.

"I'm sure our humble shopkeeper has his way, Gilles," said Vermeulen.

"Before I begin, would the four of you care for some water?" asked Joël.

The soldiers and Kyria agreed to a drink, and Joël poured four tin mugs of water. Kyria sat in the corner, waiting for Joël to display his wares. She had no idea how he would manage to please Captain Vermeulen, but she had all the faith in Joël that he would do just that.

"You have the materials needed right here?" inquired the third soldier, who introduced himself as Cornetin.

Joël cut several dasenpfears into thin slices and gave half the fruit to the soldiers and Kyria. The rest he placed in an iron pan as he heated the fire pit outside his back door with a single lit wooden log. He took a container of salt and poured out a handful onto the dasenpfear slices. Taking it to the fire pit, he placed the pan on the bolsterpiece as the heat from the flames softened the fruit and the salt popped in the juices.

"Kyria?" he called from outside.

"Yes, Joël."

"There is a small container of goat's milk on the table. I just bought it this morning at Alexsi's house. Could you bring it to me along with a spoon?"

Kyria did so as the soldiers sat down, amazed at Joël's command of the process. He spooned two measures of milk into the hot, briny liquid, grabbed the pan with a thick towel, and brought the pan into the main shop room, setting it on the wooden table with a clang.

"Fruit, salt, and milk are going to repair my greaves?" asked the cynical Vermeulen.

"It will repair the clasp," said Joël, "not burnish the front where Survanki sits."

"You know the name of our god," replied Cornetin. "Not many Merivalkans, we've been told, mention him."

"I know the name of the Great Bear whom you worship," said Joël without looking up, "but shouldn't you be more concerned to worship one who created the Great Bear himself?"

"You're bold to say that, workman," remarked Gilles.

"I agree one should always be bold to say what is true. Why are you surprised?"

"You speak of the one you call Lord Creator?" Vermeulen spoke sharply, causing Kyria to jump.

"I do. I can only hope these people in the city do, as well."

93

"Then doesn't it seem improbable you give honor to your own god?" Vermeulen looked from Joël to Kyria and back again. "When our people have conquered yours?"

"Why?" asked Kyria.

"What has the Giant Bear done that you should love him?" Joël added.

"Love?" replied Vermeulen. "What does one care about loving one's god? Is that what they exist for?"

"To be a god, shouldn't a god exist from himself? And if all comes from him, then wouldn't one expect him to care for his own? And if that god cares, wouldn't he love his own?"

"That is true," Kyria said.

"And," Joël continued, looking with concern at Kyria, "if the god, like Lord Creator, loves his people, shouldn't they will to love him in return?"

"That hardly seems the point of a god," said Gilles.

"How do you know?" Joël replied. "Did your Bear tell you?"

"A Bear reveal things!" laughed Cornetin. "How preposterous!"

"We seem to have moved far afield from my greaves," Vermeulen complained.

"Indeed," said Joël. "I'll allow you to ponder what I've said. For now, let me reveal to you how these might be repaired. The solution has cooled enough. The juice from the dasenpfear, mixed with the salt and goat's milk, will dislodge the rust from your clasps." He took a rag, dipped it in the pan, and began to rub it on the clasp. The dark brown residue began to disappear and give way to a shiny glow of the metal. With a few vigorous twists of the rag, Joël managed to click the hook from its stuck position. "There, Captain. The salt mixed with the juice caused those bubbles in the solution, which dissolved the rust. Your hook can reach the clasp loop now, good as new."

"Then why the goat's milk?" asked the captain.

"That protects the leather strap from the saltiness of the solution and ..." He began to whisk the rag the length of the strap, "... you can see it cleans the strap. The elements of the goat's milk strengthen the leather from wear."

"This is amazing!" Vermeulen shouted, his eyes wide.

"This is what he does," Kyria said, smiling admiringly.

"Let me finish the other greave, and you'll be all prepared," replied Joël. He rubbed for a half minute more on the other one, dried both with another rag, and handed then back to the captain. "Your possessions, sir."

"Joël, I stand amazed at your skill and willingness," Captain Vermeulen rejoiced. He took out a money pouch. "What do I owe you?"

Joël waved him off. "No payment of funds. Allow it to be an agreement of good will between your people and mine."

"How do you ever make ends meet?" asked Kyria. "I'm sorry, but do you ever make money?"

"Oh, I merely did not accept money today," said Joël, "but that doesn't mean I won't expect payment of some kind."

"What do you mean?" asked all three soldiers at once.

"You have said you've been granted a general holiday, no? Perhaps we can enjoy that together with others. That, to me would be payment enough."

"What?" asked Kyria.

Joël turned to her. "Kyria, I'm closing the shop for the remainder of the day. Let's find some people who want to join us."

15

The Coastal Gate creaked open and—with Captain Vermeulen and his guards keeping pace—nearly fifty citizens of Selanna headed out on a sunny, hot afternoon. Joël kept conversation with several people at once, keeping his eyes on the beach area and angling toward the cliff walk that bordered the bluffs northeast of Selanna. This particular stretch of the cliff walk would widen into a broader road that formed the main travel artery between Selanna and Branström. The latter town was renowned for its wine and farming and stood ten miles up the coast. Joël knew that the full distance would be too rigorous a constitutional for several of the fellow travelers, so after about an hour of easy walking, the entire group sat in an open field. From where they stopped, they could see out over the White Sea. As they had positioned themselves on the downward slope of the ridge, they could see Branström in the distance even as their view of Selanna was obscured by the height of the ridge to their southwest. The few clouds overhead spun lazily across the sky, and all in the assembly could smell the salty tang of the ocean.

"Joël," Henrik finally spoke up. "I want to say this, given that we have many here: Do you know when the Rhoken is to come? I will say that you are without a doubt the most unique person I know. There is no doubt you can heal with your hands and your words. Many of us have seen that. You can change the circumstances around you. I have seen that firsthand. There's no question that whatever a citizen of Merivalka might be, whatever a citizen of any nation might be, you are different. You have to know things none of us do. So if we are expecting the Courageous One to come one day, then when?"

Joël looked at Henrik, then at the crowd. The people there had stirred at the mention of the Rhoken. Even the Kronji soldiers lifted their eyes, caught between their diffidence for the Merivalkans' Faith and their desire to keep order on their holiday.

"You speak of the Rhoken as distant future, but the first truth about the Courageous One is one of humility. You should humble yourselves that Lord Creator's ways are not necessarily your own. You may expect the Rhoken to come many years from now, but are you willing to open your eyes and see what is happening around you every day? You may have expectations about the Rhoken, that he will deliver you from your subjugation." And here Joël glanced briefly and sympathetically at the Kronji guards. "But are you humble enough to admit what you may not know, that there are many different kinds of defeat, of servitude? And it would be these thresholds of your hearts the Rhoken must cross first and foremost, and other concerns are merely just that ... other concerns?"

"Are you saying that you know when the Rhoken will arrive?" asked Elaenor, who had come along.

"My awareness is not as important as your readiness to receive him," replied Joël gently.

"But we make ourselves ready every week in worship at the kopanos, every three months at the Gatherings of each Nave," said a tall rug maker named Edvin from the rear of the crowd. "We are aware of our past, and we face that all the time. How much more ready can we be?"

"The readiness I speak of comes not from the sincerity of your hearts or whatever self-deprecation you can display, friend," Joël called back as the breakers crashed onto the beach far away from them. "You can be sincere that a frozen lake will support you as you walk across it, but if the ice is merely a thin layer, your sincerity will not prevent you from falling through and drowning. In like manner, if you doubt your ability to cross the same lake, but the ice is several feet thick, you will navigate the lake well even if you are fearful on every step."

"Your point is that what matters is the lake," declared Kaleva.

"That is true," Joël nodded. "What matters is where you place your trust. How you exhibit that is important, but who you believe Lord Creator to be is much more important. Ask yourself if the outworking of your Faith reflects this! The way you pray, sing, and gather ... if someone accused you of believing that Lord Creator loves you and is for you, would there be enough evidence to convict you?"

"Lord Creator shows love to us by giving us what we need," acknowledged Edvin.

"All you need and more," replied Joël, "and he gives you your daily bread. But Lord Creator not only shows love; He is love. Imagine, if you would, a farmer who tends to his crops, prunes weeds, keeps wild animals out, and ensures as best he can that he will have a good harvest. Or a herdsman with his sheep, patiently grooming their wool and taking them out to graze. Or a quartermaster of a town like Branström or Selanna, taking supplies to people who live out of town. Does he not care for the reindeer that pull the wheel-sled? Or a mother who sees her daughter has fallen and is injured? Is her heart not broken and overflowing with compassion?"

"In each of these, you see people like you exhibiting care and love, whether it be for crops or animals or other people. You would never doubt or question their love. Yet imagine how different Lord Creator is from each of you in power. The variance between you and an object, animal, or child is paltry compared to the chasm between Lord Creator's being and yours. And yet He cares for each of you, providing food from the earth, water from its rivers, clothing from the materials produced around you. But He doesn't love you because he provides for you; He provides for you because He loves you!"

"What indeed is the difference?" asked Kaleva.

"The love of Lord Creator is not dependent upon your work, your response to him, or anything you can imagine. His love is free and infinite. Those who are condemned are condemned by their willingness to reject the grace of Lord Creator. Truly, you wish him to accept you, to honor you as His children. But if that is why you have your Gatherings, aren't you missing the truth?"

"You offer yourselves time and again to Lord Creator, every three months at the Gatherings and every week at the kopanos. But He calls you to offer yourselves to Him every day, to receive His love and grave, and to rest upon His love and grace. You must not ask forgiveness so that He will love you; you ask for and receive forgiveness because Lord Creator loves you!"

"This," said Edvin, "as attractive as you make it, seems too good to be true. Why would it be offered this freely?"

"Are there degrees of freedom when it comes to the love and grace of Lord Creator?" Joël replied. "If so, then such grace would cease to be grace."

He paused, looking around the people who were marking his every word. "The Faith tells you truly that all we see is fallen from glory, yet does not this world pulse with heartbeats of the goodness of what Lord Creator brought into being at the first? You speak truly that Lord Creator loves and provides for you, yet you seek to earn that love by wishing you could ascend once more to Vuoristad. And yet never do you wonder if the One who dwells on Vuoristad could descend to you!"

Kyria stood. "Can you not see, though, that this good news is overwhelming for us, Joël? We cannot be ruined and yet seek for Lord Creator, can we?"

Joël passed through the assembly until he stood before Kyria, placing his hand on her shoulder. "Dear one," he said loudly enough for all to hear, "you are right the news is overwhelming. But would you not expect that of truth that strikes at the deepest hopes of your hearts? Of certainty that stirs your soul because Lord Creator whispers it from the heights? The news that you cannot ascend the Mountain of God is not despair! It is the best news of all!"

"How?" Kyria gasped, on the verge of tears. "How is that good news?"

"Can a dasenpfear that has fallen to the ground fly into the tree and attach itself back to the limb from whence it came? Of course not! Can water flow up a waterfall or a mountain? Water flows downward because it must; it is pulled to the earth. And when it reaches its destination, it continues flowing. Observe when water flows over the soil of a farmer's field. It does not merely sit on the surface but it seeks even deeper dwelling, sinking into the depths and going down to the roots of the plants. That is what Lord Creator has done. Of course you can't ascend to where He is, so He pursues you with the clear, flowing, descending water of His grace. It is always flowing, always reaching. His grace is the water that flows to the lowest place; no one is beyond His reach and salvation!"

It was then that one of the women, a clothier named Lilja, smiled but nearly fell over. Several around her kept her from fainting. "Are you all right?" Joël asked.

Several moments went by and whispers passed amongst the friends surrounding Lilja. "She seems to be," said Elaenor, approaching Joël. "But the reason for her swoon is that she hasn't eaten since mid-morning and she needs food."

"Does anybody have anything?" asked Saku, whose voice startled everyone given how quiet he had been the whole time since leaving the city. "We're miles from home, and we're probably coming up on supper."

A brief scramble of all the victuals brought along revealed only a paltry amount. Kaleva and Henrik joined Saku in the collection and, turning to Joël, said morosely, "Very little. We gave Lilja a dasenpfear and a piece of trout, but she's not the only one starving, and we have only a loaf of bread, three pieces of salted chicken, and a couple of pavenders. At least there is a spring of fresh water down the path there."

"You have the food with you?" asked Joël.

Henrik and Saku held it forth, and Joël took it eagerly into his hands. "Tell everyone to stay calm and listen."

Kaleva turned away and cleared his throat, but Henrik grabbed him from behind. "You're going to tell people to prepare for half a bit each, at best? Are you insane?"

Thumping Henrik's meaty shoulder, Kaleva replied, "Brother, we saw him destroy a storm and give us safe passage back from sea. I think I'm ready to take a few things on faith."

In a matter of seconds, Kaleva had calmed the people and asked them to sit down. Joël stepped forward with the bread and fish in one hand and the chicken scraps in the other. Looking over the plain, gazing northward to where the elevation rose and the darkened summit of

Vuoristad pierced the horizon, he raised his hands and called out, "Lord Creator, my Father and the Giver of all good things, You are the One who multiplies grace that flows to these lowest places. Cause us to taste of your abundant love as we taste of this multiplied food, to the glory of your name."

Bringing his hands downward, Joël handed the bread to Kaleva, the fish to Henrik, and the chicken to Saku. "Give one to everybody."

"One?" the three men echoed in unison.

"Yes," Joël grinned.

"Joël, I have only one loaf of bread," Kaleva chuckled.

"I know. Give one loaf to everybody." And Joël's eyes were dancing with joy as he said it.

Feeling short of breath, Kaleva walked over to Lilja, bearing his loaf. She saw him approaching and waved appreciatively. "I believe I am feeling better, but having some bread for the walk back to Selanna will help."

"I know, Lilja," Kaleva said apologetically, "but one loaf is all I have."

"You must have not known how to do your sums from your school days," Lilja replied, giggling with joy.

"What do you mean?"

"Give me one and you'll still have one left over," she pointed at his hands.

Kaleva looked down at his hands and nearly dropped what he held. Not believing what he saw, he beheld two rye loaves, one of which Lilja eagerly took from him.

"I ..." he began. "I ... I."

"Hi, Kaleva," called Edvin, "might I have some bread with this chicken?"

Kaleva looked over at Saku, who had just served Kyria and Elaenor before coming to Edvin. Saku's knees were knocking at the sight of five full strips of salted chicken in his hands. Henrik was passing out a steady stream of pavenders to others. Kaleva looked again at what he held and saw that he was struggling to hold three loaves now. The grass was alive with people swarming around in the wonder of a feast created out of thin air!

In five minutes, fifty citizens of Selanna were munching contentedly on their unexpected dinner while a rotating group of helpful souls took small earthen jars and other containers to the spring for a continual supply of drinking water. Even the Kronji soldiers joined in the feast, munching on the provisions agape with wonder. Kaleva wandered back over to Joël, who was eating with Kyria and Elaenor. Taking chicken from Saku and a pavender from Henrik, Kaleva chewed on his loaf of bread, not believing what he had just experienced.

"You make a storm invisible," Saku voiced effusively, "and now you make a meal from the invisible."

"This is unlike anything before," whispered Kaleva. He turned to Joël. "You are unlike anyone before. This is truly the work of Lord Creator."

"His grace is flowing to you, Kaleva," Joël replied, "as my Father intends."

"Your Father?" inquired Henrik.

"And yours as well," Joël said, before tearing open his bread and taking a bite.

16

The crowd was in a buoyant mood as they approached the gates of Selanna, with the sun descending to the horizon's edge. With the approach of Suntide Nave, the hours of daylight in Merivalka were at their zenith, and so the Merivalkan guards at the Coastal Gate could see the returning party and had no need to ask them to identify themselves.

As Joël passed by the gate along with Kaleva, Kyria, and their friends, he took the sack of leftover food from Henrik and went up to the lieutenant of the evening watch.

"Sir?" he said. "You are in charge?"

"I am. My name is Tarmo."

"My good Tarmo, thank you for allowing our return. We had a picnic together and want this to be our gift to you and your men as our gratitude for your kindness."

"What is this?" asked Tarmo.

"Merely what was left over. Twenty pavenders, thirty-two pieces of salted poultry, and about fifteen loaves of fine bread. To be well fed, we believe, would make for happy guards and also make for a safe Selanna."

"At least at this gate, Joël," replied the usually stern Tarmo, his eyes twinkling. "I thank you, both my own thanks and for my men."

"Think nothing of it. The sack, by the way, belongs to dear Elaenor."

"I'll make sure it's returned to Jehre's bakery. Thank you!"

"Will the food multiply continually once in the guards' hands?" Henrik asked Joël once they began walking along the street toward the shipyards.

"You ask good questions, Henrik," said Joël, "but this time, the food they received will be the food they eat. No more, no less." He looked at Kaleva, who appeared stunned. "Kaleva, you have questions?"

"Plenty," Kaleva replied, shaking his head, "but of the sort I need to ponder for some time rather than ask immediately. Perhaps that would be better."

"Those tend to be the best questions," Joël agreed.

Kyria smiled and laughed. "I've never known anything to quiet Kaleva like today!"

"You there! Joël!" Captain Vermeulen shouted from the rear of the group. Joël, Kyria, and the others turned. Vermeulen strode toward Joël, hand raised.

"I wanted to thank you for your work today as I have neglected to do so until now," the soldier said quietly. "Truly, I have never seen such fine activity."

"There is no need," said Joël.

"I was speaking, not only of your work on my greaves, but for the food, also. I meant to thank you for that." He had difficulty meeting Joël's eyes. "You are truly a citizen who does all things well. You are unlike anyone here."

"I hope that, more than the gifts, you and your men have at least opened your hearts to the Giver, as well."

"The distance between our faiths is a wide distance," replied Vermeulen, "and frankly, I worship the Great Bear because it is tradition that gives hope and for no other reason. Before today, I always thought of the miraculous as an accident. But what you did, you meant to do. Forgive me for a military man being quite shaken to his inmost depths."

"There is no shame in that, Captain."

"You also are different from this nation in another respect. I happened to stand nearby when the crowd surrounded you and the young man pressed you on the matter of Merivalkan tribute to our government. It was just after we came ashore in the harbor. You remember."

"I must apologize for my brother, Captain," offered Kyria. "He was the one who instigated that."

"I do not speak to condemn your brother, but to commend Joël here," answered Vermeulen. "You handled yourself well and you peaceably quelled that situation. You are neither a wealthy merchant who profits from trade with us, nor are you a rebellious citizen who seeks to throw off our yoke. You find the new way. I appreciate that."

"I can only hope you see the new way of which I spoke today," said Joël.

"We are too far apart for that, Joël."

Joël peered into the eyes of Captain Vermeulen. "Remember, Captain, grace flows more deeply than you can imagine."

"I can only hope so," Vermeulen said. He offered his hand to Joël and they clasped. "Thank you."

The Kronji soldiers walked toward the Lakihalle as Joël's group continued walking toward the shipyard. "Making a few friends?" Elaenor asked.

"The warmth of Lord Creator's smile does not fall only on Merivalka, Elaenor," Joël replied. "Why should other nations be excepted?"

"Sir, can I speak with you?" A voice called out from the front of the group. A tall young man pushed his way through until he was face to face with Joël.

"Yes, you wish to speak?"

"Sir, my name is Osku. Osku Virtanen."

"Virtanen. Your father is the one who owns the mill on the west side of town, true?"

Osku doffed his hat. "And newly elected to the Council of Nobles, yes. He will be seated soon. I occupy a less stellar position than he does, but I am just as hungry for truth as I am for the success of our business."

"That is most noble, Osku," Joël remarked.

"I was hoping to see you today and found you had left the city for some time. Now that you are back, my question cannot wait any longer."

"And that question is?" asked Joël as others crowded around.

"You speak of the love of Lord Creator and being with him. You talk of that as naturally as eating, drinking, or breathing. So I ask you as one who pines to know: What must I do to receive this life with Him?"

"Do? That is an interesting choice of words!"

"Yes, what must I do? To receive life with the Maker of all things, there must be a key that opens the lock."

"Again, your words are fascinating. 'What must I do?'"

"Certainly. That's what I meant."

"What do you mean by 'what'?"

Osku looked down at Joël, who was a good six inches shorter than the wealthy Virtanen. "Something to do. What one thing must I do?"

"Is it as simple as one thing?"

"You've spoken in such a way that it seems to be simple, but the answer escapes me."

"Perhaps the answer is before you."

"I am listening."

"Osku, as a citizen of this city and this nation, I am sure you know what is in the Stories. You know the ways of the Faith and the good life Lord Creator set down after the Great Ruin and before the dawn of the First Age. What was it that Besno showed to our ancestors in words as deep as a dagger in the wall that rings Vuoristad? The Revered Way, the good life as the path for the follower of Lord Creator. Even a few of those truths should suffice. *You shall not take the life of the innocent. You shall not cheat those in your midst. You shall not break faith in marriage or troth or purity. You will uphold truth, speak honestly, and be satisfied with your possessions. You must honor your father, mother, and all authority.* Surely there should be no question about the good life of Lord Creator's?"

"Of course there is no question," Osku replied in a voice of quiet, guileless confidence, "but all these words, this calling I have accepted and kept faithfully all my life. What else is there to do?"

"A little humility, perhaps?" whispered Henrik, who stood back with Kaleva, Saku, Elaenor, and Kyria.

Joël said nothing at first. In fact, Kyria began to wonder if he would say anything at all but rather agree with Osku. She looked at him and saw his jaw quiver. When he finally spoke, Joël placed his hand on Osku's arm and formed his words slowly, in a voice shaking with emotion. Kyria looked and saw Joël blinking back tears.

"Very well, Osku. Since you believe you have kept the will of Lord Creator as He desires, you have asked for one thing. And here is that one thing: You are to inherit your father's business, correct?"

"I am. He is giving it to me to manage when he takes his seat on the Council."

"And along with the textile profits and the contracts you have with merchants here and abroad?"

"That is correct," said Osku, who smiled even as his voice betrayed a decrease in his bravado.

"A beautiful thing, work. A helpful thing at times, wealth," Joël replied quietly. "Osku, do one thing, and one thing only, and you will have the life you seek."

"Anything, Joël!"

"Take the mill, your wealth, and all your dreams of outstripping your father's goals. All you have and all you've been given. Take them, and sell them."

"S ... se ... sell them? Osku sputtered. "And the money?"

"Sell it all. Give the money away."

"A-all of it?"

"Every akran, Osku. Give it to the lame boy who begs down by the pier. Give it to the widow who hasn't eaten in two days so her daughter can have soup to eat. Give it to the Kronji soldier who is stationed here, far from home, wife, and child. Give it all away until you have nothing left but the shirt on your back and the breeches on your legs and the shoes on your feet. Come live at my shop, talk, eat, and listen to me, forsaking everything else. Where I might go, follow along.

And I promise you, you will have life beyond any abundance imaginable."

Kyria could not believe what she was hearing. As Joël's thick, husky voice uttered the words, she couldn't help but believe they were not merely intended for Osku, but also for her. How comfortable she had become in her family home, working and helping her father, and believing Selanna had all she could want. And yet when Joël spoke about the grace of Lord Creator, hadn't she believed that was worth abandoning everything to receive? Could she? And what did that involve?

She looked up, surprised to see Joël standing there, unmoved, while her friends let out disappointed gasps. Osku, head bent and shoulder slouched, was walking in the opposite direction, toward his family's textile mill on the west edge of town.

"What happened?" she asked.

"He chose," Joël said regretfully.

"He felt he had no choice," said Elaenor.

"There's always a choice," Joël answered, still watching in the twilight until Osku disappeared from sight.

"It's a lot to give up," replied Saku. "A lot to ask."

Joël turned to them. "There's more at stake than you can possibly imagine, my friends! But what an idol! What a power that holds him in its grip! It's so difficult for the wealthy to let go of what they hold dear and give it all up for so much more."

"If that's the case, Joël," offered Kaleva, "who can receive this life from Lord Creator? Who can gain it? How do we even have the ability? What chance do we have?"

Joël smiled broadly and extended his palms toward Kaleva, as if he had just answered a vexing riddle.

"That's exactly the truth! What chance do you have? But why do you require a chance when Lord Creator does the unthinkable instead?"

Joël took another step into their midst, gathering them into a tight circle around him, where their heads were almost touching each other.

"Call to Him, my friends, and you just might find He has been calling you all along."

He quietly turned and walked down a side lane, headed home, leaving them under the setting sun alone with their thoughts.

17

The lengthy constitutional of that afternoon and evening left Joël's back and legs both weary and sore. He took a drink from the small well behind his shop as the sliver of moon dropped behind the clouds. His friends had given him much delight over the spontaneous meal and the subsequent conversation. He thought of the looks on their faces upon his challenge to them after Osku had walked away. Kyria's concern, Kaleva's curiosity, Henrik's bemusement, Saku's wonderment, and Elaenor's reflectiveness. Their faces shuttled through his mind as his heart beat with gladness for their receptive ears. Bowing his head, Joël quietly prayed for their hearts to be equally open to the loving offer of Lord Creator.

Taking another gulp of water, Joël felt the liquid spill over his lips onto the front of his tunic. Squeezing the fabric, he dispelled some of the water from his shirt as he sat on the rough ground. Reaching to his side, he patted his walking stick as if thanking an old friend.

"You did well," he said to the stick before lying flat on the ground and looking to the sky. Some of the stars peeked through the sluggish flow of the clouds, and as Joël exhaled slowly, he called off their patterns, their kuvim.

"Koiri ... Hiiri ... Miekammi," he greeted the shimmering clusters of the Dog, the Mouse, and the Swordsman in the southern heavens that spread over the White Sea. He closed his eyes as he listened to the pounding of the waves colliding with the beach just east of the harbor. With a contented sigh, Joël stretched out on the ground with full intention of returning inside and eating a dasenpfear before bedtime. It was then that he felt the cold breeze whisk over him, one he could sense at once. This was no gentle air; a foul spirit pulsed through its current, followed by a voice that hissed in the darkness.

I am waiting for you.

The most eastward pier stood several stone's throws away from him, and as the waves thrashed against the sand, Joël bent down, his finger coursing through the granules in flowing, precise movements. With a series of whirls and flicks, he created a picture of a pavender, lightly denting every other scale to give the appearance of its rainbow-like tessellation. Smiling at his little creation, he felt an icy blast shear through the salty expanse before him. Joël stood to face the cobalt nebula before him.

"You are late, Tuona," he said at last.

The throaty cackle slipped from the bluish wisp. "I happened to be early. I said I was waiting for you. I didn't say where. It's not my fault you refused to come out into the sea."

"I've been to the sea already, as you know," Joël shot back. "Meeting me here does not give me any angst, to be by the sea, below the stars in the sky." He paused. "I am well acquainted with them all."

"Hardly a powerful statement given your present position," Tuona scoffed. "A lowly binder of material disfigurements. It doesn't seem to me that you are speaking from a ground of strength."

"Once again, declaring what you want to see and not what is actually there," Joël replied. "Hatred is not a ground of strength. Malice is not the high ground of future success. And evil will never, ever, result in victory."

"As I said before, your lowly position belies your speech, Joël," the cloud hissed.

Joël slapped the sandy residue from his hands and strode into the cobalt vapor, which divided, doubled back, and regathered several feet in reverse. "No one knows of a lowly position better than you, Tuona! The fall from the Mountain must have damaged you more than one would expect."

"I am no Fallen One, Joël! Standing here on this beach might provide you a sense of equality to me, but there is a great distance between us!"

"As I've said to some others in this city, you are more right than you know."

111

"Your parries of humor might sustain you for some time, but do not delude yourself into believing that you can ignore my power forever!"

"Spoken by one who backs away from me. And I don't not ignore your power. No one in Merivalka truly does that. But deep in the core of that cloudy veil, you know that I have willed myself to face your power, not turn away from it."

The vapor billowed, spread out, and then darkened against the glistening waves of the White Sea. Finally, there came a voice more steel-like than before.

"If you will yourself to face my power, then permit me to show you that power once again!" And the mist crackled in the air, ripping open a portal in the space surrounding them, and in a flash, both Tuona and Joël disappeared.

The Messengers packed the chamber, watching intently as Dalvig's chest heaved in worry and anger. Standing tall at the other end of the hall, Tuona cocked his head waiting for a reply from the myrioi commander. For the past hour, the two had roared back and forth at each other, Dalvig urging restraint and humility, Tuona urging rebellion and independence.

"Your words, Dalvig," Tuona spoke with mellifluous charm, "have been forthright if not desperate. But here in the privacy of this chamber, you should heed what I alone have dared to offer. Lord Creator has made the worlds and constructed the ages. His Holy King has breathed life into the creation we see around us, and the Breath of Lord Creator sustains life. But He has given life to His creation in order that it freely seek him, far from the glory He has given us! Do you not see that belittlement laid bare before us?"

"Belittlement, Tuona?" inquired Solvik, who stood at Dalvig's side. The myrioi warrior clenched his sword tightly as the question exploded from his lips.

"Yes, Solvik! Magnus and Merta are given this world, to explore it and enjoy it. We are made to serve Lord Creator and do His bidding.

Is that really enough for you? I tell you the truth, it is not so for me. Not so, I might add, for those who have already left this mountain and hide in secret, waiting for my command to march on Vuoristad itself!"

"Take care, Messenger!" Dalvig snorted, striding toward the center of the chamber and looking directly in the eyes of his counterpart. "And do not delude yourself into believing that the hosts you have poisoned might gain with you any fruit from this evil plan! We are created to serve Lord Creator, and this is not servitude wrought in chains, but it is the greatest grace and glory one could imagine! To dwell in the presence of God on this Mountain, to be created for this, is to find our true place and joy. In leaving that privilege, you invite not life, but certain death! No one reigns above Him because no one can!"

It was as Dalvig roared at Tuona that the recalcitrant Messenger glared in return. Even in the enclosed chamber, the entire assembly beheld the change coming over their once-respected comrade. The glorious golden chain-mail that covered Tuona glittered sourly and faded to gray. The Messenger's skin and muscles expanded, stretching thinly over his bones and turning a pale smoky blue, barely covering the bones, which gave the ghostly appearance of a fish skeleton. But the assembly gasped in horror at the most disturbing change, the emittance of a cobalt cloud that diffused from Tuona's abdomen and began to trickle throughout the chamber.

"No one can, Dalvig? You dare to question my power, my desire, my willingness, or those who will fight by my side? You doubt what can be? Then you doubt to your own destruction. You can no one can, but that is because no one has tried! But I will! I will ascend to the heavens! I will raise my throne above the stars that watch over Vuoristad! I will sit on the throne of Lord Creator, in the hall where the Holy King broods, and will expunge the Breath of the Lord that needlessly wafts through the Mountain! I will ascend above the tops of the clouds, and I will make myself—myself!—like the God of this world Himself!"

Dalvig could take it no more, and with fury unknown he grasped his lance and reared back to throw it at the sneering Tuona. But the moment he shot his arm backward, he sensed the ground shaking under his feet. He stared with fear at Tuona, convinced his new enemy had summoned an earthquake in the hollows of the Mountain itself to bury the myrioi forever. But the shock on Tuona's face betrayed that this was none of his doing; in no time, the shock transformed into fear as a great cracking noise sounded from the wall of stone behind the renegade Messenger himself.

With a massive rumble all around them and peals and roars from above the chamber, the wall behind Tuona was gashed wide open as if by an unseen sword! From the outside, a massive swirling wind grasped Tuona as if he weighed no more than a feather, plucking him from the chamber and pulling him into the air, suspended nearly thirty thousand feet above the land of Merivalka. The myrioi braced themselves against the wind by falling to the chamber floor, but Dalvig looked above to a beautiful and terrifying sight. The terrifying rumble, ensconced within the tempest surrounding them, emitted another crack as the stone roof above the Messengers became dazzlingly clear and transparent. The Messengers gaped as one, seeing that they were being given a view into the throne room of Lord Creator, whose figure of blinding light had filled the room, crowding out even the visible figure of the Holy King. Lifted roughly through the air by the power of Lord Creator, Tuona found himself face to face with the Almighty One, whose voice rang furious like the White Sea and as loudly as a battle-horn.

"Your deception and pride have brought you to this place, Tuona of the Messengers!" roared the voice of Lord Creator. "And from this place you will fall and receive your perpetual banishment! You and the Messengers whose spirits you have poisoned are thrown henceforth from this Mountain, which will remain forever unspoiled by your treachery!"

"Curse you, Lord Creator!" Tuona gagged and choked in desperate bursts. "This Mountain may remain unspoiled, but do not deceive Yourself into believing Your creation can resist my entreaties. Everything You hold dear I will bring to horrific ruin!"

The unapproachable light blazed white-hot, and Tuona himself wailed in agony as his throat burned in the grip of Lord Creator. The Maker of the world leaned toward the heinous spirit and growled with a voice that shook the Mountain as the other Messengers watched below with reverent, spellbound awe.

"Do so, Tuona, and you will know that I will be neither shocked nor helpless by your menace. And as for My creation, do not deceive yourself. You have no understanding of how far I will go to pursue them!"

With another twist of Tuona's neck, the blazing light of Lord Creator lifted him and shook the Messenger violently, clattering every inch of the Evil One's being. "For your rebellion, your deception, your unfaithfulness, and your pride, I, the God of this world—Lord Creator, Holy King, and my Breath together as One—cast you down from Vuoristad forever into the Shadow-Realm fit for your eternal gloom."

And with that, Tuona found himself hurtling toward the soil of Merivalka at tremendous speed. Falling through the clouds, his eyes peered through the throbbing clouds back to the throne room of Vuoristad, where he saw his opponent beholding his demise.

It is not over, Tuona thought before he met the ground with a devastating collision. *I will come for you yet again.*

Joël staggered, falling forward onto the beach, his throat scratchy and worn, his skin covered in sand and earth, and his head throbbing so badly he could barely open his eyes. Rising above him was the cobalt cloud, hissing and popping as if in anger. The White Sea lashed against the coastline in the darkness. The vision seemed to have lasted for hours, yet Joël knew that no time had passed. Pressing his hands into the packed sand as the water rushed over them, he pushed himself upwards before his knees buckled and gave way. Coughing and wheezing against the saltiness of the air and water, he gingerly knelt facing the dark mist.

"Showing me your rebellion will not deter anything, Tuona," Joël gasped. "Nor will it gather you any strength for any future battles."

"You cannot deny my power, Joël! That you must admit!"

"Power? Why does your quest come down to power? Why do you insist that must be the way? Why do you only seek to take for yourself? Why do you try to ascend to what is not yours?"

"As I said before," Tuona chuckled menacingly. "I will not merely try. I will do it. That is what power does."

"Not the power that is victorious, Evil One," Joël replied. "True power gives of itself to lift up those who are powerless. And no matter how often you offer your diatribes, truth and love do not change. If you will not listen, then be gone. And the next time you confront me will be the last time."

Joël closed his eyes and drew a deep, briny breath from the ocean air. When he opened them, the cloud had disappeared. Tottering unsteadily along the beach, Joël slowly began the way back along the harbor toward his home.

18

The days grew even longer as the weeks passed into High Suntide. The hours of market activity were more vigorous than ever, and every business was profiting in some way from the presence of the Kronji delegation. The soldiers frequented the public houses for their meals, and establishments like The Iron Bow, The Foundryman, and The Red Raven were running flush with riches. A general period of good feeling pervaded the general public, even as increased consultation and debate between Prince Dewulf and the Council of Nobles showed in the strain on their faces whenever seen in public.

Joël took a morning break from his labors and was taking a walk past the Lakihalle on toward the vikarloge, where he encountered a score of children cavorting and kicking a feather-stuffed leather ball as they played stroika. Joël stood to the side for a few minutes and laughed as the urchins energetically if haphazardly played the national sport to the best of their ability. One sent the ball spinning off his own shin over toward Joël, who tossed it back in play from the perimeter of the ground before running into the midst of the children and joining in the game.

Eno crept through the quarters of the Sun King as it anchored offshore. It was his shift to stand guard, and he decided to check on Sigrid, the Prince's niece. Dagarata, the child's mother, had remarked her daughter seemed weary and worn that morning and perhaps some extra sleep would do her good. Perhaps rest would soothe what afflicted the ten-year old girl.

Sliding through the door of the lower cabin, Eno knocked on Sigrid's door as he held his candle steady. No answer.

"Sigrid?" he called. "It is I, Eno. Your mother sent me to make certain you were well."

A crash against the door nearly caused Eno to drop his candle, and without a moment's delay, he opened it to the horrific tableau before him. Sigrid lay there, sprawled on the floor of her cabin, twitching violently with a gaping wound on her forehead. She opened her mouth, emitting a scream that reverberated throughout the ship. Eno, holding back at first, put down the candle on a table by the door. He stumbled forward to control her and pin her down. Another servant appeared at the door.

"Baudin! Get my lady, and hurry! Sigrid is ... There's something terribly wrong!"

Baudin blinked with terror as Sigrid glared at him, her eyes rolled in the back of her head, revealing white, glassy pools. The blood from her head wound trickled down between her eyes as she unleashed a scream even more terrifying than before, a second before she grabbed Eno by the throat with both hands.

"Go!" yelled Eno in a choked cadence. Baudin sprinted up the stairs toward the deck where he knew Dagarata would be. As the sun and sky came into view, he could have vouched that he saw the flittering vapors of a dark cloud of blue disappearing into the wind.

Joël sauntered down the lane leading behind the Lakihalle with the children in tow. Passing the ball behind his head, he roared with delight as the boys and girls leapt to catch it and throw it back to him. They had passed the Lakihalle and come abreast of the first pier when they heard the scream, moments before they saw Prince Dewulf and his entourage bolt from the Lakihalle in the direction of the howl that came from the sea.

A woman, red-faced with strawberry-blond hair, was yelling toward the Kronji gathering at the pier, holding forth her hands and screaming something incomprehensible. Prince Dewulf sprinted down the pier as the rowboat slammed against it, and he lifted the woman out as she kicked, yelled, and spat.

"Dagarata!" the prince shouted. As her screams continued, he roared back in her face. "Dagarata! What is it? What's wrong!"

"Sigrid!" Dagarata wheezed out the name. "It's Sigrid! She has lost control of her mind! She is throwing herself against walls, striking herself and trying to kill herself and others!"

"Where?" insisted Prince Dewulf. "Where, sister? Is she still on the ship."

"She is ... She has been tied down on the deck. Eno and Baudin managed to control her but she could break the ropes at any moment. Something has entered her ... something evil, and it refuses to let her go!"

"Elbart!" Prince Dewulf roared from the pier as the Great Steward approached. "Elbart! Where are your doctors and healers? My niece is gravely ill!"

"What is it?" Elbart asked in a more severe tone than he intended.

"Something grips her, something beyond anything my sister has ever seen. We are here as your guests ... now do something!"

Elbart was about to respond when he saw Joël enter the midst of the crowd. Ignoring him, Elbart called up to Lasjen and Dirnik, "Find Umlar and Gheren and tell them to fetch our best physicians and report to the pier!"

"Please! Hurry!" insisted Dagarata. "She'll be dead by the time anyone comes!" Wiping tears from her eyes, she looked around wildly, her eyes resting on Joël. "You!" she shouted. "Aren't you the one they speak of? The one who makes bread from the air and who causes the lame to walk?"

"Are you mad, my lady?" Elbart replied. "We are sending for a physician, not this ruffian!"

"Let my sister and I determine that!" Prince Dewulf roared back at Elbart as he tried to steady his sister's gait. "You! The one they call Joël!"

Joël stepped forward, handing the ball to a little boy as he did so. "Yes?"

"Please, good sir!" Dagarata wept bitterly. "My little Sigrid! She is gripped by an evil one, a demon of some kind!"

"He is not the one you want, woman!" Elbart and some in the crowd called out.

Joël looked down at Dagarata. "A Kronji asking a Merivalkan for deliverance? Are you sure I am meant for this?"

"Sir!" Prince Dewulf shouted, his hand going for his sword. "If you will not listen to her, listen to me, and help her daughter and my niece, right now! Get in the boat and go there!"

"The gifts of healing given to the people here," said Joël, looking out toward the Kronji long ship, "and you believe it's right to take them for yourselves?"

"You are mad, you heretic!" yelled Dirnik, who had just come into the crowd.

"How dare you!" spat the prince.

The crowd gathered closer, sure that whatever occurred, it would be nothing good. Joël continued to look out to the long ship, closing his eyes and whispering something that no one could hear. He felt someone tugging at his boots and saw that it was Dagarata.

"Good sir, please," she wailed. "Whatever crumb of hope you can grant me, I will eat it now gladly."

Joël reached down and pulled Dagarata to her feet, looking at her with kindness and love. "My lady, your faith astounds me. May what you desire be done for you!"

"What was that?" Prince Dewulf, Dagarata, and Elbart replied together over the roar of the people.

Joël released Dagarata and pulled loose from the others. He walked toward the end of the pier, gesturing to a man in a boat that had just dropped into the water. In a matter of minutes, the rowboat had drawn toward the pier, paddled madly by the wide-eyed Eno.

"Eno!" called Prince Dewulf, who pushed past Joël. "What news?"

"My Prince!" Eno cried. "My lady! All is well!"

"All is well?" The prince and his sister answered, befuddled.

"Seconds before I left to tell you we were beyond hope, all changed! Sigrid stopped quaking, took a deep breath, opened her eyes, and called out for you both! She is well! Whatever afflicted her, she has been healed!"

The Kronji entourage and many of the Selannans gathered there erupted into a wild celebration, fueled by wonder and amazement as much as gladness. Dagarata hugged her brother the prince as both wept at their blessing. It was then they looked around to thank the man who had healed little Sigrid and they couldn't find him.

"Where is he?" asked Dagarata. "Where is Joël?"

A couple minutes later, Joël entered his shop through the back door. Sitting down at his table, he tied an apron around himself and began to grate a stone to collect a spoonful of residue before mixing it with a measure of leafbitter oil in a bowl. He took a brush in his hand and dabbed the mixture onto a crack in a stone plate.

19

Kaleva slapped his hands into a bowl of water, beginning the process of cleaning himself after the day's work. Another fishing day completed, he turned to Mirko as the latter tabulated the haul from the White Sea.

"Close to a thousand, it is," Mirko chirped happily. "That should keep our pockets filled for some time."

"Provided the Kronji don't dip into them first," deadpanned Ivar.

"My brother the pessimist," Mirko shook his head.

"Regardless, we've earned it," Kaleva shouted with mirth. "If Germund is taking our wares around to our clients, we should finish with some healthy bills of sale. This calls for a celebration."

"I'm for one," said Henrik.

"As am I," Saku agreed.

"The news must be encouraging from the White Sea, my friends," Joël shouted to them from the harbor lane amidst a bustling crowd. Kaleva couldn't find him at first but then caught sight of his walking stick.

"Hi, Joël! Yes, we were going to celebrate our most magnificent catch yet this summer. It seems we missed the lunch hour, though! Will you join us for a drink together?"

"I was going to ask you the same, but if you would like to do so with the sun on our faces. Will any of you desire a northwards hike again?"

"A-drinking and a-walking?" Mirko asked. "Mischief has come from less."

"I promise you no evil, my friend," Joël promised, walking down the pier toward the ship. "And if it's a stout drink you'll be wanting, I believe Kyria has worked the lunch hour at the Iron Bow. I'm sure she could provide us something and I could persuade her to come with us."

"It would be just the thing," offered Saku. "Henrik and I could bring our wives along, also. Another Midnight Promenade is taking all their days with planning, and with the city bordering on the edge of delirium with the continued presence of our guests, they'd likely welcome a constitutional past the gates."

"If it will be many," Joël offered, "it would be need for many provisions. It shouldn't be hard to purchase a small cask of ale from the Iron Bow if we could prevail upon some transport."

Ivar stepped forward to shake Joël's hand. "If it is transport you require, I know just the thing."

Well before afternoon nave, the contingent of twelve, along with a cart laden with a cask each of ale and water and pulled by two sturdy Merivalkan ponies, walked through the Coastal Gate as Joël made arrangements with Tarmo for a return just after lakkaa. Taking the road toward Branström, the group strolled the path they had just a month before. The womenfolk finally took to sitting in the cart, talking excitedly among themselves. The wives of Henrik, Saku, Mirko, and Ivar—Matleena, Rauha, Sanni, and Ilma were their respective names—laughed and spoke at length with Kyria and Elaenor. The men walked in front—Ivar guiding the ponies with the bridle—as Joël suggested to Kaleva they take a westward trail that would veer away from Branström toward a grassy plain that abutted the Toiva River.

"There is a spring over that way," Kaleva mused, "larger than the one we used for libation when you showed us how to multiply fish, chicken, and bread."

"You mean near the base of that hill?" replied Joël. "I remember seeing it on my way to Selanna on my travels. I stayed at a farm there the night before I set foot in your city."

"Kyrt's farm?" Mirko asked.

"You know him?"

"Our uncle Juha is the chief quartermaster for Selanna, and Kyrt's holdings fall just within our jurisdiction," Ivar said. "He is the ideal patron: sends his messages quickly, pays well and on time, and thanks you profusely."

"Perhaps if we take the trail slowly," Kaleva reminded them as the approached a significant descent.

"Ponies know the ground's slope," Ivar deflected the warning, and the ponies shortened their stride in accordance with his grip on the bridle. In another ten minutes, the group stopped in the valley near the spring, which was built up more like a well. The women slid out of the cart and Mirko hammered a tap into each small cask, both of which were slightly more than a foot tall. Henrik and Saku distributed a collection of steins and the whole company settled down to a drink of their choice together.

Several minutes went by in contented and companionable silence, each of them enjoying the warm summer breeze that rippled the grass. The rain from the night before had perfumed the grass with a fragrant smell that brought out the richness of the earth beneath. So deep and agreeable was the silence that several of them jumped when Joël broke it boldly. Sanni spilled her ale into the grass from the shock.

"Who do the people of Selanna say that I am?" he asked.

"Say again?" asked Germund, who had also joined them.

Mirko gulped down the rest of his ale and drew himself another stein full. "Why the question, Joël? Are you the subject of conversation around too many tables at The Red Raven?"

"No mention of the competition, if you please," Kyria groaned sarcastically.

"It's just a question," said Joël with complete gravitas. "The people of your city know you well enough. To them, I'm more of a mystery, for many reasons. But of all the people of Selanna, you know them and myself the best. So again, I ask: Who do the people of Selanna say that I am?"

"No lie," Saku said, "some call you the Storm Prince."

"Because of what I did on the sea?" Joël asked.

"That has a great deal to do with that title, wouldn't you think?" Saku rejoined as he raised his drink in Joël's direction.

"To be honest, no one has ever gotten as mixed a response as you have, Joël," Matleena said. "Some say you're mad."

"Agreed," Ilma added. "Some have said you've been away in a secret war and have arrived full of the battle shock. Others think you a wonder-worker, both with miracles of health and miracles of shop skill."

"Even the Kronji say that, Joël," said Elaenor.

"If I might be of some encouragement," offered Henrik, "there are a number of people who say you are a prophet, a seer."

"A seer?" Joël repeated.

"Either one that is bringing about a new age or calling us back to an age of glory," Henrik replied. "Especially those who are hoping to get rid of the yoke of Canute and Dewulf. Members of the Council of Nobles would be included in this total, I'd dare say."

"Even though many of them have been unduly harsh toward Joël?" Kyria said, her memory of the Gathering of Brightide Nave still strong.

"Kyria," Joël said gently, "have patience. You do not know what might be occurring in their hearts."

"But many do say you are a seer," Rauha said.

Sanni stood, brushing grass from her clothes. "It is true, even among those who do not believe you to be a new prophet. Some say you are Besno or Ahntunen come back to life."

Joël walked toward the cart, opened the tap on the other cask, and drew cool water into his stein. He took a long drink and looked very thoughtful. "It seems that for every citizen of Selanna, there is a different opinion of me. But that is not important. Let me ask this instead: Who do you say that I am?"

"Us?" Several voices spoke at once.

"Yes, it is one thing for the crowds to chime their chords of belief or disbelief and offer their opinion. But many of you have spent enough time with me to form your own convictions. So I ask you again: Who do you say that I am?"

"The Rhoken."

The words were Kaleva's, and the looks from his friends showed him that they were shocked by his broken silence.

"You say I am the Rhoken, the Courageous One?" Joël asked him.

"I ... yes, that is what I say," declared Kaleva with a slight waver in his voice. "Look, I am not saying I understand everything about you, Joël. What you do is so incredible and shocking that it is hard for me to make sense of it. No one I've ever known—that any of us have ever known—can do the things that you've done, or do them in the spirit with which you've performed these deeds. You come here from beyond the horizon, for all we know, but you come to Selanna—not to threaten our people, but to help them. You give of yourself and your ability and your words, with no expectation for payment. A charlatan would manipulate people for some sort of reparation or monetary advantage. You do none of that. You heal Perttu, you speak boldly from the Stories at Brightide Nave, you make a feast from the invisible ... and by Vuoristad, you defeat a storm and quell it and cause it to disappear, as if you twirled it on your fingertips and placed it in your pocket!" Kaleva put his hands to his head before spreading them out wide. "To not only do these things, but to do them in this manner, you would have to come from Lord Creator, sent for a purpose! I don't claim to fully understand that reason, and I may not understand everything about you, but you have shown me enough to demonstrate who you are. You have to be the Rhoken, the one who will cause the Great Ruin to work backwards! You are sent by Lord Creator himself."

Kyria stared at Joël, then at Kaleva, and back at Joël. The words she had just heard seemed impossible, but there was a conviction about what rang in her ears, one that brought the indescribable music of truth and sense. She saw Joël put down his stein of water and walk over to embrace Kaleva.

"What faith!" Joël affirmed heartily. "How graced you are, Kaleva Reiji! So strong and deep is this truth you have uttered, and in your speaking you have not done this on your own. This has been most certainly revealed to you by Lord Creator himself. What you have just said are the words that will shake the foundations of this nation and of this world, building new ones in their place. This that you profess will unlatch the prison of those who suffer and make possible the redemption of many!"

The group stared at Kaleva with a mixture of confusion and happiness, some of them smiling at his plight. Kaleva, for his part, dropped the stein of ale from his trembling fingers.

"Me? Faith, Joël?" he sputtered. "I hardly think that's faith, and it's baffling enough to think it would move the earth like you say."

"All I can tell you, Kaleva, is that I know enough of this world to know how it will be changed by what you just confessed. And as to faith, why did you say it?"

"About you? Because ... well, because anyone who has spent time with you and has an open mind can see that what you do is different. It's unparalleled ... and even more than that, it's good. It's ... it's both right, and you do what is good. And I think no one could do that unless Lord Creator sent him. Like I said, I don't understand how that is the case, but what you do and who you are happen to be enough that I am convinced. Considering all those things, and considering what the Stories have told us from the past, you must be the Rhoken."

"The One to cause the Great Ruin to work backwards," said Kyria, the words spilling from her lips. "And how will you do that?"

"Hopefully, involving getting these wretched Kronji out of our land and out of mind," grumbled Henrik.

"Peace, Henrik!" Joël ordered. "If, like your brother has said, I have come here in unexpected fashion, and I work in unexpected fashion, then wouldn't it stand to reason that the unmaking of the Great Ruin would be effected unexpectedly? Perhaps you have been under the yoke of Kronjva so long that you have let your life experience demand a certain deliverance, rather than allowing Lord Creator's revelation of your need dictate your response."

"That is what you said, in so many words, at the Gathering of Brightide Nave," Rauha declared.

"And what I will continue to make known," Joël replied with a sweep of his hand toward Vuoristad. "Think back through the Stories to the telling of the Great Ruin. When Magnus and Merta dipped their fingers into Sivvlaka, polluting their bodies and their souls, and causing all their lineage of mankind to stand guilty before the throne of Lord Creator, were the Kronji on the earth at that time?"

"Absolutely not," Saku acknowledged. "It was Magnus, Merta, and their children at the time. No oppression, no subjugation, only freedom."

"The freedom for what?" asked Joël.

"The freedom to do what is good," said Matleena.

"To choose what is good," added Sanni.

"The liberty to love and obey Lord Creator," continued Eleanor.

"To desire what Lord Creator desired," said Kyria quietly, tears falling unbidden from her eyes.

Joël paused, looking at Kyria before going toward her and taking her hands in his own. "Yes, the Great Ruin was the nightmare that drove a sword through Lord Creator's dream for his world, for his people, and it is a nightmare from which this island and this world cannot wake up. No oppression from the Kronji or creatures like the Ehrma giants. Simply the oppression that comes from aligning one's desires with all that would oppose Lord Creator."

"You mean Tuona," Germund said.

"Tuona has worked to undermine Lord Creator's world from the beginning," replied Joël. "And even though every sin committed is a reminder of that rebellion, it does not lessen Lord Creator's love for you or anyone at all. That would mean each Merivalkan, as well as any Kronji. All of you bear the wounds perpetrated by Tuona and brought forth by Magnus and Merta."

"If Tuona is that powerful," asked Ilma, "then what would the Rhoken ... what would you have to do to overturn that power, Joël?"

It was at those words that Joël looked markedly pensive and troubled, for a moment looking at the ground and sighing deeply. Kyria looked at him and saw he bore the same film of sweat on his forehead when they had found him kneeling at Elks Hill weeks before.

"Overturning Tuona's work is beyond the reach of any of Lord Creator's people, for even though mankind brought the Great Ruin and is responsible, mankind is also impossibly polluted and so is unable to make restitution, Ilma," Joël responded finally. "I can only tell you that as the Great Ruin brought about the deepest suffering, so only the deepest suffering can overturn it and bring redemption."

"You mean suffering for you," Ivar said after a long pause. "This is something that is going to happen to you, part of being the Courageous One."

Kaleva could not believe what he was hearing. "Never, Joël! How could that happen given what you have done, and what you are doing, for Selanna? This can't be the way! Why can't people have some time to accept your message and your teaching and believe that way?"

"Haven't you heard anything I've said, Kaleva?" Joël implored him, with a slight growl in his voice and a glint of anger in his eye. "When you said I was the Rhoken, did I tell you that you had arrived at your conviction by your ingenuity or Lord's Creator's desire?"

"I merely followed the clues, Joël. I saw what you did and I came to that understanding."

"But you would not have done that if Lord Creator had not arranged those clues, had not turned your heart toward him to believe in what and whom you observed! No one ... no one believes in me unless Lord Creator brings him or her! You are a fisherman. A fish doesn't willingly jump from the sea into your boat. You catch the fish in the meshes of your net. When Lord Creator has you in the embrace of his choosing, he draws you and whomever he desires."

It was Kaleva's turn to look pensive and troubled. "I am sorry for how I responded, Joël. This is too much to consider."

"I understand, more than you know," replied Joël, placing his hand on Kaleva's shoulder.

"It's just that the idea of your suffering is too much for us to fathom," Elaenor offered.

"And," added Kyria, "what you are implying is that you will have to stand alone."

"More than you know," said Joël quietly.

The turn in the conversation had brought an eerie calm to their group, and it was with some relief they heard Joël say, "Well, I had arranged for us to be back at the Coastal Gate just after lakkaa. If we are not to wear out these ponies on the journey back, then we should leave soon."

The return to Selanna was more subdued, although after some time Joël, walking with Ivar and Mirko alongside the ponies, returned to speaking and laughing with them. Kyria sat in the cart next to Sanni when she noticed Kaleva walking, head down, next to them.

"Are you alright?" she asked him.

"Speak the truth, express your worry, and have him baffle me more than I ever dreamed possible? I'm hardly alright," Kaleva replied.

"I know," she said. "Having Joël in Selanna has been wonderful, and now I am worrying already that these days will come to an end."

"Maybe a new beginning," Kaleva offered, "although I don't know what shape that would take. It's just ..." and here his voice trailed away.

"What is it?" asked Sanni, who had been eavesdropping on their conversation.

Kaleva looked at both the ladies. "If Lord Creator has indeed sent him, it must be for Lord Creator's purposes and not our own. That can be both good and scary."

"But if we care deeply about what Lord Creator wants," replied Kyria, "shouldn't that be enough?"

"I don't know what we want," said Kaleva. "Henrik is such a firebrand at times, he wants the Kronji to be a thing of yesteryear. Mirko and Ivar want good business. You yourself know Vilius would be content being a thorn in Joël's side. We all want what's most advantageous for us and our circumstances."

"Maybe that's what Joël is trying to get us to realize," said Kyria. "Our deepest need is not what we think it is."

"And he has to suffer for it in some way?" Sanni added. "That sounds disturbing."

"More disturbing is that he seems to be facing it by himself," said Kyria.

"He never said that specifically," Sanni replied.

"No," offered Kaleva, "but I'm with Kyria. There was something about his words and the weight of them that implied that. And why should he have to bear what he faces alone?"

"Maybe he's supposed to," Kyria sighed, looking down at her hands.

"He shouldn't have to," Kaleva said, "and I will never allow him to do so. I'll be with him to the end." He quickened his pace forward to join Joël and the others as the walls of Selanna came into view.

20

Alisa grasped the water jug in her hand and moved through the door of her thatched hut. From the settlement off the Capital Road, she could look both toward the southern coast near Selanna and northwesterly toward Stahlgard. The night had brought a passing thundershower from the White Sea, which christened the many rooftops of the settlement with a soaking rain. Yet the huts held firm against any leaks, and the three hundred or so Vale-dwellers woke up to dry interiors and began cooking their morning breakfasts. Alisa walked through the dirt paths connecting the huts, nodding her greetings to the settlers on the way to the spring for a fresh jug of water.

Skipping around puddles in her summer dress and canvas clogs, Alisa breathed in the cool morning air that had all the hints of turning humid within hours. Her thirst assaulted her and quickened her pace. The distance to the spring seemed longer this morning, although Alisa knew her slow pace had much to do with that. And she also knew that diminished stride had more to do with her languid hopes.

She knew any home was a matter for gratitude, but the hut that had been in the family for generations was little more than a squatter's den. Her parents long dead, Alisa had inherited their home but little of their character. It had nothing to do with lack of devotion to Lord Creator. The Vale-dwellers worshipped him, albeit in their own way. And why approach the Maker in the Gatherings of each seasonal Nave when prayers could be made privately according to their own tradition? Why indeed, thought Alisa, would they want to join with the faithful in Selanna, Stahlgard, or elsewhere, the faithful that rejected the Vale-dwellers out of hand as less-than-worthy, as subhuman?

It was not her people's fault, thought Alisa as she saw the spring come into view. The Torchers had been repulsed unexpectedly less than two years into the Second Dawn. Their invasion had been timed with expectation of victory, not believing that an island wearied by turning back the imposing Ehrma would summon the will or strength to garner another victory. Yet the Torchers were turned back, suffering an ignoble defeat while several dozen soldiers escaped to the inland territory. Afterward they found shelter among the sympathetic and spineless of Merivalkans in the grassland. Bearers of gaunt faces and flaming red hair, the Torchers forged marriages with the women after killing the men of the countryside. The resulting intermarriages bred future "half-breeds" that many Merivalkans viewed with disdain.

But as she strolled the final yards toward the spring, Alisa knew she bore plenty of blame for her own plight. Though many women of the past had been forced into marriage by the Torchers, she herself had willingly chosen many men for herself. Unwilling to settle on one, she wanted nothing more than to lose herself for another spell with another man. Until one man led to another. And then Alisa realized she truly had nothing more. So deeply had she plunged into the ocean of her secrets that she took no heed of the gentleman walking several yards back and to her left.

"Good morning!" And the man's voice was charming and warm, full of life, music, and healing. Wheeling around and with heart beating, Alisa banged her jug against her right knee.

"Oh, good sir!" she blurted out. "You startled me!" Despite her kind greeting, she quickly looked around, desperately looking for a rock, a fallen tree branch, anything that she could use as a weapon if he meant her harm. While she could use her jug, she preferred not to smash it to pieces against someone's head.

"I am sorry for that," said the stranger, putting up his free hand while setting aside his walking stick with his other. "You seemed quite preoccupied."

"Yes," Alisa replied, still looking around, eyes darting. "Mornings can bring on my heaviest thoughts."

As if knowing what was in her mind, the man sat down in the grass. "Do not be alarmed, despite my sudden greeting. I mean you no harm. I saw the spring from the distance while taking an early morning walk and I was wondering if I could have a drink."

"A drink?" Alisa asked, with even more questions coming in the wake of those first two words. "For what reason are you out here? Who are you? Where are you from, for you are clearly not from our settlement and I've never seen you before?"

"Ah, many questions," the man laughed. "You are closer to hope than you ever dared imagine."

"Questions you haven't answered."

"Well, allow me to take them in turn," he said, lying back on the grass. "I closed my shop and came out in this direction, one I've not taken from the city, for a morning walk in a new area of Merivalka. My name happens to be Joël. Although you wouldn't believe where I am originally from, I presently dwell in Selanna, where I repair broken pots, tables, and other items. And you are right. I am not from your settlement. And you have never seen me before because I have not visited your settlement in person, nor have you come to my shop in Selanna."

"Clever, Joël," Alisa rejoined. "It is good, if somewhat shocking, to make your acquaintance and to hear your request for a drink."

"Why is that?"

"Are you admitting to complete ignorance, Joël? Do you seriously know nothing of the history between my people and the rest of this country?"

"The fact you dwell in those huts under the stars obviously speaks to exile of some sort," said Joël thoughtfully, "but does that mean we cannot speak or I receive a drink?"

"Oh, I can draw you some water. It's just shocking to me that you'd accept it. Your people accept so little else about us."

"Is the difference that great?"

"Wide enough to be barred from all Gatherings. But why should that matter? We can worship Lord Creator here beneath the sky, in a great hut in out settlement, in our own way. We know of the inscriptions of the Revered Way from Besno's hand. Shouldn't that be enough?"

Joël studied her as she pulled her jug out of the spring, the water spilling out of the top. "It depends what you mean by enough." He took the jug from Alisa.

"If you would wait until I can go home and find a cup, you can drink from that," she insisted.

"No, no," he refused, and in an instant Joël took the jug to his own lips.

"Are you mad?" Alisa shouted. "What sort of a Selannan are you to touch my jug with your lips?"

Joël lowered the jug after a long drink. "If you only knew how many times your first question has been asked of me." He wiped his mouth. "That spring offers some delicious water. Thank you."

"You're welcome," Alisa replied, her wariness receding.

"The only trouble," Joël continued, "is that in time, one grows thirsty again."

"Then I will just come to the spring again."

"For a drink that will lose its power. But what if your thirst could be satisfied for good?"

"What are you saying, Joël? You know of a liquid that would keep me from being thirsty ever again?"

"Not a liquid, Alisa, and the thirst you truly have is hardly a physical one. Your desire goes much deeper."

"I don't understand."

"You spoke earlier of the differences in how you worship, how Selanna worships, how every town and city approaches Lord Creator. Your settlement's great hut, the parpallo at the Lakihalle in Selanna. They are places in which you look for future hope. What if hope had arrived before you and offered itself?"

"Are you speaking in riddles?"

"Not at all, Alisa. You worship a shadow. I am offering you something greater. Lord Creator wants his people to honor and adore him, not so that their spirits and hearts can be cleansed, but because he himself has worked that cleansing in their spirits and hearts."

"I thought that was something only the Rhoken could offer."

"That is true."

"Are you a prophet, a seer concerning the Rhoken?"

"You are walking along the correct path, yet not quite there."

"You seem like a prophet."

"Is that what you would tell Pietari?"

Alisa blanched. "How did you know that? Have you met my ... my husband?"

"Alisa, my dear. If your heart craves what it needs, it cannot hide your secrets. I know of Pietari. And you should also admit that he is not your husband."

"Pietari ... My ... What? How did you know?" the embarrassed Alisa stuttered.

"Nor were Ensio or Frans."

Alisa tossed her water jug into the grass, disbelieving the words that had poured from Joël's mouth. She tried to speak and couldn't; she made every attempt to catch her breath and failed.

For his part, Joël rose from his seated position and approached her. Touching her shaking arm at the elbow joint, he said, "You thirst for grace, and you seek everything else that cannot satisfy. Will you not unite your deepest need with your truest search?"

"You know me," Alisa gasped, her voice barely breaking above a whisper.

"I do, Alisa."

"Not just about me. You truly know me."

Joël looked at her with a glowing smile. "Then what are you still doing here?"

And in an instant, she was racing back toward the settlement, flying down the road faster than she ever imagined.

Joël knelt in the grass, scooping the water from the spring into his mouth. The shadows that crept up behind him betrayed the approach of the guards. Looking behind him, he saw four Selannan soldiers from the North Gate staring at him in bewilderment. Flanking them were Mirko and Ivar on horses, equally confused.

"Joël," one of the guards said, "what are you doing here?"

"Niilo?" Joël replied. "It's good to see you. I was merely taking some time away from work and outside of the city."

"That's not the oddity," spoke Ivar as his horse neighed. "It's where you are that has us wondering. It is today, the day of preparation for tomorrow's Gathering, that makes your presence here so strange."

"Why is this place so distasteful to you?" asked Joël.

"I never said it was distasteful."

"Ivar, are you denying what was in your heart?"

Ivar looked pleadingly at his brother, and Mirko said, "Alright. I'll be blunt. The fact that you are here amongst the Vale-dwellers is difficult to stomach."

"Why is that so difficult, Mirko? Ivar? Niilo? Do you care to share that with me?"

"They do not worship Lord Creator the way we do," Niilo spoke up. "There are years of convoluted activity that are difficult to look past that have led to this point. It is exceedingly taxing to accept anything else. It would be hard for them to change. They are not like us."

"That is the reason why the Vale-dwellers should be avoided, because they are not like you?" Joël's voice was firm but his tone was more sibilant.

"I never said they should be avoided. We're just surprised to see you here. Not to mention what kind of woman you were speaking to in Alisa."

"I believe she knows that well enough, Niilo. But she also knows her greatest need. And that happens to be your greatest need, if you will open your eyes and heart."

"Sir!" barked one of the guards.

"What, Jaarko?" asked Niilo, who followed Jarrko's finger into the distance.

Leading the band of all the Vale-dwellers, Alisa sprinted uphill toward the spring and saw Joël as she closed the distance.

"There he is," she shouted to the settlement inhabitants as she pointed ahead. "He's the one who told me everything about me, everything I needed!"

"That one?" shouted another.

"Yes!" called Alisa, her lungs burning. "His name is Joël."

Niilo drew aside Joël as the Vale-dwellers swarmed nearer. "I came here to find you, Joël. If you are intending to stay here, I cannot offer you protection. I and my men will have to go."

"I do not require your protection, Niilo, but if you will watch for our return at the North Gate by evening," said Joël, "I will be grateful."

"You say 'our' return?" said Jaarko.

In unison, Mirko and Ivar turned with their horses and faced the guards. "If it please you," Mirko said with a nod, "we will remain with Joël."

"None of this is a good idea," Niilo insisted.

"Ignoring what is true human need is not a good idea," Ivar responded. "You may go, we will stay and then return with Joël."

The guards shrugged and turned away as the Vale-dwellers arrived. Mirko and Ivar saw a woman rush up to Joël, who turned to them and said, "I want you to meet Alisa, one of Lord Creator's new children."

21

Although High Suntide normally brought the hottest temperatures of the year, Suntide Nave began with a swirling wind off the White Sea and a fast-moving rainstorm with several lightning strikes off the shore. The cloud cover dropped the temperature into a more comfortable range, but the rain sent the Council of Nobles scrambling to cover the dasenpfear wood from the drops falling from the sky. Because of the tendency for summer heat, the Suntide Gathering was normally in the evening. By the time people were filing toward the Lakihalle after supper and the parpallo for the Gathering, the clouds moved eastward and the sun pierced the gray canopy overhead.

The day's events unfolded slowly leading toward the evening's Gathering, but with the sun in its descent toward the horizon, hundreds of people began swarming into the public area near the Lakihalle. They saw the wood stacked and ready for the fire, which they had been expecting. What they were not expecting was to see Joël leaning against the fence before the Lakihalle. Already the priests, with Umlar leading them, were in a vociferous argument with Joël. As Kyria, Elaenor, Kaleva, Henrik, and Saku moved to the front of the crowd for a better hearing, Umlar screamed at Joël, "And you will not read from the Stories during today's Gathering! Is that clear?"

"Abundantly so," replied Joël with a confident air as the citizens of Selanna pressed more closely, "as long as you are willing to publicly declare why it is you refuse me, even though I never made a request today!"

"You will not do so since you compromised your righteousness by consorting with people who do not share in the Faith!"

"Consorting!" Joël laughed. "Of course! How else are people to know of the Faith unless those loyal to Lord Creator tell them? How else would the nations come to believe?"

Gheren, the priestly assistant, edged forward to confront Joël. "They are unwilling to believe! With no disrespect to our guests from Kronjva, they have chosen to worship the Great Bear and so have disqualified themselves from hope. The Vale-dwellers with whom you dallied yesterday—if those reports are true that you did—those people have mingled the Faith with other traditions that sully their cleanliness before Lord Creator. With such people, there can be no compromise!"

"Who said anything about compromising the truth, Gheren?" replied Joël. "But are you, Umlar, the Great Steward, and his wake of supporters ... are any of you immune from wounding your own faith?"

"Again, madman!" screamed Dirnik and Elbart together. Elbart continued, "You dare speak against the Faith!"

"I do not come to speak against the Faith, let alone destroy it, but to fulfill Lord Creator's intentions from the very beginning! You have turned your hearts inward to champion yourselves, trusting in your own righteousness. You hide the sin that plucks at your hearts as one hides the imperfections in his own house. Imagine seeing your neighbor's house and viewing the furniture therein. Beds, bath basins, tables ... all kept clean on the outside. But if you lift them up, you see the dirt beneath. Trusting in your own cleanliness of heart, believing you can please Lord Creator by the sheer force and excellence of your best efforts ... all that does is mask the sin you set aside or conveniently ignore. What Lord Creator desires is that you receive and rest upon his mercy as offered in his Rhoken, not in the endless posturing you bring to your exercises of the spirit!"

"Silence!" called Dirnik, who saw Prince Dewulf and the Kronji delegation watching from the Lakihalle.

"You will not silence me!" Joël cried in return. "For you will hear of the truth of this distinction, of choosing to trust in your own merits or the grace of Lord Creator. There were two men who walked into a kopanos to pray to Lord Creator. One was a priest who had read conscientiously from the Stories, ritually cleansed himself, and wore the exact garments with alb and belt. The other was a Vale-dweller who had entered the town through the water trench under the walls. He was known for being a petty thief in his settlement, defrauding his mates, and being an untrustworthy soul.

"The priest lifted up his eyes to the ceiling of the kopanos, as if he could see beyond it, looking northward to the summit of Vuoristad itself. He said, in a polished, mellifluous voice, 'Lord Creator, I give you all praise for the way you have made me to serve and honor you, and that I am not of the ilk of other folk. You know the sort: the habits of those who cheat, who rebel against the law, who commit unfaithfulness against their husbands or wives, and also the defrauding nature of this Vale-dweller. I give of my income to you; I pray six times a day. This is my offering to you.'

"Yet in contrast, the Vale-dweller lay prone on the ground in his foul and damp clothing, his tears staining the stone floor of the kopanos as he shook with grief and humility. He would not even look upward, instead shutting his eyes tightly and striking his fists against the ground. He wailed, 'Lord Creator, my dear Father whom I have defied, have mercy! Have mercy upon me, for I have sinned!' And his words died away in an avalanche of weeping."

Joël looked around the crowd, his eyes resting upon Kyria, Kaleva, and the others briefly before continuing. "I tell you all," he shouted out, "with all certainty: The Vale-dweller himself went home to his hut that day with Lord Creator's heart beating for him and his smile warmly upon him. That is the grace of Lord Creator! The one who exalts himself," and here he looked at Umlar and the rest of the Council of Nobles, "will be brought low, but the one who sees his lowly estate and cries for mercy will indeed be raised up by the very hand of Lord Creator!"

"You fool!" Umlar roared at him, the spittle flying from his mouth and flecking his graying stubble. "You do not come to fulfill the Faith but to defy it!"

"Wrong, priest!" Joël snarled back. "Your words show that you worship the hedge you have built around the Faith rather than Lord Creator himself! But in order that you might realize who I am and the truth I speak, I give you this."

He extended his walking stick toward the parpallo in the grass, with the dasenpfear wood stacked neatly inside its parameters. As the many who gathered there watched, the wood smoldered with white smoke, then flickered with a reddish tongue before erupting into a blaze that shot into the evening sky. For his part, Joël took up his stick and walked through the crowd, which exploded into peals of thunderous shouts as they thronged around him. Even Petric left his position with the Nobles and joined them!

The scene was chaotic, and the reprimands of Umlar, Gheren, and the other Nobles were powerless to dent the roar of the assembly. Elbart and Dirnik were moving forward to accost the priests for their lack of control when Prince Dewulf came up from behind and clutched them by the hoods of their cloaks.

"Is this a common occurrence at your celebrations?" the prince inquired, wearing a sarcastic grin.

"We will tell you the brief and true answer, sire," Elbart said in a low growl. "And that is no."

"Oh, I would think the evidence leans in the other direction," replied Dewulf. "But it is unsettling that a mere man can just enter this assembly and set a wood pile aflame and carry your people off with him in a frenzy."

"This troublemaker is not beyond our arm!" insisted Dirnik.

"I would hardly worry about this Joël's words," said the prince, "given how they seemed to put you in your proper place. And I do confess a great deal of respect for this Joël."

"Then why are you unsettled, sire?" asked Elbart.

"Because, Great Steward, our lands and commonwealths that we hold and govern, even from afar, must be orderly expanses and not pits of denizens given to turmoil!"

"My lord ..."

"Steward, tomorrow we sail for home across the White Sea. I fully intend to find my father the king alive upon my return, even for a little while. Upon his death, I will be Kronjva's king, with full intention that all my realms be domains of quiet decency and order! And if your city and your nation bear the marks of turmoil that I am seeing more and more, the kindness of my father will erode and you will meet with my iron hand!"

"By your mercy, Prince ..."

"Elbart, I have made myself abundantly clear. If my father Canute meets his end over the coming months, I intend to return throughout my realms to establish my kingdom. By all means you can expect me to return to Merivalka at Late Harvestide or Early Snowtide. If your land is a harbor of calm, you have nothing to fear. But if you cannot control one man in your midst, I make you no promises, other than I will not fail to act."

Prince Dewulf released the men from his grip and turned back to his fellow Kronji watching from the Lakihalle. Dirnik watched him in a rage, but upon turning to Elbart, he saw the Great Steward wore a calculating look on his visage.

"Elbart, you can't seriously be thinking this is a good thing?" he asked.

"Not a good thing now," Elbart said wistfully, looking with a critical eye to the burning woodpile, "but that doesn't prevent us from turning this to our advantage later."

"You speak of Joël's following?"

"I speak of Joël himself. Let this play out for now, but soon, we could have an opportunity."

THE SACRIFICE

22

Following the events of Suntide Nave, and after the Kronji left to return to their homeland, life in Selanna settled into an extended calm, the first of its kind since Joël's arrival. Even the next Gathering at Harvestide Nave occurred without any interruptions or miracles, and Joël merely stood by quietly as Umlar, Gheren, and the other priests led the citizens of Selanna in the requisite responses, songs, and prayers. In the weeks following the Gathering, farmers in the area surrounding Selanna took to their fertile fields to reap new harvests of beets, cabbages, peas, radishes, and turnips. The booths in the Great Market Road swelled with victuals that flew off the counters as fast as people could purchase them. From across the White Sea, messengers bore news of the quiet and peaceful death of Canute the Eighth, ending his reign as King of Kronjva. With the accession of Dewulf to the throne, citizens openly discussed what this meant for the future of Merivalka. Although opinions were varied and debated passionately, the one consensus was that no one knew for sure what the coming months and years would hold for their nation.

Meanwhile, Joël continued his labors, extending his efforts to include one project of a repaired mast for one of Kaleva's competitors, as well as several tables and chairs from The Foundryman that were broken in a fight at that pub. Word about Joël spread into the countryside, and farmers brought feeding troughs in need of repair, as well as tools and implements that had seen better days. In all cases, Joël was not only able to restore all things to working order but he also made them better than they originally were.

He was applying some homemade adhesive to a wooden mixing bowl that belonged to Sanni when a hand rapped loudly on the front door of his shop.

"Please come in," Joël called out, and Lars pushed through the doorway and walked into the main work area, hauling a large wooden box.

"Good evening, Lars!" Joël said, smiling. "How are you this evening?"

"M' mind's full as m' heart," replied Lars. "Haf' a project for you, though it's no' th' most i'portant thing compared t' others."

"Well, we can speak about all of it," said Joël, setting the mixing bowl aside for the adhesive to dry. "Let's talk about your box here."

"Th' box i' one of my storage boxes for cloth an' yarn an' thread. I' holds jus' fine, but I like th' idea of m' customers being able t' lif' th' lid and i' no' slide off, like this."

He lifted the lid of the storage box, showing the loosened hinges, as well as the front clasp.

"As one who cares, sir, I'm someone who's partial t' appearances, an' I don't think there's anything wrong wi' that."

"No, indeed, Lars," Joël answered. "You are entirely right to care. I assume you don't mind until after Prayers tomorrow night before I begin?"

"I don' mind. I wasn't expectin' i' for a couple days."

"You seem troubled, Lars? Are you alright? Is Perttu still well?"

Lars smiled briefly. "Perttu is well, th' li'l rascal. Ev'ry day he mentions your kindness in helpi' him walk ag'in. It's the latest news from north o' town."

"North of town?"

"Yes, sir," Lars brushed a tear away from his eye. "It's a friend o' th' family, and o' others. A farmer up near th' Toiva died yesterday. Dear frien'. One o' his workers was a schoolmate o' mine."

"What happened?"

"That's th' strange thing. Was harvestin' an' got nicked on th' leg with a pick. Didn't heal right an' fever set in. Died last night an' set hi' wife into a right wailin'. Since he wa' north of town in th' country, they're bringin' hi' body in to the kopanos on th' north edge of th' city. Part o' Evening Prayers tomorrow will be his fun'ral, I'm told."

A lump formed in Joël's throat. "What was his name?"

"Kyrt, sir. Hi' name is Kyrt."

Joël groaned, placing his face in his hands. "Kyrt? From the farm near the Toiva?"

"Yes. He's th' one. You know 'im?"

"I did," said Joël, his words dropping heavily from his tongue. "On my travels here when I first settled in Selanna, his farm was where I stopped the night before I came to the city. He was a fine host and a humble man. Oh, Kyrt! You're saying he's dead?"

"I am, sir. Fun'ral tomorrow, like I said. Evening Prayers in th' kopanos, th' one that sits two blocks from th' North Gate."

"The one on Kings' Lane. I know it."

"Yes, well. Thank you for takin' on th' box. I can come back in a few days. Sorry for botherin' you, Joël."

"You've been no bother, Lars," Joël responded as he left. The door closed, and Joël sighed before placing his head on the table and shutting his eyes tightly to the pain of the news.

The moon hung in the eastern sky in docile fashion, a marked contrast to the roiling emotions in the kopanos in the shadow of the North Gate of Selanna. Commiserations and condolences had passed from members of the congregation to Kyrt's widow, Helene. The wishes were heartfelt in spirit but limited in power. Childless, Helene had no heir who could work the land alongside the hired hands. Her own physical ability to participate in the planting and harvest was severely constrained by the strength taken from her every day, in the blood and fluids that her body could not retain. No physician in all of Selanna could heal her malady, and she had only returned to their home from her mother's house five weeks ago. After months away in Gerta with the longing prayer that bathing in the hot springs would save her, she returned to the farm as weak and languid as before. All the savings that Kyrt had set aside in their hope for a cure was nearly gone. And now Kyrt was gone.

The prayers muttered by Umlar floated in the air of the kopanos, meant to bring tender comfort but lacking in power. The congregation joined in, forming a well-meaning defense against the pain that Helene alone could bear. *All alone now,* she thought, *with nothing to carry me onward. I have nothing left.*

It was as Umlar moved to the conclusion of the prayers that the doors opened, and all in the kopanos looked to the source of the sound of the entry.

Joël walked down the center aisle that split the benches in half, striding with purpose and quivering lips toward the bier upon which rested Kyrt's linen-shrouded body. Hired hands Karno and Gard stood open-mouthed as they saw this man—whom they remembered well from his one-night stay—coming with intentional steps toward the table where Umlar stood. The priest, of course, was furious but controlled, not willing that his services should denigrate into chaos.

"You!" he whispered stridently to Joël. "Have you no shame, even here when we commend this man to the care of Lord Creator?"

"I do not come to bring more sorrow," Joël replied aloud, turning to face the assembly in the candle-lit interior. He looked over the crowd and saw those he knew well. Kaleva. Kyria. Elaenor. Henrik and Saku and their wives. Finally, he gazed at Helene. "I have come to bring a foretaste of the hope that will wash over this entire world when my Father renews it!" His words were drenched with joy and pain together, and as he said them, Helene fell off her bench, stumbling toward Joël. Karno and Gard moved toward her to lift her up, but she waved them off. In a flurry of crawling, she scrambled across the floor until she grasped Joël by his hands from her knees.

"Sir," she gasped, "are you the one my husband always spoke of? The one called Joël? Because, sir, why could you not have been there for him?" And her words died away in a river of chokes and sobs.

Slowly, Joël took his right hand from her grip and touched Helene on her head. She looked up and saw the last thing she imagined she would see from this mysterious yet compelling man.

Tears. Tears hot and salty were pouring from his eyes. Joël was blinking furiously as the drops came unbidden down his cheeks. In that instant, he took her by the shoulders and pulled her upward, her legs dragging beneath her, and she clutched in desperation at his wrists.

"You and I," Joël said in a voice that, while calm, seemed to shake the room. "You and I know grief deeply, Helene. And while it shall continue to grip this world, I will give you a pledge of Lord Creator's promise to work it backwards. First, for your body."

Feeling herself slip from his grasp, Helene dug her fingers into his wrists more tightly, sure she would fall. But she didn't. And then, a strange sensation began to flood her body. The warmth rose in her arteries and veins; strength returned to her legs and she stood firmly upon the ground as Joël placed her into a standing position. In an instant, Helene felt her circulation stabilize, her heartbeat quickening, and she knew that her unhealthy blood flow had ceased! Looking around at the astonished congregation, she saw they were just as amazed as she was, and the amazement was one shot through with joy! Only the high priest Umlar showed any disapproval, for whatever reason.

"What is the meaning of this?" he screeched at the loss of order. "Can you not come to any assembly without a devilish need to occupy the center of attention?"

"I believe my new friend Helene is the center of attention here, Umlar," Joël replied without looking at the priest. "But truly, the heartbeat of this work is the power and grace of Lord Creator himself working through me. Yet the promise is not complete." He let go of Helene's hand and walked toward the bier that held Kyrt's enshrouded body. "Karno. Gard," he commanded the two men. "Please unfasten the shroud."

"Demon! Spawn of Tuona!" roared Umlar, who had lost all patience. "You have forfeited both reason and all union with Lord Creator!"

"If you claim I am a demon, O priest, then bear witness to what is to come this minute!" Joël snapped back. "Go to your fellow Nobles and tell them what has happened. But do so with a full report after you have seen this!" He drew next to the dead body as Karno and Gard moved aside and looked at Helene. "My dear, I promised to show you a small bit of the Great Ruin turned backwards. It was first for your body. Now, I do so for your husband's."

The reality of the promise sunk in with the many dozens gathered in the building. Kyria grabbed Kaleva's arm and whispered, "He can't possibly mean what I think he's saying!"

"I do believe he does mean it, Kyria," Kaleva replied, as Joël reached upon the bier and laid his hand upon Kyrt's heart.

"Kyrt, my friend," Joël commanded, "the one who gave me food and shelter and first friendship on my journey to this city. Dear friend and beloved of Lord Creator: I say to you, arise!"

The collective gasp of the assembly upon the last word muffled the initial sound of the shuffle of Kyrt's arms and legs, but to the surprise of everybody, there was no mistaking the movements of his limbs. Then came a few twitches, a quick convulsion, and finally a magnificent yawn from Kyrt's mouth. Suddenly, the farmer sat straight up, rubbed his eyes, and found himself face to face with Joël, Helene, his fellow workers, and dozens of others in a candlelit room!

"Helene! Joël! Joël! You're here! You're ... wait! Where is 'here'?"

He had no time to wonder, for the crowd exploded in a spasm of celebration and cheers. Karno and Gard pulled him off the bier, ripping the shroud to pieces. Helene, her own body now whole, embraced and kissed Kyrt with a ferocity she could previously only dream of. And the many others clamored and whooped around Joël, who was nearly tackled by Kaleva, Kyria, and their friends.

"Joël!" shouted Kyria in the jumping human bundle around him. "What was that?"

He smiled, taking embraces from Henrik and Saku and Kaleva stood stunned. "Merely cutting into the depths of the Ruin, Kyria. It is the power of Lord Creator."

All around them came shouts.

"Lord Creator has come among us! His messenger is here!"

"The Rhoken has come!"

"Joël, Joël! The Courageous One is here! All praise to Lord Creator!"

The crowd spilled into the streets, calling out the wonders they had just seen to anyone there. Running down the Kings' Lane toward The Foundryman and past houses and alleys, the word went out about the miracle of resurrection had just beheld with their own eyes.

Yet not all ran with happiness or hope down the Kings' Lane. One form took the early turn down the Great Market Road, headed straight toward the Lakihalle, where he lit a beacon to call the Nobles to meeting.

"If you cannot control his actions at any gathering, small or great," bawled Dirnik, "perhaps we need to remove you and put another high priest in your stead!"

"Spoken like someone who is unwilling to listen!" Umlar shot back. "I was there. I saw it all! Now because we have tolerated him in our midst, the people are more captivated than ever! My lord, Great Steward." He turned to Elbart. "Sir, the people are solidly behind every action Joël takes. Every word he says, every miracle he performs. He threatens to overturn our history, our heritage, and our standing as a nation. Whatever it is, to do nothing is not possible."

"What indeed has he done?" asked Petric. "Has he assaulted anyone? Has he harmed anyone? Has he compromised our city or nation, truly? Is he in any sense a danger or threat? How does he deserve this slander?"

"Get over yourself, Petric," snarled Lasjen. "You command no army, rule no city, nor shepherd the souls of many. This is much to risk."

"Silence!" ordered Elbart. The Great Steward rose from his chair and walked between Petric and Lasjen. "We will not delay our plans further! I will not have our city or nation put at risk. Today, I received final word through messengers from Kronjva that Pri-- ... King Dewulf will be coming in Early Snowtide around the time of our Winter's Liberation feast. The last time Dewulf was among us, he told

Dirnik and myself that chaos would be the last thing he wants to see. We cannot afford to let Joël cause disorder that brings us down."

"And you think that allowing this to continue will work?" asked Dirnik.

"You misunderstand me," replied Elbart. "If the people can grow to love Joël in such a short time, we can use this passion to turn them against him. We can time it with a heavy hand at the right time, when Dewulf is among us."

"I will not be part of this!" declared the shocked Petric. "None of you can rightly say this is good! This is a trap." He pulled his cloak around himself and stormed out of the Lakihalle in protest.

"We have been part of this since the day that heretic came amongst us," shouted Elbart. "And this trap is one that will work. And when we have all turned against him ..."

He paused, gashing the air with his index finger for emphasis. "We kill him!"

23

The air turned from brisk to outright cold as the days of Early Snowtide brought plunging temperatures to Merivalka. The coastal cities and towns such as Selanna, Stahlgard, and Branström remained slightly warmer, if one qualified an unfrozen harbor as warmer. During the evenings, snow flurries fell from the sky as the citizens of Selanna preserved their vegetables and meats in the saltboxes of their homes. Meals grew heartier and people looked forward to the Winter's Liberation feast that marked the pride of days past when the Ehrma were driven from Merivalkan shores.

Kaleva and his crew took the White Sea less and less as the waves grew more tempestuous several miles from Selanna harbor. Much of their time was spent mending nets and refurbishing the ship for the days once Late Snowtide passed them by. The percentages of their sales were still coming in from the markets, and the profits they would enjoy remained steady even as the daylight grew shorter.

With the lessening sunlight, lakkaa came earlier in the day; in fact, the workday ended a couple of hours before dinner, and the pubs swelled with more and more people. It was one such day that Kaleva suggested a pub dinner to Henrik and Saku, suggesting they bring along their wives as well. Upon returning to their houses, Henrik and Saku found Kyria bringing a bag of potatoes to the women, and so they prevailed upon her to come along.

The sight at the Iron Bow, however, was not one they planned on beholding. Kyria saw her father Olav distributing drinks while simultaneously holding court with a heated discussion around the central tables. Two things were clear, though. First, the people surrounding the tables were highly opinionated. Secondly, Joël was speaking in response and not giving any ground in the argument. He looked up and saw Kyria's group enter the Iron Bow.

"Kyria! Kaleva! All of you! Hello!" he called out with vigor, although even in the dim light, Kyria could sense a trace of weariness in his eyes. The party approached him just as Vilius stood with a stein of ale in his hand and, raising it forth, said, "Beg your pardon, Joël, but let us move past this distraction. We saw you wandering the streets before you entered this fine establishment, and we all saw your deep distress. To be burdened in spirit is hardly the picture of health as we come upon this week's feast of Winter's Liberation. You practically had tears running down your face as you surveyed this city up and down. My father here has politely asked you what has caused such a shift in your emotions, and many of us around these tables have dared to go further. No one doubts that you have taught with fervor and done greater things beyond human comprehension while in Selanna. But once again, we press upon you this entreaty: As none of us still know where you come from, we have no understanding of who has sent you. By what authority do you come into our city and bring a teaching that neither upholds Kronji power nor our own nation's ambitions of freedom?"

The murmurs and ayes around the tables rose forth, and in response, Joël rose from his seat to face the crowd. Kyria and Kaleva looked at him, shaking their heads and wishing him quiet, knowing their requests were futile.

"You have posed a question of authority, Vilius," Joël replied at last, "and I say this to all of you: What would you do with one who comes with authority from above, from the summit of Vuoristad? Has it not happened before, only for you to drift from such a one, or to reject him outright?"

"You have asked a question, a straightforward question that cloaks a twisted motive. And so I answer you with a story for ears willing to listen and believe, while those that reject Lord Creator's word will be cursed. There was a farmer whose land bordered the fragrant waters of the Toiva, and his territory bore the abundance of wheat and rye that proved a delight of bakers the nation over. As he had matters to attend to in a distant area, he placed hired hands in charge of his land, with instructions to nurture and grow the grain, to love the land as if the soil was their children. In time, to appraise their progress, he sent one of his servants to his property. The servant was to build a wall of protection around the farm, keeping it safe from those that would destroy; in return, the hired hands were to give him some of the wheat and rye. However, once the wall was built, the hired hands brutalized the servant, kicking him in the ribs, shaving him bald, and throwing him off the property with no grain given out."

"Months later, thieves and robbers approached the farm, intend on stealing some of the grain and burning the rest. The farmer heard of their plot and sent another servant, who attacked bravely and ran off the robbers. But the hired hands, unexplainably angry with the farmer, beat this servant worse than the first one, and sent him away battered and bruised."

"Finally, the owner of the farm sighed and said, 'How can I reach those men? How can I truly help them? I know! I'll send my son, my dear son, my only son, whom I love. A delightful young man to live amongst them, to work and till the land to its abundance so that they will be convinced of my generosity and kind heart!' So he sent his dear, only, and beloved son on the long journey to the farm. And when the hired hands saw the son coming over the lush hills, walking down the road that skirted the Toiva River, they gathered together and said, 'Look! The fool has sent his son as a way of pacifying us. As he is the heir, if we do away with him, then the land will be ours to do with as we please!'"

"And so they did, torturing the son worse than they had the previous servants, before putting him to a savage death on the parpallo. Their celebrations and shouts reached the heavens, and even from a great distance away, the farm owner heard the cries of apparent victory. Now do you think the farmer gave up and surrendered to the hired hands? No! Before the embers and ashes of his son had cooled, he rode hard across that great distance and destroyed all the hired hands, giving them a death far more brutal than what they gave his son. With no one to work the land, he called out into the darkness, and without explanation, people of all kinds throughout the nation walked toward the farm, and people beyond the sea sailed toward the land, which he gave over to them as if it had always been theirs."

Joël ended his story and leaned over to collect his walking stick. Walking through the crowd toward the door, he passed Kyria, Kaleva, and their friends before turning around.

"Be careful whom you reject," he shouted above the disagreeing patrons, "lest you find the farmer riding toward you because of the way you have treated his emissaries." And pulling his cloak about his shoulders, he disappeared into the streets as the shouts of the people followed him into the distance.

Kyria turned to her friends, grasping Matleena's arm. "I don't like the sound of this. What is going on?"

"I don't know," said Saku, as Rauha shook her head.

"Me neither," Henrik added.

Kaleva put up his hand. "We're not going to get an understanding unless we find out here. Come on. Follow me." He waved them onward, toward Olav Halmo.

Elbart poured himself a glass of wine from the crystal bottle, wiping his eyes from the exhaustion of the day. King Dewulf was arriving in three days in Selanna Harbor. The Winter's Liberation feast would capture the enthusiasm of Selanna in five days, an ironic moment to celebrate past independence while under the rule of another nation. And still that troublesome Joël managed to make his city a roiling tableau of anxiety for him. Elbart yawned, noting he had not enjoyed a restful night of sleep for a week's time. Perhaps the wine would help.

It was as he sat in his chair in the Council Hall that he heard a knock from the side entrance. A servant entered, his frame bent and apologetic, bearing a paper in his hand.

"What is it, Olli?" Elbart called in the moonlit gloom.

"Begging your pardon," the servant said, his voice low and meek, "but someone brought this note for your lordship. I asked him what the nature of his visit was, as he merely said, 'Make sure the Great

Steward receives it, for it is a matter of extreme importance and future success.' And then he left."

"Leave it, Olli," Elbart replied. "You may go."

Once the servant had left, Elbart took the paper in his hand. It was folded once, unsealed. Unable to read the script in the darkness, Elbart lit a candle on his side table and looked at the words that leapt like a long-desired dream off the page.

Our hopes of independence and my shares of profit now diminished, we can still establish our order and authority in this land both with the favor of the people and those we live under. All that is needed is to leverage the people against Joël, and, after an incident from this evening, the time is ripe and I am willing to assist. If you and your allies wish to take this step, you know where to find me.

The walk had been short from the Lakihalle once the others had come. With Dirnik, Lasjen, and Umlar following him up the stairs on the west side of the shop, Elbart stepped onto the landing, lantern in hand. He put forth his hand and knocked loudly on the upstairs door three times. Only a few seconds passed before the door opened soundlessly and the owner of the house and the shop below nodded in comradeship to the men assembled outside.

"Meeting this late means we require stealth and speed," said Elbart.

"Those both we have, sire," said Vilius as he waved the nobles in before closing the door behind them.

24

The landing of King Dewulf's entourage, along with a more sizable contingent of the Kronji army, did nothing to abate the enthusiasm for the Winter's Liberation feast through Selanna. The highlight of the Merivalkan calendar, the once-yearly banquet of smoked trout and pavender, roasted potatoes and turnips, and the candied and spiced dasenpfear dispatched its smells throughout Selanna as families and friends gathered together around tables in memory of the freedom won at the end of the First Dawn. The food, ale, and wine would flow as freely as the remembrances of the victory over the Ehrma under an overcast and frigid Early Snowtide day.

It was at afternoon nave that Kaleva, Henrik, and Saku walked down the Avenue of the Commonwealth discussing the plans for their celebration of the feast that night. Drawing near the harbor lane, they noticed Joël standing outside his shop. There was no light coming from inside, and as they came nearer, they saw Joël was locking the door.

"Joël," said Kaleva. "Did we find you at a bad time?"

At first, the men thought they had spoken to the wrong person, as he made no response other than leaning against the front door of the shop. But in the gathering twilight, they could make out the silhouette of the walking stick, and when he finally turned silently to them, they saw for sure it was their friend.

"Good afternoon, men," Joël replied at last. "I was locking up my shop."

"Locking your house, as well," said Henrik, "since you live here."

"That is true, also. I am sorry. I am not well, and upon the moment of the feast, sad to say."

"You really don't look well, Joël," Kaleva offered. He stepped closer and saw that, while there was nothing physically that caused him to believe Joël was ill, there was an uneasiness of spirit that stemmed from deep within Joël's very being.

"Yes, well. That does seem odd. I assume, not to change the subject, that you are headed to your celebration of the feast?"

"We were, Joël," answered Saku, "but with whom are you to celebrate the feast?"

"As of now, I guess it's myself."

"That cannot be, Joël," Kaleva shook his head. "Come with us. We'll be gathering together at sundown, I with my brothers and their wives. We might even be able to convince Kyria and Elaenor to come. I am sure we might give Kyria an excuse from feasting with the Halmo clan and others in the boisterous Iron Bow. And I'm sure Elaenor wouldn't mind the option of dinner with friends."

"That ... yes. Feasting with friends does seem like a gathering I would favor. I would be very glad of such moments tonight. Thank you."

"You know where our house is, Joël?" asked Henrik. "The west end of the harbor near our ship and the West Tower? I can tell Matleena to set another place for you."

Joël closed his eyes, only opening them after some effort. "Excellent, my dear friends. I will see you there."

As was tradition, the table was bedecked with a clean white cloth, stoneware jugs and cups, and earthenware plates with the dasenpfear insignia. The fish had been smoked in the outdoor fire-oven, and Kyria had helped Matleena and Rauha with the potatoes that she had brought just the day before. She mentioned that, as several families had joined together for a feast at the vikarloge, Elaenor had managed to excuse herself to join with Kyria and the others, and so Matleena managed to squeeze another place setting for her. In all, eight places ringed the table.

The friends sat down, with the food and drink before them, and a disturbing hush settling upon them. None of the friends would dare speak a word about it, but it seemed to them that Joël's presence carried much anguish. His eyes remained closed, his body leaning forward toward the table, as if an invisible weight pressed him down.

"Joël," asked Henrik, "would you do the honors of returning our thanks to Lord Creator?"

Again with much effort, Joël's eyelids fluttered open. "I will, Henrik. Thank you for asking." And they all joined hands as the cold wind increased outside.

"Lord of snow, Lord of storm," began Joël, "We come before you tonight remembering your glorious grace in the rescue of this land and this people years ago. Truly, you passed over the sins of your people and showed mercy as you rescued them from the Ehrma. As the earthquake of ages past brought the giants to their knees to vanquish them, so may the earthquake of your severe mercy bring your people to their knees again to recognize their need of your forgiveness. Only with great loss can there be great gain, Lord Creator. May these friends around this table find that grace to be true in the coming days as you prepare them for a future under your warm smile. May you bless this food to our bodies that you have created for your glory. In this hope and your name, we make this prayer."

"We make this prayer," repeated the others, looking around and finding stunned faces.

The meal was a prolonged affair, with many attempts at conversation that ultimately centered on the reflections of the past year. The recollections varied, but the common thread was the place of Joël in the stories. Kaleva and his brothers retold the memory of when they first met Joël at the harbor docks. Kyria and Eleanor laughed when they told of Joël's ability to fix Jehre's bread table, and Kyria continued with the retelling of how Joël fixed Captain Vermeulen's greaves. The others brought up the walks to the country, the sudden feeding of the crowd, and finally told with happy tears the amazing night when Joël had raised Kyrt from the dead.

Joël said little throughout but was attentive to their stories, wearing a smile on his face as his friends shared their appreciative thoughts of his arrival and stay in Selanna. The fish was consumed and the potatoes were mostly gone. All that remained was a loaf or two of bread along with a pitcher of water.

"Joël," said Kaleva, "what are you thinking?"

"I am thinking about how wonderful it has been to be here," Joël replied.

"You know that you always have a place at our table, Joël," said Matleena. "You are ever welcome here."

"I would include your table, Matleena," Joël answered, "as you are a gracious hostess. But I specifically meant Selanna. It has been good to dwell amongst you."

"May I ask," said Saku, "why the use of the past tense?"

Joël did not answer, fixing his eyes on the bread and water. Finally, he took a loaf of bread in his hands and tore it in half. Then he took the pitcher of water and poured it into his cup, to the brim, spilling several drops over the top.

"Bread that is torn, water that is poured out," he said, moisture forming in the corners of his eyes. "How true this is, how very true. Only by being torn and poured out can hope come to my people."

"Joël!" Elaenor called out across the table. "Are you alright?"

Her strident voice seemed to arrest Joël's attention, and he looked at her with kind, shining eyes.

"I am only saying that this is no mere feast like in years past," he said quietly. "This is a new moment in your lives and the life of this nation, of this world. You are on the verge of Lord Creator drawing near to open the gates to his presence in ways you never dreamed possible. But his drawing you all, his making atonement to cleanse your hearts, comes with great anguish.

"It is anguish that is unspeakable, my friends. It is a road that I must walk myself."

"No, you can't," said Kaleva suddenly. "We can't allow this, Joël. We can't allow you to suffer alone."

"This is not a path for you to take right now, Kaleva," Joël replied, waving him off and reaching for his walking stick. "You are most welcome to come with me when I leave, but I must go forth." He pointed to the window looking over the street. "The darkness is more than what you see outside. It inhabits those who would seek me out, who would offer me up."

He grasped his walking stick and turned toward the door. "If you wish to come with me, I would be glad of your presence now. But it is the path that I must follow."

Vilius peered from the alley as the wind whipped into the street. He saw Joël leave the house, followed by several people he knew well, one for most of his life. He heard nothing of what they said, but he didn't need to. The direction of their trek told him exactly where they were going. He waited until they were out of sight, then stepped out of the alley, headed in a southeasterly direction toward the Lakihalle.

As agreed, he rapped five knocks on side door, which led to a storage room off the court atrium. The knocks identified his presence and the door opened immediately. The darkness kept him from seeing anything, but Vilius knew immediately that he stood face to face with the general of Merivalka's army.

"They left," he said, "and I can lead you to him."

Lasjen looked back over his shoulder and barked out. "Assemble the guards to move immediately." He turned back to Vilius and invited him in, waving his hand toward a chair that stood by the interior door.

"It's your new seat for a new noble," Lasjen said with a cruel smile.

"My thanks," Vilius replied.

Lasjen put his riding gloves on as Elbart approached from behind. "Make haste," ordered the Great Steward, "and bring him back with all speed. We have a long night ahead of us."

25

With Kaleva having negotiated for a later return through the North Gate, six figures slipped through, their feet crunching over the gelid grass as Joël led the way. Moments later, by the light of Kaleva's lantern, the shadowy rise of Elks Hill came into view, and Joël took them to the highest place of that elevation.

"Joël," said Elaenor, "is there something you need us to do?"

"Anything," echoed Kyria. "We'll do anything. It would also keep our minds off the cold."

"It is rather frigid, yes," replied Joël. "Making a fire might be just the thing. If you wish, set the wood up in that stone pit near the tree that lies on the south side of the hill."

"But won't you join us?"

"I shall remain here on the summit so that I might pray."

"But the fire will be at the base of the hill."

"But I can see Vuoristad from here, and that is from where my help will come."

Kaleva, Henrik, and Saku approached Joël. "What do you need from us?" asked Kaleva.

"Stay and watch," Joël said evenly. He looked at Henrik and Saku. "Your wives will be well?"

Henrik nodded. "They trust us with you. They needed to clean up after the dinner."

"Very well," Joël replied. He pointed toward Selanna. "If anyone comes to pay us a visit, they will come from the city. If you are going to tend the fire with Kyria and Elaenor, please be watchful and stand firm if anyone approaches."

"Do you want us to prevent them from coming near?" asked Kaleva.

"We'll do as you ask," Saku added.

"Just stand firm, but if anyone comes near, it is because they are meant to. Do not resist them. If anyone comes for me, it is by design. And now, Kaleva, Henrik, Saku, I wish to pray."

The three men shuffled down the hill to its base, where they helped the women gather branches. The stone pit sat next to a spruce tree, one of many that ringed the hills in the area. In little time, they had a fire going and Henrik and Saku set themselves to tending it as Kaleva peered into the distance.

"Do you think something is happening tonight?" asked Kyria.

"I hope not," answered Kaleva, "but Joël doesn't sound hopeful."

Elaenor spoke up. "I don't think hopefulness is the issue. Joël seems to know something is happening, something that is hardly ideal at best and horrific at worst. But I don't know if he is hopeful to avoid it. It just ... I don't know. It seems to just be ... there."

"I feel like he is leaving us in some way," groaned Kyria. "There is something about him lately that makes me believe he will not be with us anymore. That, with his painful look, and his story at the Iron Bow ... all of that makes me believe that he is pulling away from us."

"And yet he wanted us to come with him tonight," said Saku.

"That's true," added Henrik. "That doesn't seem like he is pulling away from us."

"I hear what you are saying," saying Kyria, biting her trembling lip, "but I feel this night is something of a goodbye. I hope not. Since he came to Selanna, life has been ..."

"Been what?" asked Elaenor, reaching over to take her friend's hand.

"Different. Not just in a good way, but the best way. It's as if, for the first time I've ever known, Lord Creator smiles on me, on us. And it's all because Joël is here."

Kaleva stood, then suddenly crouched down. "He might not be here for long." He pointed toward the North Gate. "Look."

The others followed his gesture and saw movement in the distance. "Who is that?" asked Saku.

"I can't say for sure," said Kaleva, his courage seeping away, "but the odds are they include guards from the Lakihalle. I saw the epaulets on their uniforms and those are swords they carry. And they brought some others who don't want to be noticed under those hoods."

"Saku, Kaleva," said Henrik, "go warn Joël. I'll stay here with the ladies." He instinctively moved in front of Kyria and Elaenor, his broad shoulders and solid girth hiding them from the view of the advancing intruders. Saku and Kaleva scrambled up the hill, where they found Joël prone on the grass, face down toward Vuoristad and convulsing.

"Joël," Kaleva whispered. "Joël! Soldiers and others are approaching. We need to get you away from here to another place."

Kaleva and Saku gripped Joël under his armpits, trying to heave him up into a standing position, but Joël's legs gave way and he slumped back to the ground. Saku took him by the shoulders and tried to lift him again when Joël let loose a cry of pain that resounded over the countryside. Pitching forward toward the ground, Joël wailed and emptied the contents of his stomach. Sweat poured from his body. Kaleva came to his side and waved the lantern in his face. Looking down at Joël's hands, he gasped when he saw the carved palms, marked by the bloody scratches that contrasted with Joël's fair appearance.

"Joël, we need to get you away!" he pled with him. But Joël only shook his head vigorously.

"No," he whispered. "No!" He grabbed his walking stick and pulled himself upward, lurching around as if in pain. "My time. This is my time." He fell, his eyes glazed and unfocused, before pulling himself up. "My friends, my time has come!"

Kaleva took a step to prevent him from moving any more when he saw the glint of the guards' armor. His legs gave way as he made out the gleam of the swords, and the polished shine of the sheaths and greaves. It was when he saw the non-uniformed men come around the soldiers that his heart gave way with his legs. They doffed their hoods and in that moment Kaleva knew the darkness had truly come.

Elbart. Dirnik. Lasjen. Umlar.

There was only one that remained with head and face obscured, and Kaleva could not see who it was. Nor did he wait to find out. Already he felt the tears hot against his skin, could hear the voice of Saku echoing in the distance, and sensed the raw, spiked grass crunching beneath his feet. Sprinting into the far countryside, he felt the frosty air pour into his lungs, nearly paralyzing them with cold if not for his desperation to flee from the danger behind him.

After what seemed like hours, though he knew it was only a few minutes, he slipped and fell headlong into an array of stones, bruising his arms and bloodying his face upon impact. Turning over, he looked up at a cloudy sky that blocked out the stars. Sitting up, he looked back, barely seeing the corona of firelight from the other side of Elks Hill. It was then that he felt the shame wash over him like a tidal wave from the White Sea, and he wept, his body racking with the sobs that broke from deep within.

I promised that I would be with him until the end, he thought. *And here I am, denying him at this very moment!*

"We call forth the one named Joël!" called out Elbart, his voice ringing like a bell through the night air.

"No," demanded Kyria. "Not until you tell us why you've come for him!"

"Kyria, enough," came a gentle voice halfway up the hill. The figure, slumped with halting steps and leaning on his walking stick, stumbled past Kyria and came face to face with Elbart, Dirnik, and the other Nobles.

"I am Joël."

"Joël, citizen of Selanna and resident of our domain," Dirnik read from a paper illumined by a servant's lantern, "you are required herewith to come forth in our custody, to face trial before the Council of Nobles on charges of treason, civic disturbance, criminal activity, and the wanton and deliberate teaching against our Faith. The trial will begin one hour after you have arrived in the holding cell of the Lakihalle."

"You cannot do this!" screamed Henrik. But Joël stayed him with a stiff hand across his chest.

"Peace, Henrik!" Joël ordered, his voice restored. "And that goes for you, Kyria, Elaenor, and Saku. Return to your homes. And pray."

"Prayer will not serve them if they use it in support of you," Umlar snarled.

Joël said nothing to Umlar, instead looking at the one to his right on the edge of the company. The man's hood was still drawn over his face, and he dipped his head as if to avoid recognition.

"The currency of your soul was a seat at the Council's table, was it not?" asked Joël, to which the figure suddenly turned away, walking back toward the gates.

Elbart nodded to the guards and called out, "Let the prisoner be taken forth!" to which one of the guards came forward and sent a vicious greave-covered forearm cracking into Joël's chest, sending him crashing to the ground.

It was several minutes later that Kyria stopped crying, and with Henrik and Saku's help, she was lifted up and taken to Elaenor's house and laid on a bed in her friend's room. Her head swimming, she drifted in and out of sleep, for how long she couldn't say. When a shaft of moonlight pierced the darkness, Kyria sat bolt upright in bed, clutching the blanket that had been laid over her.

Low voices were coming from downstairs, and with effort, Kyria fumbled in the dark until she found the latch on her door. Feeling her way along the wall, she came to the back entry that came out on the loft set above the bakery. Looking down, she saw candles lit and Henrik, Saku, and Elaenor talking in low tones. Elaenor looked up as Kyria began descending the stairs.

"Are you alright?" she asked Kyria, coming near and embracing her friend.

Kyria shook her head, slowly at first, then quickening the motion until she burst into tears. Henrik and Saku drew to either side of them, waiting patiently until Kyria's crying ceased. Finally, both men slipped on black cloaks, passing an extra one to Kyria.

"We're going," Henrik said in a voice husky with recent weeping.

"Going where?" asked Kyria.

"To the Lakihalle," answered Saku, his jaw clenched and his eyes burning. "We're going now."

Elaenor swallowed hard. "They'll never let us in, Saku."

"We don't have to get in. We don't even have to stop them," Saku said in a huff, pulling on a pair of thick gloves. "We're going to be there, because we will not let our friend down."

Stumbling out the door of the bakery with her friends, Kyria pulled her own cloak around her to ward off the bitter cold. It was when they shuffled on their way over icy streets toward the Lakihalle that she finally noticed Kaleva was not with them. And that was when her tears returned.

26

The crepuscular glow of the court atrium flickered with the glass-encased candles. The winter gale whipped outside as the Nobles arranged themselves in their chairs. Only one chair remained empty, but not for long, as the door from the Council Hall flew open and Petric came striding through, hot with anger.

"To what end," he roared, "does this Council break the laws of our city and land? For what purpose does this Council put forth an accusation against a citizen when the entire Council has not been told in advance? In what possible fashion did any of you believe this was right and just?" He wheeled around, his eyes flashing fire at his fellow Nobles. "Because of this impudent maneuver, we have citizens coming through the streets and hovering outside this hall, hoping to hear anything of your dealings! In the middle of the night! You have accused this man of madness, but that is the question I must pose to each of you: Are you mad?"

"Silence, Petric," Elbart ordered in a languid tone, bringing a cup of wine to his lips. "We have a number of witnesses regarding the public behavior of this Joël. Given his obstinacy in these actions, not to mention the timing of his sayings with King Dewulf here the past four days, we must deal conclusively with this bludge. So if you would be so kind as to take your place among us, rather than strafing against us, Petric, we can bring him in and begin."

"Begin what?" Petric badgered. "A sham of a trial?"

Ignoring him, Elbart signaled two soldiers. "Go, and bring in the prisoner!"

Joël shivered in the dark wooden cell, which afforded a small window view to the sky, bringing in the salt of the ocean on the brumal wind. The flickering candle tossed ghastly shadows on the walls as Joël sat on the bench, awaiting the summons to continue this fateful night. He

171

heard the murmuring of the crowd flocking around the Lakihalle, some chanting for his demise, some asking questions, and others whispering support for him that countered the defense of the Nobles. He placed his head in his hands and prayed.

Father, maker of this world, I ask that you buttress my spirit for the hours ahead. The pain of what is to come is more than I can bear, but I know it must be, because I will not see those I love fall into destruction's grip forever. I know what must happen, and you know what must happen. In the anguish that must be, may there be cleansing, and if this array of suffering could be avoided, you would make a way. Even now, I hope that there could be another way. But I know your desire, and I will seek that, as well, above all else. And so I commend myself into your love.

The footsteps down the hall grew louder, but they were drowned by the caustic cackle Joël heard within the cell walls.

"Ha, ha, ha!" said the throaty, flinty voice, oozing from the cobalt mist that wisped in front of Joël. "Again, all for love. The glorious hope that sends you to your doom."

Joël said nothing, pulling himself up and standing, his knees holding but wobbly.

"Your altruism would be admirable if it had a purpose, Joël, but your love blinds you. Once you are gone, there is nothing standing in the way of feasting on this world as the meal of cruelty I have long desired," the mist throbbed in the gloom. "You have given all, and still I have won!"

The footfalls grew louder, but before their bearers came into sight, Joël's eyes flamed with light, his blue irises flaring with gold and silver flecks in a magnificent sheen. He did not flinch, but rather he stepped into the mist itself, forcing it to scatter from shock.

"You and I have very different definitions of victory, Tuona," replied Joël. "You have always been thirsty for tearing down, for maiming the glorious, for breaking apart what is good and whole. And this you will always do. And you will do so tomorrow with me. But here you shall advance, and no more. Your final thrust against me will be your fatal, foolish one. Be gone, Tuona, and take your lies with you!"

The mist evaporated. The cell door clanged open and the soldiers stood before him. One of them placed chain-cuffs on Joël's wrists to bind him.

"It is time," the man said. "Follow us."

27

"Joël," called out Dirnik, playing to the hilt his assigned role as prime prosecutor, "you have been summoned here tonight to face witnesses and evidence of four charges of law breaking that have been levied against you! First, there is the charge of treason; this is followed by a second charge of civic disturbance of the city and citizenry of Selanna. Also, you stand accused of criminal activity, all of which leads to a severe spiritual assault on our city, as well: wantonly and intentionally teaching against our Faith. Do you have anything to say in your initial defense?"

The Nobles looked at Joël, expecting oratory of a caliber that would force them to navigate their response carefully. All evening, they had been rehearsing their measured reactions to any of Joël's possible defenses and counter-arguments. The one possibility that occurred was the one they had not thought possible.

There, in the middle of the court atrium, with the Nobles silent and the crowds outside arguing, each side against the other, Joël stood, looking down at the floor.

And he said nothing.

"I asked," yelled Dirnik, his voice cracking, "does the accused say anything at all in his defense?"

Joël looked up from his chains and fixed his eyes on Dirnik. And still he said nothing.

"Continuing on," said Elbart, signaling Dirnik to bring forth witnesses.

"To the charge of treason," Dirnik announced, "we have several witnesses from the days of Early Suntide. The specific day is when Prince Dewulf—as he was then known—and his ships landed in Selanna. You were accosted by Vilius Halmo as to your loyalties of whether Selanna should pay tribute to Kronjva or not."

"I recall that day," Joël replied hoarsely. "Vilius Halmo did ask me that question. I also find it interesting that Vilius is nowhere to be seen."

"The issue of Vilius Halmo's presence is immaterial!" barked Dirnik. "Your answer directly assaulted both the subordinate authority of Merivalka and the primal authority of Kroňjva."

"So you say."

Almost to a man, with the exception of Petric, all the Nobles thrust their fists in the air and snarled at Joël, who stood quietly, showing no concern.

"You have heard it from his own mouth!" Dirnik bawled out, sweeping his hand toward the prisoner.

"We have heard it," interrupted Petric, "but his words have no scent of treason. I was nearby that day, and he clearly continued his statement by saying all we have belongs to Lord Creator, and that it was imperative we turn to him before we lose our true freedom."

"Your commentary is noted," said Dirnik with great irritation, "but it is the judgment of the court that this bludge's intent was to foment treason!"

"Isn't judgment to come after the collective assessment of evidence, and not before?" Petric snapped.

Ignoring him, Dirnik went on. "You also stand accused of civic disturbance of our fair city. Everywhere you go, you stir up questions and trouble that create a backlash against the good and necessary order of this realm. Several people, including many in the Iron Bow from several nights ago, heard your pointed, irascible, and scornful story that accused our land of hating the prophets and killing the Rhoken!"

"It is as you say," said Joël, swallowing hard. "Although your intent is truly to condemn me not matter what, and although you mistake a solemn reality for an accusation, you have judged the story correctly."

"Again, we hear it for ourselves!" said Elbart, rising from his chair. "And in fomenting disorder, you place our nation at risk under Kronjva rule! That alone is cause for condemnation!"

"Lies! All lies!" roared Petric.

"The charge of criminal activity is a serious one, as well," spoke Lasjen for the first time. "When you first established yourself here, coming before the nobles to purchase a shop for your trade. You paid well above the asking price for the shop, but you refused to reveal the source of your wealth."

"If you listened to everything I have said, and to my claims of who I am, you would have no confusion," said Joël.

"Silence!" Lasjen shouted. "You wear none of the clothing or regalia of other nations, come from a place you never identify, and work for practically no money in your residency among us. No one can survive like that without resorting to other means for survival! There is no doubt you must be robbing from others!"

"And unless you have conclusive evidence, Lasjen," Petric growled as he shot out of his chair, "stay your accusations!"

Two soldiers immediately barred Petric's path, forcing him back to his chair. At the end of the atrium, another guard drew near to Elbart and whispered in his ear.

"In a few minutes," Elbart replied to the guard, "and I will see him outside." He signaled Umlar to rise.

"Finally," said the high priest, "we have the heresy and unspeakable destruction to our Faith from this madman here! The evidence is overwhelming. At the Gathering of Brightide Nave, he declared that all the Stories point to his coming and reveal him to be the Courageous One! In public, he forgave a little boy's sins as if he was Lord Creator himself, and then—in this room before us!—he claimed the divine power for himself! From the reports of eyewitness, we have evidence of witchcraft as he uses dark magic to quell a storm on the sea and to create food from the air! And he brings the word of Lord Creator to the half-breeds of the Vale-dwellers! You!" Here Umlar approached Joël, pointing a wrinkled, shaking finger at him. "You have defiled our land, besmirched our city, and attempted to destroy our Faith! Far from Lord Creator's own, you bear the work of Tuona himself wreaked among us!"

"Of the two of us, Umlar," Joël replied, "the one who does the work of the Evil One is you."

In response, and in spite of Petric's attempt to calm the eruption, the Nobles screamed in horror at Joël's claim. Umlar's eyes flashed with fire, and his assistant Gheren came forth with a brass censer. Swinging it forward, Gheren smashed the heavy container across Joël's face, cracking his jaw and splitting the skin, revealing a deep cut that exposed blood and bone. Joël fell with a thud to the stone floor.

"Tell us, Courageous One," Gheren yelled, "was that Tuona's work, as well?"

"Quiet!" called Elbart. "We have heard it from his own mouth! There is no need to bring forth any more evidence. We have the responsibility to bring accusation and convict him, but as King Dewulf is here as primal ruler, we must bring Joël before the Kronji for sentencing. The truth is before us and I call for the conclusion of wills: Do we find the prisoner and accused one, Joël, guilty of the charges given?"

Several voices cried "Guilty!" at once, extended by agonizing screams. It was when they faded that Petric stood and walked to the center of the atrium.

"I recognize that my voice will not sway your opinions," he said, his voice quavering. "Nor will it save you, Joël. And it might cost me my position on this Council. But the accusations tonight have been brought against an innocent man. If we wish to expose sin and guilt, my fellow Nobles, then we must begin by looking at our own hearts and our stubborn unwillingness to heed the possibility that Lord Creator has visited his will and his grace before us these past months in the person and work of this Joël. Because of this, I will not be a party to the verdict you desire, and I will vote most clearly against your guilty declaration!"

"You are one against all," said Dirnik, "and the verdict passes."

"And history will judge between us, Dirnik," Petric answered, "and it will find you deficient in its balances."

"The argument is ceased," declared Elbart. "Take the prisoner to the vikarloge and go at once to our royal guest quarters. Entreat the

King and his court to come as soon as possible with all apologies for awakening him. The Kronji have the right of sentencing. Bear him forth!"

Mirko pulled back from below the window. As he had the best ears of the group, he had been chosen to listen to the proceedings inside the Lakihalle. Several other groups, some friendly toward Joël's chances, others more hostile, clustered around the perimeter of the building.

"Condemned on each of the charges," he said sadly when Ivar lowered him to the ground. "He never had a chance, as the Council was against him from the beginning."

"The entire Council?" Kyria said, aghast.

"No, Petric stood firm, but he was only one voice among the rest."

"Mirko," said Henrik, "what is happening now?"

"They are taking him to the vikarloge, where he will await sentencing by King Dewulf."

"Oh, no!" Elaenor cried. "There will be no mercy from him!"

"I'm not so sure," replied Saku. "Remember Joël healed Dewulf's niece before. That could buy him some mercy if ..." His words trailed away, and his friends followed his eyes to the town square and a stumbling, cloaked figure leaning against the wall near the parpallo.

"Kaleva!" said Kyria, and in an instant, she was running toward him. She and the others met him together, and Kaleva fell into their collective grasp.

"Kaleva, brother," Henrik spoke, his irritation coming through in his voice, "where were you?"

Kaleva stared at them, eyes unfocused, with a disagreeable smell coming from his mouth and clothing.

"Dearest brother," Saku shook his head. "You've been drinking."

"Drinking my shame into what should be my grave," said Kaleva, "not his. I failed, my friends. I insisted I would be with him till the end, and I failed him."

"You there," called someone from down the street, pointing at Kaleva, "you were with the man called Joël, all of you!"

"He was," said a woman. "The one called Kaleva, the sailor. You're thick as thieves, all of you, with that bludge! Making friends with troublemakers and criminals, are you?"

"He's no criminal!" Kyria yelled, her better judgment leaving her.

"I can't take this," muttered Kaleva.

"You're his friend," the woman accosted Kaleva. "Took him sailing, did you? Did you all? When he stopped that storm?" And here she waved her arms about, mockingly, piping her shrill voice as others laughed.

"You spiteful li'l bludge," Lars spoke at long last. "He ha' done no 'arm an' you act worse 'an those nobles!"

Kyria and Elaenor turned from the woman, knowing their anger would serve no purpose. But in the confusion, they saw the sobbing Kaleva had once again slipped away, careening down the street in the direction of his house as other curious citizens came running toward the Lakihalle.

Elbart sniffed the frosted salt breeze from the White Sea as he stepped through the back door onto the stone patio to the rear of the Lakihalle. Rubbing his gloved hands, he approached the figure on the edge of the patio. "Well?"

Vilius turned around. "I have traded blood for an honor that I can never deserve. I have brought forth a man for charges of treason when I myself am the traitor."

Elbart rolled his eyes. "It's too late for that, wouldn't you say? When you wrote us about this possibility, and you promised your work in moving the people more against Joël, this was the price for your success. Now you are plunging into a bath of guilt, yet why should that be my concern?"

179

"I never saw it until he came forth on Elks Hill!" Vilius insisted, tears pouring down his face and wetting his scanty beard. "Nothing can take it back. The way he looked at me when he spoke there!"

"The same eyes looked at me, Vilius," replied Elbart. "And nothing happened."

"Then we are different, the two of us," Vilius wept, turning toward the sea as he clutched the balustrade.

"We certainly are," said Elbart, walking stealthily toward him, both reaching out to the unsuspecting young man and calculating the steep drop to the rugged path below.

28

It was another three hours before the Kronji made their appearance in the main hall of the vikarloge. Joël was led from an anteroom before King Dewulf and his guards. With no sleep or food, Joël felt his strength fading in this hour before sunrise, yet he stood firm before the Kronji. His eyes fell upon Captain Vermeulen, who returned his quiet gaze with one of shock and dismay. Finally, Elbart passed by Joël and approached Dewulf, who sat on a cushioned seat behind the platform where Umlar would read from the Stories.

"O King Dewulf, Ruler of Kronjva and the Northern Realms! In humble reliance upon your grace, we strive to keep proper order here in Selanna, capital of the land of Merivalka. Although our efforts are tireless, we confess to having in our midst the occasional troublemaker. But matters more serious arrest our attention early this morn. This Joël, who is a relative newcomer to Selanna, has taken it upon himself to spread treason, to foment civic disturbance against the quietude of our city, to engage in criminal behavior, and to sully our Faith, all of which constitutes a cumulative threat to your good rule, O King!"

"What is the evidence against the accused?" asked Dewulf in a skeptical tone.

Dirnik and Elbart swept forward together and spent the next ten minutes giving Dewulf a carefully worded statement that captured everything that had been said in the court atrium back at the Lakihalle. Dewulf's posture showed clear irritation by the business at hand so early in the day. Yet stalwart in his position as king, he listened intently, his eyes never leaving Joël. Finally, the Great Steward spoke his conclusion.

"And thus, O King, we beg your decision to find solidarity with our conclusion of wills, and to further the necessary tranquility of our city and your domain by sentencing this man to death."

The word death hung in the hall of the vikarloge, and King Dewulf raised his head at the mention of the word. Captain Vermeulen looked at his sovereign with a worrisome glance. From outside came the shouts, threats, and pleas of a crowd mixed in their opinions, a crowd that had grown as the news had spread throughout Selanna during the night.

"The desire for quiet and order is a noble one, Great Steward," Dewulf said after much deliberation.

"Thank you," replied Elbart, too hastily.

"I was not finished!" barked Dewulf. "You heard it from my own lips when our delegation was here previously. My iron hand would meet your nation viciously if Joël stirred up any more trouble that left these shores ungovernable. It is certain there is unrest here. Of that, there is no doubt.

"But what I have trouble seeing is how much of this is due to the man Joël himself. He heals and speaks in cloaked stories and performs miracles ... miracles that even I can attest to and express my deepest thanks. The reaction I hear outside cannot be defined clearly. There are cries for his death, but are such roars from those he has harmed or from those he has offended by his words? There are also pleas for clemency and release. My question is this: Is the unrest we see in Selanna these days and especially this morning a natural reaction to Joël as a man, or might they be a manipulation of those gathered before me?"

"Your Majesty ..." began Dirnik.

"Please, quiet yourself, Dirnik," Dewulf sneered caustically with a dismissive backhand into the air. "I tire of your bombast. You have brought your version of evidence. I want more."

King Dewulf rose from the chair. "I wish to speak to the prisoner myself. The rest of you, excepting my house guards, shall leave the hall and move to the public area north of the Lakihalle. Vermeulen, I ask that you assemble the soldiers under your immediate command to set up a barrier behind which Joël and I may come back to the Lakihalle when we are finished."

"Very good, my Sovereign." Vermeulen bowed slightly and left, gesturing to others to accompany him.

The early morning sunrays had begun their initial invasion over the tops of the Selannan homes, piercing their ornate lead-framed windows with a vibrant shine. In the kopanos, Dewulf took ten steps and stood face-to-face with Joël.

"Is this the way it is?" Dewulf asked him quietly.

"All that is comes from my Father's hand," replied Joël.

Dewulf frowned. "That is not what I meant. Come, you must realize that. We are alike, you and I."

"If you understood what is, then you would not have said that."

"Joël, I can admire your peace and calm in the midst of this chaos, not to mention the abuse you have received and that deep cut on your jaw. I can believe that you are a good man, and I am hardly inclined to deliver you to the wiles of the mob that gathers. I am also disinclined, as you know, to believe this rabble about their hope in the Rhoken. So I ask you, between us, are you indeed the Courageous One?"

The cuffs scraped against Joël's wrists, and he lifted his head, belying the pain he felt deep within, to meet Dewulf's face.

"You yourself have said so."

"Joël, I am trying to seek your good. Surely you can understand how others might pursue the benefit of their fellow man. No one can reasonably watch your actions without realizing you have come to do good. I am King of Kronjva, Ruler of the Northern Realms, the Sovereign of Sovereigns, and even I consider myself in debt to you in some way from when you healed our little Sigrid. So why do you insist on claiming to be what you say?"

"The Sovereign of Sovereigns?" Joël said, his voice croaking dryly.

"That is my title."

"All titles of mankind, Dewulf, are man-made. True power and glory—all that crowns mankind from great to small--come from Lord Creator. I have come, not merely to heal and speak and do miracles, but to bring a kingdom greater than and beyond yours to this world, one which works back the darkness of sin from the very beginning."

"To bring a kingdom?" laughed Dewulf. "Greater than mine?" He cackled. "The Nobles just might be right. You must be mad! So you are not merely the Rhoken, but a king, as well!"

"As before," Joël rasped, "you yourself have said so. Accept it or reject it, but all I have said and done is a beacon to the truth."

"Truth?" sneered Dewulf. "You speak of truth? What is that, in the larger measure of things? If you wish to be a king, Joël, you must put aside ideals such as that. As a ruler, what matters is both my power's extent and its preservation. Right, wrong, truth, falsehood ... these things are all shifting stones. All that matters is who rules and writes his name in history. And today, that is me."

"You say it is you."

"Look at us, Joël. Which of us do you believe has the true power to change the other?"

"My answer would only shock you, and you would not believe me anyway. But you have no power unless it is granted to you from Lord Creator."

King Dewulf sent a blast of air, hot with frustration, from his nostrils. The vein that ran down the middle of his forehead, which enlarged when he became angry, was pulsing now. Calming his breathing, he placed his hand on Joël's shoulder.

"Joël, I do not wish to condemn you. I am not in the habit of punishing innocent people. If you believe yourself to be a king of an imaginary land, who am I to stop your desires? I ask you as I did before: Look at us. Look at us, Joël. I rule in reality, you rule to whatever extent you believe. We are men. We believe in ourselves. We are not really different, you and I."

Taking one step back, Joël allowed the hand of Dewulf to fall from his body. The blood staining his jaw and neck from Gheren's strike, Joël cleared his throat and spoke calmly but powerfully.

"You know not what you say, O King. We are nothing alike in this clearest respect. You, as monarch, demand the blood and sweat of your subjects to expand your rule. But I willingly would spill my own blood to bring the freedom of my kingdom to my subjects."

Joël looked at the embittered face of Dewulf, and concluded, "And that is why we are nothing alike, you and I."

Dewulf clenched his teeth, his words measured yet laced with anger. "Guards, bring the prisoner with me. We go to the grounds of the Lakihalle, and this one will see who has the power now." He swept his cape around him and strode toward the door as guards took Joël by either arm and began the walk into the early morning chill as snowflakes swirled in the air.

29

The snow fell increasingly as the crowds, numbering in the hundreds, pressed near the soldiers that formed the barrier needed to protect Dewulf and Joël as they walked toward the public grounds on the north side of the Lakihalle.

"Cursed cold!" muttered Dewulf as they stepped through the gate. "You had best pray for a quick affirmation from the crowd, or you should settle on an agonizing walk to a brutal death."

"Death I do not fear, O King," said Joël.

"All mankind fears death, troublemaker."

"They fear what kills the body. What matters is what destroys the soul."

"My body and soul are not the one facing destruction, Joël," Dewulf growled as they approached the parpallo, with Vermeulen, Elbart, Dirnik, Lasjen, and Umlar standing nearby.

"You have no idea," Joël spoke sadly, "the depth of falsehood you just professed."

Ignoring Joël's chastisement, Dewulf strode to the head of the crowd that bordered the dais. The assembly swelled to over a thousand citizens, several rows deep into the streets, and covered with a dusting of morning snow, clamoring for action, although a few shouted for mercy. Toward the rear of the assembly, Kyria stood with the others from the night before, hoping for the best but fearing Joël's doom.

"Citizens of Merivalka! Subjects of my realm!" began King Dewulf. "I bring before you the man known as Joël. Your Council of Nobles brought me this man as one run through with treasonous speech and desire, who stirred up dissent and disorder, who robbed and cheated, and who poisoned your religion. To the final charge I merely refer him to you, as that is no matter for which I, as of Kronji stock, feel passion. But the Northern Realms are to be marked by order, peace, and coexistence under my hand. When I hear of reports that tranquility is being disturbed, I stand to action. When I find such reports are true, I bring justice.

"But after examining him before the Council of Nobles, as well as privately, I do not find him guilty of the charges against him that pertain to Kronji law. Whatever your complaints may be, nothing deserving of death has been done by this man. I am willing to punish him as a sign of my authority, but upon that, I will release him!"

The Nobles, Petric excepted, shaking with cold, immediately sprang from their shivering positions with rage. "No!" screamed Elbart.

"No!" shouted Dirnik.

"Injustice!" screamed Umlar.

"We will not stand for this!" added Lasjen.

While Kyria and the others expected the Nobles' contention, they were shocked by the enmity and indignation of the crowd, which shouted nearly as one voice, "Guilty! Guilty! The man is guilty!"

"He came upon us to criticize our Faith!" called out one.

Another shouted. "His parables and riddles are put forth to shame us and set us against one another!"

The roar grew to titanic levels. Dewulf glared at the hundreds before him, fists clenched. "All your words speak disorder and hatred! You are the wretched ones! I thought he was the one you called the Rhoken!"

"We have no Courageous One here!" the crowd yelled, drowning out the roar of the White Sea. "He is not the one to save us!"

"Destroy him!" cried Umlar.

"Take him away to die, King Dewulf," said Dirnik, "and then you will have your peace! Do you think you will have it otherwise?"

Dewulf wheeled around, coming nose to nose with Joël and grabbing him roughly by his bloody tunic. "Talk to me, and retract whatever you need to survive! Do you not realize they mean to destroy you, that they are leveraging my command for order to gain that? All your work here, all you've done for them, even for me? You are willing to throw that away? This is your last chance!"

Joël leaned his head to where his mouth nearly reached the lobe of King Dewulf's ear. "No, King. This is your last chance."

Shaking his head and scowling with rage, Dewulf turned away from Joël and back to the Council, holding up his palms and spreading them wide.

"I am innocent of this man's demise," he thundered. "Do with him as you will!" And turning on his heel, he walked off the dais as the crowd shrieked into a frenzy.

A hand touched Kyria's arm at the back of the crowd. Through her tears, she could see who it was. "Kaleva!"

"This is what I've done," he wept as Henrik and Saku gripped and embraced him. "This is the result of my cowardice."

"No, it isn't," insisted Elaenor.

"It is the result of the Ruin, the Great Ruin, Kaleva," said Kyria as she threw her arms around him on the ground. "And that cowardice and sin has touched us all."

No sooner were the words out of her mouth than the command of Elbart rang through the morning air. The words chilled her more than the swirling wind and cut her to the heart.

"He has come among us as one to be trusted and heard, and he will die as a criminal and heretic!" the Great Steward bellowed. "Force him through the North Gate, to Elks Hill, for the one who has no place with us shall be put to death outside the city walls! Take him there, the parpallo and wood with him, and **let him be burned!**"

30

The Great Market Road turned into a gauntlet, with the rabble of citizens lining both sides to mock, jeer, spit upon, and strike Joël as he stumbled along the thoroughfare toward the North Gate. Lurching unsteadily, Joël looked severely exhausted, and the burden of dragging the parpallo behind him only slowed him even more. The tightly-bound rope cut deeply into Joël's waist and hips, rubbing the skin raw and drawing blood that matched the cut on his jawline. His white tunic was smeared with red by the time he lurched and wobbled to the gate, which two soldiers opened. As he tried to pull his sturdy load behind him, Joël suddenly fell, earning a cry from Kyria and Elaenor following nearby. Sadly, it also brought laughter and jeers from the Council-sympathetic crowd. As Joël pushed off the ground to get back to his feet, one of the soldiers ran forward and kicked him viciously in the ribs, sending him back to the ground gasping for air.

"No!" screamed Kyria as she was held back by Mirko, Ivar, and Lars from the crowd. Desperately, she tried to pry herself loose and couldn't. Yet even as she was restrained, she saw Captain Vermeulen approach the Selannan guard and chop him from behind with a marital punch with his arm greave.

"None of that!" he snarled. "Just because you have wrongly condemned him does not mean you take liberties at his death!"

Stunned, Kyria, Kaleva, and the others watched Vermeulen lean down and place his arms around Joël, lifting him upward onto his wobbly legs. Even more unbelievably, Kyria saw Vermeulen appear to whisper something in Joël's ear. Whatever the words might have been, Joël responded by stepping forward once more, Vermeulen with his arm around his waist, supporting him as his lurching movements took them onward to Elks Hill.

Although the crowd surrounding the dais was more than a thousand souls, Kyria and the others now believed twice that number clustered around Elks Hill. The priests stacked dasenpfear wood on the parpallo and then lashed Joël to the pyre with chains. Elbart nodded to Umlar, who stepped forward with a bowl of oil, facing Joël for the final time.

"Traitor, troublemaker, criminal, and heretic," the high priest spat, emphasizing each of the words as the crowd roared its assent to each vocable. "You have defiled this city, the jewel of Lord Creator's world and the treasure of his eye, with all you have done. Your body and soul are beyond saving, but this city is not. By the cleansing power of this oil, we wipe away the bitterness and the evil you have wrought among us. By the flammability of this oil, we will cleanse the spoilage you have brought within us through the fire that consumes!"

Umlar brought his hand from the bowl and swatted Joël with the oil-laden brush, again and again. The crowd rent the air with their cheers, bringing a fresh round of tears to the eyes of Kyria, Kaleva, and their friends.

"My heart," whispered Kaleva as he sank to the ground. "My soul."

Gheren stepped forth bearing a lit torch, gleaming in the air under a sky that had turned mysteriously darker for morning nave. He came within two feet of the parpallo, a vile smirk playing on his lips.

"Hardly the Courageous One now, eh, heretic?" he asked.

Joël laid his head back, his eyes straining through the clouds that parted briefly, and looked at Vuoristad in all its distant majesty. Gathering all his strength, his chest heaved and he opened his mouth and groaned.

"Lord Creator, Father, Beloved ... I beg you ... do ... not ... hold this ... against them. Even now ... forgive them."

He turned back and saw both Gheren and Umlar before him.

"Die, heretic," Umlar screeched. And Gheren threw the torch upon him.

The flames rose quickly, smoke rising, and Joël's screams pierced the skies. The crowd roared their approval at first, then subsided as they sensed that something, somehow, was truly wrong, either in the manner of this death or their response to it.

"Please, Lord Creator," prayed Saku and Henrik.

"End the suffering," pled Kyria.

Kaleva said nothing, as his tears flooded the tundra at his feet.

Suddenly the cries from the flames grew stronger, even though unintelligible. But through the tongues of fire, all there could see movement, thrashings of desperation. It was not as if Joël was attempting to get free of the chains, but as if he was being crushed by an invisible hand. Finally, Joël cried out with all his might.

"Why? ... Why, my Father? ...Why have you turned your back on me???"

As the last word escaped from Joël's mouth, a clap of thunder sounded from the skies, the earth shook and gave way, and the flaming pyre exploded in blinding light! The assembly fell together to the ground, frozen in fear.

Finally, they began picking themselves off the grass, and to their amazement, they saw the fire extinguished, the wood blackened and charred, and the reddened, burned body of Joël wrapped in chains, completely still. Umlar approached the still form and pressed his hand to the neck area. Turning around, he emitted a smile laced with worry toward Elbart.

"The heretic is dead."

Dalvig looked from the window in the throne-room across the breadth of Merivalka, taking in the horrific scene on Elks Hill as if he stood in that very frozen glade. The blinding light had nearly robbed him of his own sight, and the reverberation of the earthquake had even given Vuoristad a slight tremor.

It was then that Dalvig had two shocks. The first came when he happened to look at the base of the Mountain, where the Wall of Iniquity stood. Open-mouthed, Dalvig looked down at the exact place where Besno—at the beginning of the First Age—had inscribed the principles of the Revered Way, the commandments of the good life that no one could perfectly live. Until now. To Dalvig's awe, the Wall had been split in the middle of Besno's inscription, and where there had been stone there was now a broad space!

"Lord Creator!" called Dalvig. "The Wall! The Wall is broken! Whatever Joël has done, the Wall ..."

He stopped as he looked at the unapproachable light surrounding the throne of Lord Creator. The golden brilliance was now muted, its shine having become a throbbing gray. And from the morass came a sound Dalvig had never heard before.

"My Sovereign," he asked, "what is it?" And suddenly he saw. There on the ground beneath the now-flickering light, he saw the puddle forming, slipping down the emerald steps on the platform.

Tears, Dalvig realized. *Lord Creator, the Maker of all, weeps.*

31

Elbart's annoyance turned to vehement frustration as the day progressed. King Dewulf had angrily told him that any responses among the populace after Joël's death were now the responsibility of the Great Steward, and any unrest meant the full wrath of the Kronji army. In the meantime, the Selannan guards had been summoned to the Council of Nobles, who were locked in argument over what to do regarding Joël's burial.

"What is the harm in bringing the body to a private area and burning it again to ashes?" asked Umlar.

"A secret re-burning?" Dirnik yelled at him. "Taking the corpse from an open place to behind closed doors? To risk questions of conspiracy and meddling? No, thank you, Umlar. Leave your priestly functions at the door and leave the governing to the rest of us!"

"Agreed," said Lasjen. "This requires a burial in a marked grave."

"With a public seal," said Niilo, the guard from the North Gate.

"What was that?" asked Elbart.

"Begging your pardon, sire," replied Niilo. "A public seal of the Council would verify the burial took place. Then we wouldn't worry about any shenanigans taking place."

"Other than his rabid, misinformed followers stealing his body," agreed Lasjen. "Or ..."

"Or what?" asked Elbart.

"Nothing, sire. Only that if what we saw at Joël's death this morning was anything beyond our natural world, one can't help but wonder other forces are at play."

"To do what? Bring him back from the chains of death?" laughed Dirnik. He was about to continue his harangue when a knock sounded on the door of the council hall. Two soldiers opened the doors and Petric walked through slowly.

"Ah, Petric!" Elbart said mockingly. "Have you returned to the fold in abject repentance?"

"I have not," declared Petric. "Nor do I desire to return to a group so wantonly set against true justice. You may take my seat and ask another to serve."

"Palo Virtanen will take your seat as he officially sits among us at the start of the year. We can always call another election."

"I thought Vilius Halmo seemed to have been granted some sort of assurance of joining the Council, given what appears to be his role in securing Joël's arrest."

"He seems," Elbart said with a guilty tone in his voice, "to have taken leave, and none of us know where he has gone."

"Just like that?"

"Petric, are you here to complain of the inner working of the Council as it stands or is there an actual request in our future?"

"I have come to ask for the body of Joël, so that I might bury him."

"You?" scoffed Elbart. "You seem to rid yourself of the good graces of the Council more deeply than I imagined."

"Whatever you believe him to have been, he deserves a burial that accords with the loyalties of those who cared for him."

"A dozen bludges hardly appears to be a bloc worth rewarding," Umlar chuckled.

"Peace, Umlar," said Elbart. "This would happen to meet our need of disposal. Petric, you have the Council's permission. Where are you intending to bury him?"

"There is a plot in a garden bordering Elks Hill that is part of a modest purchase of my grandfather's," said Petric humbly. "It faces north. You know the one."

"Indeed, I do. Very well, under one condition. There must be a contingent of four guards to accompany you. One from the Lakihalle, one from the Western Gate, one from the North Gate, and one from the Coastal Gate. I, too, will stand by and will seal the grave with the

Council seal, and there will be four guards standing for the first week after the burial. Is that clear?"

"Abundantly so," said Petric.

"Let us go, then."

The guards and Elbart notwithstanding, the modest numbers that joined Petric at Elks Hill brought abundant supplies for a remarkable burial. Kyria, Matleena, Rauha, and Sanni brought all the spices they could carry. Kaleva, Henrik, and Saku began the process of digging a proper crypt in the earth. Mirko and Ivar bordered the crypt with stones collected from their many traverses to their uncle's quarry on the western side of the city. Elaenor and Ilma assisted Petric in arranging the linen shroud around Joël's body.

"I wish we could do more," Kyria sighed, placing the spices upon Joël's skin.

Elaenor wiped her hands. "It doesn't bring him back," she whispered, looking with caution at Elbart and the soldiers. "Yet this does have a ring of goodness about it."

"I agree," said Petric. "Even though my heart is heavy, I do believe we are doing what we can, and that must count for something."

"Petric," announced Kaleva, leaning on his shovel. "We have finished."

Walking in the darkness and bitter cold back to the North Gate of Selanna, Kyria wiped the fresh tears from her eyes. She had felt the last vestiges of hope flit away when Elbart sealed the stone pallet on top of the grave. Hearing another draw to her side, she felt Kaleva place his arms around her, securing a heavier cloak over her shoulders.

"Thank you," she said kindly.

Kaleva smiled for what seemed like the first time in ages. "It is the least I could do." He exhaled slowly and rubbed his sore back. "How I wish I could see him once more to beg his forgiveness."

Kyria took his hand in her own. "I know for sure he would grant it, Kaleva. And you are not the only one who wishes to see him again.

But the pain of knowing we won't is more than I can bear." She looked back at Elks Hill once more before continuing on as the North Gate rose before them.

THE RESURRECTION

32

Niilo stretched and prodded the fire twice before rubbing his hands. Morning nave would mean two full days since the death of Joël, and already Niilo was impatient that the rotating squads of guards would find relief sooner than later. Having volunteered for the last night watch, he was restless for when sunrise would come and they would be relieved by another quartet from the city.

Stretching once more, he swatted his fellow guards awake and in a few moments, they were stumbling around, rubbing the sleep from their eyes and grasping their swords and shields to appear vigilant should their relief arrive a few minutes early. Niilo judged by the sky they were still a quarter-hour from going home. His eyes turned from the eastern horizon to the north when he felt it.

It was slight, but noticeable. The rumble at his feet was no dream.

"Niilo, did you feel that?" one of the others said.

"Quiet!" Niilo ordered. Then he knelt, placing his hand to the frosty ground. "There it is again."

Why he looked upward and looked toward Vuoristad, he could not tell, other than a force greater than his will had maneuvered his eyes to peer into the distance. A pinpoint of light throbbed from the summit of the Mountain of God and, instead of fading away, brightened. Niilo shielded his eyes, amazed that the light was not only burning more brightly, but it was expanding, as if it was hurtling through the air in their direction.

"Sir," another soldier cried out. "What is that?"

Niilo started to turn and order his fellow guards to stand firm when he realized his own knees were knocking together. Looking up again at the shimmering white shaft of light hurtling through the sky, Niilo drew his sword, only to have another deep rumble from the earth knock it loose from his hand. Kneeling to retrieve it, he craned his neck upon hearing the shrieks of his fellow guards and he saw the terror shearing through the clouds.

A shining figure, terrible and majestic in appearance, cut through the brisk air with astonishing speed, a radiant lance in his hand. Niilo tried to scream a warning, but his voice caught in his throat as the figure smashed into Joël's grave with tremendous force. The stone pallet shattered into countless pieces and the hill burst into a cloud of earth and frost, lifting the guards into the air and depositing them roughly to the ground over a hundred feet away.

33

Kyria tossed and turned in her bed, unable to return to slumber. The sadness that gripped at her heart was immeasurable. The news that her brother Vilius had fallen to his death outside the Lakihalle had melted the hearts of her entire family, and her father's angered accusation that it could not have been accidental filled both her and her mother with consternation and sorrow. But strangely, even the death of her brother could not outstrip the grief she felt over the loss of Joël, and the memory of his execution brought even more tears to her eyes.

Looking out her window, she could just make out a sliver of the distant sky. Rolling over in her bed, Kyria cracked open the glass pane just slightly more, sniffing in the cold air.

Strange, she thought to herself. I could have sworn the pane shook a little.

Just as she completed that thought, she saw it, the light piercing the northern sky and growing in its brilliance. Transfixed, she saw it move through the clouds, mesmerizing her as a beacon of luminescence. Suddenly, she realized it was headed toward Selanna.

It was just as the light disappeared in the area of Elks Hill that she heard the magnificent collision and the reverberating roar of the earth. As if anticipating a glorious hope, Kyria leaped from her bed, clumsily throwing on a woolen dress over her nightclothes, in the next minute clattering down the stairs before bursting into the street and sprinting toward the North Gate.

Niilo peeled himself out of the dirt that covered him, checking himself for broken bones and finding himself deeply bruised all over. His ears throbbed from the noise of the impact and wondered what sight he had just beheld. He was looking around for his fellow guards when one of them shouted toward him.

"Sire, come quickly!"

Finally reaching his feet, Niilo was shocked by the distance between him and Elks Hill. Stumbling over the icy terrain, he sprawled to the ground where the guard stood. "What?" he shouted.

"That," the guard said in a shaking voice, pointing with an equally unsteady finger.

Niilo stared in horror at the sight before him. Pebbles from the broken border stones and shards from the stone pallet lay everywhere, and dirt and grass lay in all directions. But the shocking display lay deep within the grave.

"By the raging Sea," Niilo mouthed in fright. The crypt was completely empty, dug out in the same dimensions as when Joël was laid therein. And Niilo's heart nearly stopped when he saw the empty shroud laid at the base of the crypt, folded neatly, and leading away from it was a series of footsteps heading eastward.

34

Surprised, but gladdened, that the North Gate stood ajar, Kyria, Elaenor, Matleena, Rauha, Sanni, and Ilma pushed through the doorway and slipped out of Selanna. Henrik and Saku had gone to Kaleva's house to wake him, and both their wives had used that opportunity to leave their houses unnoticed, where they had joined Kyria in the streets when she was at a full sprint. Stopping to alert the other women, their group swelled to a half dozen, which they admitted would be strength in numbers if they were noticed north of the city.

"Why was the North Gate undefended?" asked Sanni, out of breath.

"I can't speak to that," gasped Kyria, equally tired, "but I would wager all I had that it has something to do with the earthquake and the light that I saw."

The sun flooded the tree-lined pathway that Joël had trod two days previously, the light dancing through the denuded branches. Kyria ran ahead, thinking of an excuse to share with the guards why they were present. She scrambled around the base of Elks Hill to its north side, when she saw no excuse would be necessary.

There was not a guard to be seen.

Moreover, the gravesite had been decimated by a powerful force. Hearing her friends catch up to her, Kyria sprinted forward to the crypt, slipping on pebbles and stone shards, realizing that the pallet no longer lay on the crypt. Her feet sank in the dirt that surrounded the plot, and it was by great effort that she was able to reach the site and hurl herself before it. A cry escaped from her mouth and the other ladies gathered around her.

The shroud lay in the crypt, folded as if ready to be stored for further use. And the footsteps, tracing east, were there for all to see.

"By Vuoristad, what does it mean?" asked Matleena.

"Is he gone?" inquired Rauha.

Elaenor dropped to her knees beside Kyria. "Kyria, have ... have they taken him?"

"No one," bellowed a majestic voice behind them, "has stolen him. For he has stolen the keys of the Great Ruin, and he now sets it to work backwards!"

Screaming, the ladies turned and faced the voice. A shining figure, clothed in white gold chainmail and gripping a fierce lance, stood before them. For his warlike posture, they thought him first to be an enemy, but the more they looked, a friendly smile played at the corners of his mouth.

"Dearest ones, why are you here?" he asked.

"We ... we ..." Elaenor tried desperately to catch her breath and her sanity at the same time. "We were coming to pray and leave gifts at the gravesite. But now it seems to be missing. Joël's body ... it's gone!"

The shining one threw his head back and laughed, a hearty roar that shook the trees around them. Facing the ladies again, he declared, "Of course, he is not here! Why indeed would you seek those who draw breath among the corpses? And it's not 'his body' that's gone ... it's him! Joël himself is gone!"

"Gone? Joël?" asked Ilma, who suddenly found her voice.

"Where?" Sanni pressed him. "Where have you taken him?"

"Taken him?" chuckled the figure, his eyes twinkling. "I have merely been sent by Lord Creator himself to destroy this tomb. What do you think those footsteps mean?" And he pointed with his lance to the impressions in the dirt.

Kyria's eyes widened. "You mean ..."

"Yes, dear heart," said the man, "why would I have taken Joël when he has clearly walked away from this earthy prison? He is not here! He has risen. He ... is ... alive!"

Elbart threw his goblet across the room, snatched Niilo and pushed him against the wall, driving his forearm into his throat. "Say it again, Niilo! I want to make sure I haven't misunderstood you."

"It's true," Niilo hacked against the strain of Elbart's arm against his neck. "Everything. The blinding light. The earthquake. The collision of the figure with the grave itself. And everything we noticed afterward. We were unconscious, for how long I couldn't say. But I swear to you, the crypt is empty and the shroud is folded up. It's as if we never buried him!"

"And the seal?" asked Dirnik.

"I could not find the seal itself," Niilo stammered in wracked gasps, "but there was red wax, melted away and cooled on the hill below the crypt. The seal was red wax, sire, was it not?"

Elbart had turned back to his seat, brooding, seething, his entire world crashing down around him. By all rights, he knew this event would create more disorder and chaos than he dreamed imaginable.

Contain it, he told himself. *Dewulf doesn't need to know. No one outside this room needs to know. There is no sense stoking the fire of the masses.*

"We could press the idea those friends of his took the body," he said finally.

"Overpowering trained guards?" sputtered Niilo. "It would take no time for the people to see through that?"

"And he was dead and buried," grumbled Umlar. "We had two different physicians verify his death and we all, plus Petric and that whole company, can swear he was buried."

"This," Elbart wheezed, like a drowning man desperately seeking air, "is a disaster. We cannot let word get out. This is a disaster."

The rest of their company having gone back to tell the men, Kyria stayed behind at Elks Hill to collect her thoughts. The shining figure had disappeared unnoticed, as suddenly as he had come. The crypt was empty, but so was Kyria's heart, for where indeed had Joël gone?

Perhaps walking about would abate the cold. It was not a bad patch of ground, thought Kyria, and Petric's family had chosen the site well. Springtime flowers would fill this glade with plenty of color in a few months, and the view of Vuoristad was truly spectacular. She was gripped by a sudden pang of jealousy for this easy enjoyment of nature; her own father's investment in city property kept them primarily within the walls. She sighed again, remembering Vilius and his mysterious death. They would have to do something with his business now, but grief demanded more from them at this point. She shook her head at the thought of grief, for what squeezed her heart now was the mysterious disappearance of Joël.

So deep in her thoughts was she that Kyria leapt in fright when she saw a man, observing the damage, walking towards her. Her heartbeat slowing, Kyria chastised herself for her panic. *It must be the caretaker,* she told herself. *Petric is well off enough to afford someone to tend the grounds.* She slowed her breathing, as the man, clad in a thick woolen hooded cloak, smiled at her.

"Good morning," he said.

"It may be," she replied. "But I am not so sure."

"All mornings are new beginnings," he answered her. "This one just happens to be better than others. That is why I couldn't help noticing why you are crying."

Kyria nodded, disturbed and yet somehow comforted the man was that sensitive to her pain. "It's just that Joël, who was buried here the other day, is gone. Is he taken? Do you know? Has he walked away without saying goodbye? What?" She shook with renewed pain and fright. "What has happened?" And she unwittingly pitched herself forward and found herself embraced by the caretaker.

"That cannot be," he said gently.

"Why?" Kyria wept, sorrow rising within her. "How would you even know?"

"Because Kyria," the man said once more in a voice soaked in kindness and love, "why would I walk away without saying goodbye to you?"

Mouth wide open, Kyria stepped back, not believing why she hadn't seen it before. The man put back his hood, and there, with no doubt, stood Joël.

"Joël!" cried Kyria, clutching him by the hands. "You are alive! You're here! You're real! You're ... but how?"

"Raised by the command of my Father, Lord Creator, dear one."

She looked at his throat, his hands, and his arms. "Joël, your body. There are still burn marks everywhere."

"Yes, dear Kyria. To leave no doubt that the suffering and what I have accomplished through it are true and real. And now, you must hurry. The others have already run back to tell the men of the empty crypt, and the men will have abundant questions. Right now, they are all together in the upper room of Henrik's house, where we had dinner together. Your task is to go to all of them. Tell them you have seen me with your own eyes and touched me with your own hands. Tell them that I am alive, and that I will always be alive."

36

"This is wonderful news," said Saku, "but I'm with Henrik and Petric. It sounds too good to be true."

"We are telling you the truth," insisted Elaenor. "We saw the evidence with our own eyes. The shroud is there. And footprints leading away from the crypt. What more do you want?"

"Why indeed would we disbelieve the ladies?" asked Ivar. "What reason would they have to lie to us?"

"Ivar speaks wisdom," added Mirko. "And remember, the lot of us men, other than Ivar and Petric, saw Joël calm the storm. We saw him make food from nothing. We saw him heal Perttu. By Vuoristad, we saw him raise Kyrt from the dead! Why would this news be in the realm of the impossible? Kaleva, you've been morbidly silent. What say you?"

Kaleva turned from the window, seeking any arrival from Kyria but ostensibly looking out for an accusing pack of soldiers intent on arresting them if the reports were true about Joël's disappearance. "I wish it true. And I agree with Mirko. There is no reason why this couldn't happen." He bowed his head. "I just don't believe I deserve good news like this."

Sanni walked the length of the room, pressing a cup of milk into Kaleva's hand. "Dear friend, none of us deserves this. Who indeed earns this wonder and grace we've enjoyed through him?"

A shuffling of feet in the street turned Kaleva's attention back to the window. "It's Kyria," he said, "and she's coming this way."

"I'll go downstairs and unlock the door," said Matleena, and the rest heard her steps on the stairs, a latch opening, furtive and excited words from below, and a thumping up the same stairs. With radiant smiles and intense gasps, Kyria and Matleena plunged into the upper room.

"Kyria!" said Henrik. "What news!"

"It's true!" she beamed. "It's true! It's all true!"

"What's true?" asked Kaleva, crossing the floor and standing in front of her.

Kyria grabbed both of Kaleva's arms. "He's gone from the grave! Even better than that ... he's alive!"

"Alive?" they all cried at once.

"Joël? Alive?" Kaleva gushed. "How do you know? Because of the footprints?"

"Because of him, Kaleva. Him! I saw Joël, and he spoke to me! To tell all of you that he is alive!"

Kaleva took no notice or care that the North Gate was abandoned. In truth, he was grateful for it. He had always done well in the races outdoors during his school days, and since he regularly ran on the beaches west of Selanna Harbor on the days he wasn't fishing, he was in good physical condition to endure a dash to Elks Hill.

He pulled up at the familiar sight, which bore none of the arrangement of two days before. As his breath, visible against the air, poured out of him, he saw the rocky splinters and the empty crypt, the stolid red wax that was all that was left of the Council's seal, and the frosty earth piled in every direction. He crept closer and saw the cavernous space below, and there, arranged at the floor of the crypt, was the shroud.

Kaleva felt his arms and legs give way, and he fell backwards, lying on the ground as the wonder of the moment washed over him. He turned his face, catching the glimpse of the summit of Vuoristad, and the tears began to flow.

"How," he breathed. "How is this possible? For us? For me?" And he was weeping again.

37

All the friends remained in the upper room of Henrik and Matleena's house through the evening. With the workday beginning at next sunrise, they wanted to be somewhat refreshed for it. At the same time, they did not believe the events of the day warranted their showing their faces in public. Voices from the streets betrayed the citizens' confusion and excitement over the news and rumors, but Petric—who had stopped by for a visit—warned they should probably not add to the wonder, especially as the Council guards might be making the rounds and asking questions. Germund had arrived with similar entreaties but, unlike Petric, remained dutifully with them.

After Petric left, Kyria sat with Elaenor at the table. They had helped Matleena in the kitchen and distributed food and drink to all. For her part, Kyria's thrill was beginning to wear off, and even though she hadn't eaten, she seemed to be in a place beyond hunger.

Kaleva placed a mug in front of her. "You need something, Kyria," he said kindly, and so she began to fortify herself with copious amounts of tea.

It was Ivar who suddenly spoke up as dinner was passed around the table. "So I missed all the excitement when Joël conquered the storm at sea. What exactly did happen?"

"Of all days for you to be sick, brother," laughed Mirko.

"Indeed," said Henrik, "although I missed the excitement because the mast clubbed my head and I lost consciousness."

"It was a mad scramble," said Saku, "And I was sure Kaleva was going to leap from the wheel and throttle Joël."

"I wasn't going to do that," Kaleva quietly chuckled, taking a sip of tea, "but the truth was I did wonder that he had lost his mind by staring into the storm and spreading his hands as if he would be catching a lightning bolt."

"None of us could catch our footing," sighed Germund, "and every married man swore his wife was about to become an unknowing widow."

"And Joël looked into the teeth of the howling wind and rain, lightning and thunder clapping around us," said Kaleva with a faraway look in his eyes, "and he cried out, 'Silence! Be at peace!' And it was over."

"Be at peace!" came the voice of another from the door to the stairs. "Good words for all of you, my friends."

Mugs and cups dropped on the table and around the floor as the friends let out a collective yet joyful gasp. There, standing in their midst, leaning on a familiar walking stick and dressed in a bright blue tunic under a thick cloak, was none other than Joël himself.

"Joël!" cried out Elaenor, followed by Kyria, and all the rest. With laughter, they each embraced Joël in turn, before Kaleva stood there, face to face with him.

"Joël," he repeated. "I'm ... I'm ..."

"Let me help you with completing that thought," Joël laughed heartily. "Hello, dear friend!" And they embraced fiercely, Kaleva's tears staining the shoulder of Joël's tunic.

"I cannot believe it is you," said Ivar.

"Indeed," said Joël in response, "but as I have showed Kyria before, I can show you now, so there is no reason to doubt or disbelieve." He opened the collar area of his tunic. "See the burn marks there." He pulled up his sleeves. "And there." He lifted his tunic to display his waist. "And see there the imprint of the rope by which I bore the parpallo. All this you see, my friends, so that you know it is I who truly died. I have truly risen. And I am truly among you."

"Are you staying with us now in Selanna, Joël?" asked Henrik.

"For a few more days, and then it must be farewell for a time."

"Farewell?" asked Kyria, who nonetheless sensed that must be the case.

"When you saw me locking my shop the night of the feast, I was closing it for good," said Joël. "My work in Selanna, and throughout

211

Merivalka, is now done. I have finished what I was sent to do, to destroy Tuona's work and set the Great Ruin to work in reverse. I must return."

"Return?" asked several voices at once.

"To where I came from. But I will not leave you alone. The Breath of Lord Creator will fall upon each of my followers and friends. In fact, as you are listening right now, He is already falling upon you to do His will."

Several moments passed without a word before Kaleva said. "So are you leaving soon?"

"In a few days," replied Joël, "but I will meet with you when that happens. Do not search for me, but I will find you and others."

"Is there nothing you want to do now?" asked Saku.

"Well," smiled Joël, "A new body doesn't mean I can't eat. I could have some of your excellent trout or pavenders."

The friends laughed aloud, and even Kaleva looked happier. "Well spoken," he said with new music in his voice. "You came to the right group for a good supply of fish."

38

"Tell me again why we're doing this crazy excursion?" asked Rauha.

"Kaleva's idea," said Mirko from the other boat as he paddled maniacally. "For some reason, he believes that an icy evening's sail is all the joy one can hope for."

"Did you invite Germund, Ivar?" asked Kaleva.

"I asked him," replied Ivar as the boat bobbed on the waves, "but he wanted to go north to Kyrt's farm for the day. Besides, Joël had already seen him at his home for a final talk. The same goes for Lars and Petric. They went past Elks Hill two nights ago when they saw Joël and spoke with him for an hour, which they described as a fine goodbye."

Both boats skirted the eastern shore of Merivalka, moving up the coast toward Branström. "Kaleva," Mirko called out. "Where are you wanting to put in?"

Kaleva squinted through the snowfall and pointed. "Over there, south of the glade near the spring. We can pull these boats to shore and walk the path the rest of the way."

"Doesn't it slope upward?" Henrik gasped, waggling his arms.

"By the Sea, brother!" laughed Saku. "You knew we'd have to paddle and steer this contraption! The sail would only be so much good. And you're complaining about a little walk up a slight grade."

"Sometimes I believe the men complain to see if we'll grant them our sympathy," Elaenor whispered to Kyria.

"Sometimes? I always believe that!" Kyria laughed in response.

The friends were able to gently guide their boats to a slight bump against a sandbar, and then the men leapt out a pulled them further on to shore. Taking baskets of fish, bread, dasenpfears, and carrots with them, they made the climb toward the spring.

"Unlike the Toiva, the spring is bound to be frozen," said Ilma, "so I am glad we thought of bringing some water with us."

"You are forgetting the ale and wine," added Sanni, "which I am sure will keep us slightly warm."

"A picnic returning to the scene of Joël's miracle," said Henrik, "when he fed many. Who can forget it?"

"Is that why you chose this place, Kaleva?" asked Mirko.

"Actually, I chose it because its low setting amongst the hills will give us some relief from the wind," replied Kaleva, "and at this time of year, we should have it to ourselves."

"Then why is there smoke coming from just over the hill?" asked Ivar, pointing west.

Kaleva looked in the direction of Ivar's finger and saw it, billowing dark smoke. And then he smelled it, a crackling fire and the smell of potatoes and leafbitter together.

"It looks as if someone is already there," said Kaleva, quickening the pace and moving up the grade until he could peek over the ridge and see the culprit. Looking back at his friends with a smile on his face, he shook his head. "I don't believe it, and yet strangely, I do believe it!"

The entire group stepped over the crest of the hill and beheld the sight of Joël tending a fire, over which sat a pan laden with the potatoes and leafbitter they had just smelled on the wind. Catching sight of the group, Joël waved and beckoned them forward.

"Greetings, dear ones!" he called out. "I told you we would meet again! Come by the fire and warm yourselves!"

"We've brought food, Joël," shouted Saku, holding up a basket and pointing to ones carried by Sanni and Matleena.

"All the better!" Joël replied. "There is enough room on the fire to place another pan on the bolsterpiece. I assume you've brought fish."

"A meal among us wouldn't be without it," said Kaleva.

"Excellent," Joël clapped his hands and set another pan on the fire. The group distributed the fish over the pan and placed the bread on the edge to just barely harden the crust.

"We've brought water, ale, and wine, Joël," said Kaleva, gesturing to another basket.

"This is indeed a fine feast," Joël smiled before suddenly gripping Kaleva by the arm. "Henrik, Saku, can you both tend the fire for a few minutes?" He lowered his voice. "Kaleva, my friend. Come with me."

The two of them stood at the top of the ridge, gazing down upon the laughing friends by the fire. "You have the finest friends, Kaleva," Joël said as they both breathed in the air from the White Sea.

"You have been the best friend, Joël. More than a friend. One who has changed me forever. I am sorry I wasn't a better friend."

Joël looked at Kaleva and leaned on the top of his walking stick. "You truly believe that?"

"I do. I am sorry."

"I didn't mean that. I meant about me being the best friend."

"You are."

"You would devote yourself to me?"

"Yes, Joël."

"You would?"

"Yes."

"Absolutely?"

A pang struck at Kaleva's heart. "I know I ran from you that awful night. If you have truly changed me, I believe you will help me run away no more."

Joël smiled broadly. "You have been the one that I desired to change first when I entered Selanna, Kaleva. You have acknowledged your need of me, and you will always have my grace and the Breath of Lord Creator. And now, as you have confessed your need of me, I ask you to look at your friends."

Kaleva looked down at his friends. Kyria especially was rolling in the snowy grass with laughter; she turned on her side, saw Kaleva, and waved. He waved back.

"I see them, Joël."

"They now have need of you. Selanna has need of you, of all of you. And so does all of Merivalka and the nations beyond its shores. This is not an end. It is a beginning, and I entrust it to you."

"To me?" Kaleva's knees turned to water. "To one who escaped when you were in deepest need?"

"The path of suffering was set for me since before I came to Selanna, Kaleva. You could do nothing to prevent it. In truth, it was set at the Great Ruin itself. I have died, taking the Great Ruin upon myself. I have risen, shattering the Great Ruin's hold upon Lord Creator's world. And now, I pass the transforming hope to all of you, with you to lead them, to flood the worlds with my grace."

"I cannot think of a reason why you should choose me, Joël," said Kaleva, head bowed, "but it is enough that you have said so, and thus I accept."

"It is because you search your heart and know your unworthiness that I declare you will be used for this task. But it must wait until after we eat! Come, let us join the others."

The meal, leisurely and full of laughter and stories, passed for two hours. In time, all the food was eaten, the water drunk, and the ale and wine bottles capped for the return trip. The fire died down to its embers, and Henrik and Mirko gathered a supply of dirt to pour over the glowing wood and put it out. Placing the bottles in the baskets, Kyria looked around and saw everyone stretching from their extended time of lying on the grass. It was then that a thought struck her and before she could prevent herself, she spoke it aloud.

"This is goodbye, isn't it, Joël?"

The words, sadly uttered, brought all their motion to a halt. The sun beamed down in its late afternoon descent upon Joël, who walked over to Kyria and placed his arm around her, leading her through their midst.

"It is," he said. "this is the moment of farewell. Not an end, but a beginning, my friends. And I wish to share these last moments with you." He pointed northwest with his walking stick. "Come, let us go over there, nearer to the river. The path continues some distance and there should be enough light for your return journey."

After fifteen minutes of walking, Joël stopped at a lane that continued into a grove of trees. From both the familiar sights and the sound of cold waters nearby, Kyria knew they must be close to the chilled waters of the Toiva. Here, Joël turned to face them in the middle of the road, leaning on his all-familiar walking stick.

"My friends, just nine months ago I arrived in Selanna. While my arrival in the city was fraught with much mystery, what is not a mystery is the love I have for all of you, and you for me.

"The Great Ruin smeared Merivalka with guilt and corruption that the people could never remove, and because of that, death of the soul spread to all. Lord Creator could have rightly destroyed all mankind, or at least punished it severely. And justice had to come. Of that, there was no doubt.

"Yet Lord Creator could not bear to crush those whom, for reasons known to him, he loved. A king can judge by destruction or judge by cheap favor, but he must judge. Yet he chose another way, to judge by the mercy of coming among the offenders as a king most holy yet most humble, to live, to gather, to heal, to woo his beloved sinful ones to him again, and to proclaim his grace.

"It was for that purpose that I came into Merivalka, and to Selanna, my dear friends. You know me as Joël, and I have revealed myself to you as the Rhoken, the Courageous One. But before all time I was and am the Holy King, Son of Lord Creator, who came to dwell, to die, and to live again."

"You have come to save," Kaleva said.

"And save you have," added Kyria.

"Indeed, I have," said Joël, "and I have completed my dwelling among you. When you see me again, you will have come to Vuoristad to stay with me forever. But you now go in my strength and my authority, taking this saving grace to Selanna, to all Merivalka, reaching onward to Kronjva and all the Northern Realms and beyond."

"How will we do so without you?" Saku said, hardly believing this departure was happening.

"By the very Breath of Lord Creator that I have given you," replied Joël, "and remember, even if I am no longer amongst you, I am always with you, until the last breath of all that Lord Creator has made."

With bittersweet smiles, each of them came forward for one last embrace with Joël. To say there were no tears would be deceptive, and Kaleva and Kyria wept the most as they came forth at the end. Surprising them both, Joël drew them together and held them tightly before whispering in both of their ears.

"Be at peace, my dear ones."

"We are at peace, Joël," said Kaleva.

"Always at peace, Joël," Kyria sobbed, "as long as you are with us."

Releasing them both, Joël turned and walked toward the grove of trees, which now bore a thick mist within it. At the edge of the forest, Joël turned back to them, waving one last time, and then he vanished into the trees, hidden from their sight.

A strange calm came over the friends gathered on that lane, with the icy waters of the Toiva sounding beyond the trees in the distance. Finally, Mirko rubbed his hands, came forward, and stood at Kaleva's side.

"Well, my friend. What next?"

"We follow him," Kaleva replied, "to the very end."

Dalvig stood beyond the mist, watching Joël come toward him in deliberate strides. The Messenger's lance gleamed in the twilight, and as Joël approached him, Dalvig extended his hand to him, and the two clasped them together.

"Welcome home, my King," Dalvig said. "And well done."

Joël nodded and smiled. "For grace and kingdom, Dalvig."

Dalvig bowed. "For grace and kingdom." He turned alongside him, and together he and the Holy King walked toward the glorious sight of Vuoristad.

"Merivalka's Hope"

(a creed written by Joël's followers years after He returned to Vuoristad)

We trust wholeheartedly in Lord Creator,
Ruler of Vuoristad, Who constructed the worlds and the ages,
And Who fashioned all things both seen and hidden.

We trust wholeheartedly in Joël, the Holy King,
The eternal Son of Lord Creator;
Who gave life to all of His Father's creation
And descended from Vuoristad in tenderness and mercy
After Tuona deceived humanity in the Great Ruin.
This Joël traveled through the breadth of Merivalka,
Lived in Selanna, repaired the broken possessions of others,
And demonstrated through word and deed that He was the Rhoken,
The Courageous One destined to turn back the Great Ruin,
To bring grace that justifies and transforms,
Grace that flows to the lowest parts imaginable,
Seeking the rebels and making them beloved children.
By the Council of Nobles, He was condemned,
And was handed over to death by King Dewulf of Kronjva.
On Elks Hill, He was burned on the parpallo
And died as He experienced the rejection of Lord Creator.
He was buried at Elks Hill, but not for long,
For on the third day, Dalvig the Messenger was sent by Lord Creator,
Destroying the crypt and releasing Joël from death into resurrected life.
He met with His followers before traveling back to Vuoristad,
Claiming His throne, with the promise to renew all things one day.

We trust wholeheartedly in the Breath of Lord Creator,
Who unites, guides, and cherishes the followers of Joël
With an unquenchable, holy, and resilient grace.
The Breath has spoken through the Stories of the Faith,
And He, together with Lord Creator and Joël the Holy King,

219

Is forever praised and glorified.

We trust wholeheartedly
That Lord Creator has called us into His royal family,
A forgiven, cleansed, and eternally loved people,
Washed in His water,
Sustained by the bread of His Stories,
And revived by His Breath.
And one day we will inhabit the Mountain of God,
Living and reigning with our Holy King, Joël,
In the everlasting world to come.

In this we wholeheartedly believe.
In this God we truly hope,
For grace and kingdom.

Discussion Guide

This guide is a section-by-section attempt to help the reader(s) understand and respond to the key themes of Christ's life and ministry as played out in *Joël*.

As there are Biblical events referred to, one might find it helpful to have a Bible available during individual study or group discussion.

The Great Ruin

- How does the cobalt cloud's deception compare and contrast with the serpent's in Genesis 3?
- Why do you think Lord Creator is cloaked in unapproachable light and appears resolute, while the Holy King is visible and displays significant emotion?
- At the end of the chapter, the Holy King responds to Dalvig's question by saying, "We love them simply because we love them." Among many Christians, there can be a strong undercurrent of belief that God loves us because he wants to demonstrate how valuable we are to him. The Holy King expresses that divine love is a choice independent of human worth. In fact, love happens *despite* what humanity has done. What is the difference and why is that difference so important in our connection to God?

The Arrival

Chapter 1
- What are some of the defining characteristics of Selanna in this chapter?
- It's too early to say for sure, but what role do you anticipate Kyria will play as the story develops?
- How does the collective mood of the city change through the chapter?

Chapter 2

- At the beginning of the chapter, the traveler leaves a path to help others in a time of need. How does this compare to what God does throughout Scripture?
- Sometimes we restrain ourselves from asking God for help in specifics, and our prayers might be more general. Here we see the traveler help in a specific, critical time of need for Kyrt and his hired hands. How is this instructive for us?

Chapter 3

- Given what happens in Matthew 4, Mark 1, and Luke 5, what significance is there that we encounter fishermen here in this chapter?
- Henrik and Saku are somewhat cautious about Joël, mainly because his clothes and identity are such a mystery. What does this say about our faith when we are like this, that something/someone should make sense before we will trust them?

Chapter 4

- Why do you believe that so many nobles are hostile to Joël?
- How is Joël's desire to live, work, be generous with his time, and not worry about money so instructive to us?

Chapter 5

- What do the lives of Elaenor's grandparents display about the character of Merivalka?
- What does Joël's activity back at his shop show about the value and dignity of human work?
- How would you describe Joël's conversation with Kyria and Elaenor? What questions do you think the ladies still have as they head home?

Chapter 6

- How would you characterize Vilius' attitude toward Joël? Is it skepticism? Or is he finding it difficult to assess Joël? Or is it something else? How do you justify your answer?

- Why do you think Joël tells Vilius he is both close to and distant from his goals of freedom and happiness?
- Why do you think Vilius believes Lord Creator has abandoned Merivalka?

Chapter 7
- Of what event in the Gospels does this chapter remind you? Why?
- How would you characterize the assembly's understanding of faith? What do they believe about themselves? About Lord Creator?
- What do you make of the fact that Merivalkans have the dasenpfear as the national emblem but they use dasenpfear wood for burning in the Gatherings?
- Joël seems to realize his address to the crowd will be a significant moment. What do you think this reveals about him? About his activity in Selanna?
- What do you think holds Umlar and Elbart back from taking action against Joël?

The Calling

Chapter 8
- Of what event in the Gospels does this chapter remind you? Why? What Biblical character (or characters) is Petric meant to resemble?
- Petric says that Joël intrigues him, yet much of what he says is a mystery. Do you find yourself identifying somewhat with Petric? Why or why not?
- Why do you think it is hard for people in Merivalka to comprehend that Lord Creator would come to them rather than demanding they approach him?

Chapter 9
- Of what event in the Gospels does this chapter remind you? Why?
- Do you sense any characters in this story resembling Biblical characters yet?

- What characteristics of Joël's do the fishermen notice through this experience? What do you believe Kaleva is starting to realize at the end of the chapter?

Chapter 10
- Why do you think Kaleva feels anxiety about Joël's presence? Where in the chapter might you draw that conclusion?
- What do you believe is the importance of the men sharing a meal in this chapter?
- What is so profound about the way Joël desires to know about Kaleva's life? How do you think this conversation affects Kaleva?
- What has changed within Kaleva at the end of this chapter? Why do you say that?

Chapter 11
- Of what event in the Gospels does this chapter remind you? Why?
- How would you describe the difference in Vilius' and Kyria's reaction to Joël? How does this compare to Matthew 10:34-39?
- In what way is this incident the most startling and significant work yet since Joël arrived in Merivalka? What are some clues from the story that give you that impression?
- What does Joël implicitly claim about himself when the Council berates him in the court atrium? Why is this so surprising?
- Joël says he has not come to Selanna to *show* the way to Lord Creator, but because he *is* the way to Lord Creator? Why do you believe he makes that distinction and why is it such an important one?

Chapter 12
- Why do you think Joël left Selanna to go pray? What does this show?
- What do you believe is significant about the clash between Tuona and Joël? Do you believe this is typical? Is this foreshadowing something for later?

Chapter 13
- In this chapter, we see in greater detail that Merivalka is under the control of another nation. How does that change the mood in this chapter, if at all?
- What is your assessment of Prince Dewulf? What role and activity do you predict he might play, and why?
- Of what event in the Gospels does this chapter remind you? Why?

Chapter 14
- Kyria seems to have a different mindset concerning the Kronji soldiers than much of the city. What reason do you think accounts for this?
- Why do you think Joël treats Captain Vermeulen and his company the way he does? What seems to be his strategy for doing so?
- Notice the way Joël does the repairs and compare this to Colossians 3:23. What are your thoughts here?

Chapter 15
- Of what event in the Gospels does this chapter remind you? Why?
  What are some differences to that event?
- There is a considerable crowd that assembles to come along. Yet we are not told how they gathered this throng? How do you believe so many people came along?
- Joël speaks about the Rhoken, grace, and redemption. Why do you think the crowd here is more receptive than others have been?

Chapter 16
- During the return into Selanna, there are four different encounters with Joël (Tarmo, Vermeulen, Osku, Joël's friends). How do you think each encounter affects the people involved?
- Considering Joël's conversation with Osku, of what event in the Gospels does this chapter remind you? Why?

- How is Joël's redirect of Osku's rejection to Kaleva, Kyria, et al, both a warning and an invitation? Who do you believe at this time is starting to understand Joël the most? Why?

Chapter 17
- Joël feels weary and sore at the beginning of this chapter? Do you find that odd? Encouraging? Why?
- Why do you think Tuona wishes to meet with Joël on the beach? What significance might there be to that location, especially as you read the remainder of the chapter?
- We are given a look back at an incident that occurred before the Great Ruin. What are the desires that Tuona mentions to justify what he seeks?
- What significance is there that this confrontation with the Messengers occurs within Vuoristad itself?
- What does Lord Creator's reaction show about how he views rebellion against his will? What are the words he uses to describe Tuona's activity? How is that instructive to us?
- The vision seems to have an overwhelming effect on Joël. Why do you think that is? Where is this adversity going to lead? What is your reaction to Joël's frailty after the vision?

Chapter 18
- The scene of Joël playing with the schoolchildren seems to occupy a passing role. Do you think it is more important than it seems? What do you think it is mean to signify, and where can you base that in the Gospels?
- Of what event in the Gospels does this chapter remind you? Why?
- Does Joël's response to Dagarata seem bizarre or harsh at first? What is he trying to get her to do or believe?

Chapter 19
- Why do you think Joël enjoys the company of his friends when he speaks with them about important matters?
- Of what event in the Gospels does this chapter remind you, especially with Kaleva's responses to Joël? Does this clarify what Biblical character Kaleva might resemble?

- Joël says that salvation happens "[w]hen Lord Creator has you in the embrace of His choosing." What does this mean?
- This is the first time Joël brings up the idea of suffering for the sake of others. How does that change the perspective of his friends? How does that change your perspective of him at all?

Chapter 20

- Of what event in the Gospels does this chapter remind you? Why?
- Contrast what Alisa believes about herself with what Joël tells her is truly important.
- Niilo refuses to stay with Mirko, Ivar, and Joël. Is this because of what he needs to do as a soldier or is it for other reasons? And if the latter, what do you believe those reasons to be?

Chapter 21

- The Gathering of Suntide Nave brings another argument between Joël and several of the Nobles. What story from the Gospels does Joël's story of the priest and the Vale-Dweller sound like?
- Alisa' experience in the previous chapter might seem isolated if not for Joël's story here. Why do you think Joël chose the Vale-Dweller to be the recipient of grace in this story?
- Notice how Joël describes the reaction of Lord Creator to the Vale-Dweller's prayer. How would your life change if you consistently believed God viewed you that way?
- It seems clear that Joël and the Nobles are at odds; it seems equally clear the Nobles are at odds with Prince Dewulf. But how do you think Dewulf views Joël? What seems to be Dewulf's most important priority?

The Sacrifice

Chapter 22

- Months have gone by since the Gathering of Suntide Nave. There seems to be a relative calm in Selanna and throughout Merivalka. Yet little noticeable activity doesn't mean nothing is going on. How does this relate to your faith journey?

- Notice Joël's reaction to Lars' news. What does this response remind you of from the Gospels? How did that event turn out in the end, and is that providing any foreshadowing here?
- Why does Umlar react so harshly to Joël's presence?
- Why do you think Joël stresses that his work is turning the Great Ruin backwards? Where else have you heard something like this before?
- Joël's activity here is like two miracles from the Gospels. What are those miracles and what similarities and differences are there between the Gospels and here?
- Elbart and other nobles find someone willing to help them deal with Joël. Is the individual's identity a surprise, or can you track throughout the story how things have led to this point?

Chapter 23
- What is the connection between the colder weather and the decreased receptivity of people's hearts to Joël?
- What do you believe is the point of Joël's story? What parable from the Gospels compares to this?
- Elbart and other nobles find someone willing to help them deal with Joël. Is the individual's identity a surprise, or can you track throughout the story how things have led to this?

Chapter 24
- What event from the Gospels are you reminded of in this chapter?
- What is the significance of Joël locking the door of his shop?
- Notice the words of Joël's prayer. Is there a reason he blends together historical remembrance and future hope with present hardship?

Chapter 25
- Although this chapter seems to be a parallel to the Garden of Gethsemane experience of Christ, there are both similarities and differences between the two. Which ones in each category do you see?
- Are there characters in this scene with whom you identify? Who and how?

- Why would Joël's friends go to the Lakihalle if they realistically cannot do anything to help him?

Chapter 26
- Petric's actions before the Council of Nobles are meant to parallel which person from the Gospels? At what point do you think Petric has come to believe Joël, and on what basis do you believe that?
- Of what does Joël's prayer remind you?
- Why do you think Tuona continues to badger Joël? What is the common truth whenever Joël responds to Tuona?

Chapter 27
- Which group from the Gospel do the Council of Nobles represent here?
- Of the four charges the Nobles accuse Joël of, which do you think means the most to them? Why?
- Of the four charges leveled against Joël, which do you think King Dewulf will be concerned with the most? Why?
- Look at Matthew 26:57-68. What are some similarities and differences with this scene?

Chapter 28
- At the beginning of the book, the leaders of Selanna appear somewhat intent on being freed from the rule of Kronjva. Now they appear content to maintain their place under Kronji authority. What has changed and why?
- What do you think is Dewulf's intent in speaking with Joël alone? Why does he want to establish how similar they are?
- Why does Joël resist Dewulf's statements? Is it because he is intent on his sacrificial role, or because Dewulf needs to hear some brutal truth, or a mix of both? Why do you say that?
- In what way (if any) do you think this moment will make impact on Dewulf in the future? Why?

Chapter 29
- How would you characterize Joël's demeanor in this scene? Why is that so important?

- The crowd has become viciously hostile to Joël. What do you think accounts for this serious and sudden change?
- Why do you think the penalty for Joël is burning? What is that meant to display?

Chapter 30

- Why does Joël wear a white tunic for his march to the execution site?
- What do you think Vermeulen believes about Joël at this point? What Biblical character's role is he playing in this scene?
- What does Joël do and say before the torch is thrown upon him? What is the significance of this?
- What is the significance of Joël's last words?
- What was it that truly ended Joël's life?
- What is the significance of the broken wall around Vuoristad?
- The Bible is silent about God the Father's reaction to the death of the Son. In this story, Lord Creator weeps. How would you describe your reaction to this scene? Why do you say that?

Chapter 31

- What conclusions do you draw about the Council's discussion?
- What is so interesting about Petric's appeal and the location for burial? See John 19:38-42.
- What do you make of the statements of Elaenor and Petric at the gravesite?

The Resurrection

Chapter 32

- The Gospels all report that the stone had been rolled away from Jesus' tomb, but only Matthew gives some (sparing) details about how it happened. Here in the novel, the moment of resurrection brings with it a destruction of the tomb. Why?
- It seems from the details that Dalvig is the one who obliterates the tomb. He was the chief Messenger who disputed with Lord Creator after the Great Ruin occurred. What has happened with Dalvig in the meantime?

Chapter 33

- When she hears the roar of the collision near Elks Hill, Kyria immediately sets out to discover what is happening. The text also mentions something she *feels* within her. What do her actions and emotions show about what she believes?
- When Niilo finally sees the empty grave, there are some notable details. Why are these so important?

Chapter 34

- Why is it interesting the women are the first to see Joël's empty grave?
- Dalvig says, "[I]t's not 'his body' that gone...it's him! Joël himself is gone!" Why does he make a distinction between the body and the self?
- What does the Council's argument reveal about their hopes?

Chapter 35

- What Biblical character's role does Kyria seem to play here?
- Why do you think Kyria is the one to whom the risen Joël reveals himself first?
- Joël tells Kyria to "[t]ell them I am alive, and that I will always be alive." Why is the "*always*" a critical word in that sentence?

Chapter 36

- What is the reason why Kaleva has a hard time believing the good news is true? What does this reveal about us?
- Elks Hill is the site for Joël's time of prayer, Joël's capture, Joël's death, and Joël's resurrection. Why do you think that location plays the role it does?
- Before he died, Joël looked to Vuoristad. After he reaches the empty crypt, Kaleva gazes at Vuoristad, as well. Is this a coincidence, or is there meaning to this? And if there is meaning, what do you think it is?

Chapter 37

- What are Joël's first words to his gathered friends? Why are these words so necessary and meaningful?

- Joël will forever bear the cuts from the parpallo rope and the burn marks from the flames on his body. Why does he claim this is necessary? Why is this helpful for his friends?
- Joël says, "I must return." Yet he leaves the Breath of Lord Creator with his friends. Why are both of these truths so important?

Chapter 38

- Henrik notices their picnic will take place at the site of Joël's feeding miracle. Is this event intentional or coincidental? Why?
- Of which event in the Gospels does this remind you?
- What is Kaleva's response to Joël's call to lead? Why is this the right response for Kaleva? For us?
- Why is Joël's "amongst...always with" distinction important?
- Joël reveals his true, full identity before he leaves his friends. At what point in the story did you make the connection?
- Kaleva and Kyria are the final ones to say goodbye to Joël. What does this reveal about them?
- What do you think will happen with Joël's friends now that he is gone?
- The verbal exchange between Joël and Dalvig at the end mirrors an exchange between Lord Creator and Dalvig in "The Great Ruin". Why are "grace and kingdom" meant to be the lasting truths of the story as Joël and Dalvig walk toward Vuoristad?

LUKE HERRON DAVIS is the author of *Joël*, the first volume of the Merivalkan Chronicles trilogy. He presently serves as the chairman of the Bible department at Westminster Christian Academy in St. Louis. A teaching veteran of nearly twenty years, he has also penned several crime fiction volumes in the Cameron Ballack Mystery series. Luke lives in Saint Charles, Missouri, with his wife Christy, son Joshua, daughter Lindsay, and their retriever Gretel.

www.ingramcontent.com/pod-product-compliance
Lightning Source LLC
Chambersburg PA
CBHW030534030726
47495CB00004B/984

9780998400051